THE GIRL FROM SHANGHAI GHETTO

THE GIRL FROM SHANGHAI GHETTO

JOHNSON WU

Loons Press

THE GIRL FROM SHANGHAI GHETTO

Copyright © 2022 by Johnson Wu

FIRST EDITION

This is a work of fiction. The names, characters and incidents portrayed in it are the work of the author's imagination or are used fictitiously. Any resemblance to actual persons, living or dead, events or localities is entirely coincidental.

Library and Archives Canada Cataloguing in Publication

ISBN 978-1-7387821-2-3 (Hardcover)

ISBN 978-1-7387821-1-6 (Paperback)

ISBN 978-1-7387821-0-9 (eBook)

ISBN 978-1-7387821-3-0 (AudioBook)

Printed and bound in USA

Published by Loons Press

F
WU
JOHNSON

DEDICATION

To

My grandmother, who taught me conscience and decency.

My father, who taught me courage and perseverance. He fought a Japanese soldier with his bare hands in WWII.

My mother, who taught me to be industrious and humble. She introduced me the area that once was called the Shanghai ghetto.

"If there is a God and future life, there is truth and good, and man's highest happiness consists in striving to attain them. We must live, we must love, and we must believe that we live not only today on this scrap of earth but have lived and shall live."

-----*Leo Tolstoy, War and Peace*

CONTENTS

PROLOGUE

July 17, 1945
Shanghai, China

Nina was running for her life, panicking.
There were hundreds of aircraft like birds in the high clouds
above her in the Shanghai ghetto. Those big birds were cracking their
engines, making horrible noises, roaring down toward her head. Then,
suddenly, bombs were flying everywhere, exploding in front of her. It
was horrendous.

Nina had been on her way to a friend, but now she had to race back
home. She had never experienced such an air raid in the Shanghai ghetto
before, even though the war had been going on for years. Before the
bombs hit the ground and explode, the bombs' high-pitched whistling
sounds terrified her. Houses and buildings were on fire. The people in
the street were screaming in fear.

The blast from the explosions was deafening and blinding. Nina
became so frightened that she ran as fast as she could. Smoke filled the
road like a pungent cloud. The strong fumes irritated her nostrils. Her
ears were drumming, and her eyes filled with tears. Nina kept running
past her best friend's apartment. She was extremely shocked by the
ear-piercing whistle right before the bomb fell into the middle of her
friend's building. A plume of smoke with fire was rising from the site
immediately. Her legs began to tremble when she saw human legs and
arms flying in the air and dropping on the street.

When she got home, Nina crawled underneath the dining table for shelter. Nina worried desperately about her girlfriend, whether she had been wounded or killed in the explosion. Meanwhile, Nina had to endure the awful smoke and the dreaded sirens from outside.

Under the table, Nina expected the next airplane to carry bombs that would destroy her building. It petrified her. Then the bombing seemed to cease, and there was a moment of quietude. The sudden silence after the horrible explosion made Nina even more nervous.

Soon, an airplane roared over, with machine gun stuttering sounds. Then a bomb hit straight on some buildings across the street. An enormous explosion shook their apartment building with immense noise. Nina guessed the Japanese army's oil tanks might been bombed. She could smell repugnant gasoline and see the vast smoke outside. A chip from the bomb flew into their window like a brutal bullet. It dropped on the pillow, jumping ferociously to her foot.

All at once, Nina felt like the world was coming to an end.

PART I

THE RHINE RIVER

CHAPTER ONE

November 9, 1938
Berlin, Germany

Nina Friedman held her Papa's big hand and hurried home at dusk. Her ponytail waved in the chilly air as they walked in silence. Nina saw the pigeons flapping their wings in the cold breeze. She was puzzled by how crimson the streets and buildings were, wondering if all this color could be from the sunset.

Suddenly, the metal-like screech of a siren broke through the fragile evening air, shivering Nina's heart. She felt Papa squeeze her hand. Nina clenched her teeth as the shrill of the car buzzers came closer and closer. Then she saw a black Mercedes-Benz cruising along the street. She could see the miniature Nazi swastika flag pronged on the car's fender. The vehicle roared over the dead leaves and dust on the street, disappearing around the corner. Nina tried to keep up with her Papa, her small legs moving as fast as they could on the frigid street.

Albert Friedman was born in Berlin thirty-nine years ago. He was a tall and thin man with a distinguished appearance, a reddish face, and a high-bridge nose. Albert was proud of his nose and always called it his enormous proboscis with a joking tone. But he never imagined a time when this nose would bring him so much trouble. He always walked fast, swinging his arms wide, taking large steps. Albert rushed home after working an entire day with his daughter at his musical instrument store in downtown court. He kept worrying about the siren wailing on the way home.

"Mama, we are home." Nina hugged her Mama's leg.

"Sweetie, it's cold outside." Mama bent down and kissed Nina's cheek. Nina had crystal clear pale blue eyes and light chestnut hair, just like her Mama, Alona. Two cute dimples on her pink cheeks enhanced the charm of her smile.

"Honey, you look exhausted today." Mama took Papa's black coat.

"Yes." Papa's voice was low and deep. He squeezed a smile at Mama.

Nina was happy to be home, warm, quiet, and with the pleasant smell of food. They lived in a decent apartment building. Mama kept their home immaculately clean. There was a piano sitting in the living room. A violin was the centerpiece of a collection of landscape paintings hanging on the wall. Several family pictures were on top of the upright piano. Nina was positioned in the middle in most of the photos. One picture was of Nina as a baby, in her Mama's arms by the Rhine River in Cologne. Mama still called Nina "Baby" once in a while, even though she was already eight years old.

The three of them sat around the table and ate dinner in a strange silence. There was no usual chatting tonight. Papa looked nervous. He seemed reluctant to initiate any conversation about the tensions in the street. Nina was sensible enough to discern the odd atmosphere at the table, so she kept quiet for a while.

Finally, Nina broke the awkward silence. "Mama, can I play piano after dinner?"

"Sure, Sweetie!" her mother smiled at her.

Nina played a simple piano piece called the "Fluttering Leaves". Her playing was exquisite. The

melody of the beautiful music floated in the room with a gentle rhyme. It spoke of the spectacle of the autumn leaves, dropping and flying in slow motion. So many leaves spread all over the picturesque mountains with a gentle tempo. The red, green, brown, and yellow leaves across the river were fluttering, keeping pace with the larghetto of the music.

Nina's delicate fingers were flying over the piano keyboard. She played each note with a gentle and solid strength. The colorful leaves seemed to be slowly drifting down and down. Nina did not know that every time she hit the D note on the keyboard, the music vibrated in her Papa's heart until she saw tears streaming down his cheeks.

"Doesn't the music remind you of the beautiful life we once had when we were young, living by the Rhine River? Do you remember the glamorous life we used to have?" Albert kept asking his wife.

"Yes, I remember," Alona held her husband's hand. She understood Albert was sad because their remarkable life slipped away since Hitler came into power. The harsh reality of the increasing antisemitism in Berlin became a constant worry.

"Almost every note you played was so touching. Thanks, Sweetie!" Papa stroked Nina's shoulder.

"Mama, can I play more?" Nina murmured.

"We'll play it tomorrow. Let's go to bed now," Alona said.

"Good night, Papa, Mama!" She was an amenable girl.

Nina heard some dogs barking before she fell asleep. She hid her head under the quilt. "Why are the dogs barking so much tonight?" Nina worried and tossed around in her bed.

Bang! Suddenly there was an enormous burst of sound near Nina's bed.

"Ah!" Nina jumped up, screaming, "Papa!"

"Nina!" Papa and Mama rushed into her bedroom together.

Someone had thrown a stone through the window. Papa found shards of the broken glasses all over the bedroom floor.

There was chaos in the street. It sounded like someone was smashing something. People were shouting, and dogs were barking. Nina felt the air was filled with terror.

"What are those noises?" Mama asked.

"That must be the Nazi SS," Papa said.

"What are they doing?" Mama peeked out from the broken window.

"There is nothing good coming from those people," Papa couldn't see what was happening. The street lamp was too dim.

He turned to Nina, who was trembling. "Sweetie, don't worry!" Papa said, holding on to her.

"But why, Papa, why," Nina asked.

"Those bastards smashed our window. They have targeted our apartment," Papa said.

"We need to be more careful," Mama whispered.

Nina could still hear people yelling in the street, and the sounds of things being crushed continued. She was scared, not only for herself but also for her parents.

"I already saw the signs that something will happen tonight," Papa murmured. Nina understood Papa referred to the sirens and Nazi cars they had encountered on the way home before.

"Listen," Mama held her husband's arm.

Footsteps thundered on the wooden stairs just outside their home. Boom! Boom! Boom! Deafening knocks shook the front door.

"Papa," Nina looked petrified. She was almost jumping out of her skin.

"Sweetie, we will be fine," Papa embraced Nina firmly. Then, while trying to calm his daughter, he instructed her to hide behind the stairs.

At that moment, the bang on the door became much more violent. Nina crouched into the tiny space. Her heart beating was almost as loud as the pounding on the door. She was terrified.

Before Mama could unlock the door, it was flung open by force.

Two Nazi SS men pushed into the apartment. One was fat with puffy eyes, and the other was skinny with a toothbrush-style mustache. They were all in black.

"What are you looking for?" Papa asked even though he knew these men only meant trouble.

"We are looking for you," the short SS man said.

The mustached SS man squeezed into the room to hit two framed family photos on the wall with a stick like a baseball bat. The glass over the photos was smashed, falling onto the floor. Then he struck a glass bottle engraved with the Star of David on the table. For the sound of broken glass, Nina covered her mouth to muffle her crying.

The mustached SS shoved Mama with such force she fell to the floor with a moan.

"Stop it!" Papa ran over to help Mama.

The room was full of ugly noise as the mustached man crushed Papa's favorite violin on the end table. "Kill the Jews," he shouted.

"Stop it!" Papa cried. Papa stepped forward to try to stop him.

The man stared at Papa and yelled, "You Jews are rats!" Then, he ran to the kitchen and shattered the china and glassware, making a more terrible noise.

At the same time, the puffy-eyed SS was searching for any valuables in the house. He was like a hungry animal looking for food. He opened every drawer and searched through every cabinet. His fat, filthy hands overturned the contents of the drawers, pulling the clothes out of the wardrobes and throwing them all over the room.

"Don't take that!" Mama almost shouted at the puffy-eyed SS when she saw him taking her most precious treasure. She had inherited it from her grandmother. It was a necklace made of perfect pearls.

As Mama tried to grab the necklace back, the SS deliberately pulled it forcefully, breaking the strand. The pearls spilled all over the floor with a dreadful sound. He then shoved Mama to the floor.

"Ouch!" Mama fell and bumped her shoulder on the corner of the table.

"Mama," Nina came out from her hiding place behind the stairs and stopped her crying. She crouched down beside her mother, who was still on the floor in obvious pain.

"You stop!" Papa glared at the puffy-eyed SS.

The mustached SS ran over and beat Papa with his stick. Papa raised both arms to protect himself until he was able to grab the stick and throw it away.

The mustached SS hit Papa's face with his fists savagely. Blood dripped from Papa's nose onto his white pajama.

Papa was so infuriated that he fought back. He used all his strength to hit the SS man. Papa's fists pounded on his face. The mustached SS struggled.

Papa gained the advantage over the mustached SS. Papa grabbed and pushed the man, pinning him on the wall with his hands behind his back. Helpless, the mustached SS called to his partner for help.

The man with the ugly puff eyes responded by grabbing Nina, threatening to hurt her if Papa did not release his fellow.

"Papa," Nina cried out. She held in her tears even though her arms were hurting where the man squeezed her. Nina glowered at the SS. She found he was the ugliest man she had ever seen, a big gap between his front teeth with ugly puffy eyes.

"Let her go!" Papa released the struggling mustached SS and ran to Nina. Papa had never had such rage with his piercing eyes and red face. The puffy-eyed SS showed his true self, a coward, and let Nina go.

"Nina, go to your Mama," Papa said

"You Jews are rats!" The puffy-eyed SS cursed.

"You Nazis are pigs!" Papa shouted back.

The SS responded with a hard punch to Papa's belly. Papa let out a loud scream.

"Papa," Nina wanted to run to support her father. She bit down on her lower lip to give herself courage. She wiped away her tears and stepped toward her father.

"Don't come close, Nina!" Papa said.

Just at that moment, the mustached SS punched Papa hard in the nose. Blood gushed from his nose and mouth. It covered his face, pajamas and even splattered on the wall.

"You are under arrest," the two SS tied Papa up with a rope.

"Arrest, What for?" Papa asked.

"For you being a Jew," the SS said.

"Papa," Nina cried out.

"You little Jew," the puffy-eyed SS approached Nina again.

"Nina," Mama pulled her daughter back desperately, putting her arm in front of Nina to protect her.

"You watch him," The mustached SS ordered his partner, pointed at Papa, and then launched into another round of smashing the furniture in the house.

A beautiful vase in the corner of the room was struck, exploding like a bomb. Then, the SS continued his rampage, whacking the piano with a force that the keyboard made a horrible ear-piercing noise.

"My piano," Nina screamed. She could not bear to see her beautiful piano destroyed.

The puffy-eyed SS saw Nina's distress and suggested to his partner, "Let us throw the piano out from the window."

Nina and her parents watched the two SS awkwardly carry the piano to the window, and then they heaved it up and pushed it out.

The piano crashed down the cobblestone street, making crazy sound like a series of cannons going off.

"My piano," Nina's voice was full of anguish.

Mama hugged her closely. She could not comprehend this madness.

The two SS men started pushing Papa out of the apartment without warning.

"Where are you taking him?" Mama demanded. She ran over to her husband.

"To jail," The mustached SS man sneered, looking proud of himself with a malicious grin.

"Papa," Nina noticed that Papa had lost a shoe in all the chaos. She found it and held it out for him, but she couldn't reach him as he was pushed out the door.

Papa struggled to free himself from their grasp, but it was hopeless. Finally, he turned and shouted out to his daughter, "Nina!"

"Albert," Mama raised her arm and came forward to give her husband his coat.

The puffy-eyed SS shoved Mama again. She wobbled for two steps and fell down for the third time. Mama's head hit the table corner with a sickening thud.

"Papa," Nina called out in despair.

Papa was gone.

When Nina turned around, she found her mother lying on the floor. Her eyes were closed, her left arm had flopped in an awkward position, and she did not move even when Nina called to her.

"Mama," Nina cried, crouching down beside her mother.

"Save my Papa! Save my Papa!" Nina pleaded with her mother on the floor. When she realized her mother was not responding, the pain she felt was unbearable. She was terrified by the thought of losing her father and mother on the same night.

CHAPTER TWO

November 10, 1938
Berlin, Germany

"Wake up, Mama! Wake up," Nina shouted. She shook her mother's body, crying desperately.

Nina knew she had to do something to save her mother. She went to the kitchen to fetch some water. With trembling hands, she slowly dripped the water into her mother's mouth. Finally, her mother opened her eyes. It was like a miracle, and Nina cried, this time with relief and joy.

"Mama," Nina called.

"Don't cry, Sweetie," Alona's face was still pale, and she tried to raise her left hand to touch Nina's face.

"Mama, is your arm hurting?" Nina rubbed her mother's left arm.

"I can't move it," Alona said.

Nina fed more water to her mother. She wanted to comfort her. She understood Mama's left shoulder was severely injured.

Nina had to help her mother get up from the floor. Alona was almost helpless.

Alona looked around at the devastation in her home. There was no place to sit. The SS had almost destroyed everything. They had smashed tables, chairs, cabinets and overturned the sofa. The only thing to sit on was the piano stool. So Nina led her mother to it, turned it right side up, and helped her mother sit on the stool.

The house was silent and almost tranquil. However, any peace was disrupted by the noise from the street, on and off.

"Sweetie, I am a little better now," Alona said.

"Mama, do you want more water?"

"I am fine. You are a very brave girl," Alona held Nina's shoulder with her right hand. "I need you to look around and to listen. We need to know if we are safe here. You need to protect yourself."

"They took Papa away. They took him away, Mama," Nina tried hard not to cry again, remembering her mother said she was brave, but she was very worried about her father. "Why did those people take Papa away, Mama?" Nina asked.

"It's hard to explain, but they are like Hitler, and they hate us because we are Jewish,"

"I hate Hitler!" Nina's face was red.

"Shush!" Alona put her finger on her lips. Then, with a careful glance at Nina, she indicated she needed to be quiet and listen. They were not out of danger yet.

Tap-Tap-Tap-Tap! Footsteps could be heard coming from downstairs again. Alona's heartbeats were as hard as the boots stomping on the stairs.

The noise increased. It seemed there were even more SS men invading their home.

"We need to go right away," Alona told Nina.

Alona feared that the SS were coming to arrest her too. She feared mostly for Nina's safety. Alona had to make a decision quickly. She knew they had to escape but to where? They couldn't go down to the front door. The SS were already there. The only way to escape was to go to the upper floors.

"Sweetie, Let's go!" Alona held Nina's hand. More noise came from downstairs.

"Okay, Mama," Nina nodded.

Alona noticed Nina pick her rag doll "Mini" from the floor and hide it in her pocket. It had been a special gift from Nina's grandmother.

Tap-Tap-Tap-Tap! Alona still heard the footsteps from downstairs. Her stomach churned, and her scalp tingled. She held onto her daughter and ran. They moved up to the third floor of this old apartment building. Obviously, the noise from downstairs pushed them to move up faster.

Alona held Nina's hands and gave her encouragement. Nina bit her bottom lip as always when she faced any challenge. Nina had told her Mama when she bit her lips she could somehow feel encouraged and overcome her fears most of the time.

Finally, they reached the sixth floor. Nina panted heavily after climbing so far so fast, without stopping.

"Are you all right, Sweetie?" Alona whispered to her daughter.

"Yes, Mama," Nina's eyes sparkled in the night light.

Alona never released her daughter's hand. She could feel the little girl tightening her grip on her hand. She sensed Nina's tension.

"Sweetie, we are doing well." Alona tried to ease her daughter's fear, although her own heart was pounding like a running rabbit.

"Mama, I'm not scared." Nina pretended.

"Let us go to the other end of the corridor," Alona said. "There was an attic loft there. I saw it once when they were repairing the building." Nina followed her mother, trotting along the corridor to the base of the attic. They stopped as confronted by a steep iron ladder.

The noise from downstairs became louder and louder. Nina knew they had to hurry.

"Mama, I can climb up." So Nina grabbed the iron ladder and started to climb up to the attic.

"Sweetie, this ladder is too steep for you," Alona said. She found her daughter's hand trembling.

"I'm not scared." Nina's foot was on the first step of the ladder.

"Wait a minute," Alona groaned with the pain from her left shoulder.

"Mama, your shoulder," Nina turned to her mother.

"Don't worry, Sweetie, Just a little pain," Alona reassured her. "Listen, Sweetie, you need to be very careful and grasp the iron bar firmly with each step," Alona knelt down. She clutched Nina's left shoulder, giving her a hug.

"I know, Mama," Nina nodded again and started to climb up.

Alona held Nina up for the first three steps. Nina kept climbing up, step by step. She knew her mother was there, watching her and supporting her. At last, Nina reached the attic and clambered into it.

Alona could only use her right hand to grasp the ladder and climb up. Nina was so glad to see her mother coming up from below. They hugged each other tightly in the attic.

"We must be quiet," Alona said. So she led Nina to hide in the corner of the attic. But she still had to close the attic's small wooden door.

Bang! The attic door slipped from her fingers and slammed down to the floor, making a loud slapping sound. Alona knew now the attic was not a safe place to hide because the SS would have heard the bang.

"What do we need to do now?" Nina worried.

"Look around. There must be a way out. God will give us another chance. When one door closes, another door always opens," Alona told Nina.

They soon found a dim light coming from a distant corner of the attic near the ceiling.

"There's a window over there," Nina said.

"Let's go," Alona advised Nina. "It should lead to the rooftop."

"Mama, could you let me go up first again?" Nina begged her mother.

"Look around first, Sweetie," Alona said, checking the ladder. It was a wooden ladder, just as steep as the iron one but not as tall. However, it did not look very stable. But, there was no time. They had no choice.

When Nina climbed the first two steps of the wooden ladder, it squeaked. It startled Nina and stopped her from moving up.

"Mama," Nina said, frightened.

"That is okay, Sweetie. I'm right here. Keep going slowly," Alona said.

Nina bit her lower lip and resumed moving up, one step after another.

But at the top, Nina could not open the window at all. She had to come down. Nina almost cried. She was exhausted and frustrated.

"Sweetie, you are a brave girl," Alona held Nina's hand. "Let me go up to check it," Alona touched Nina's head.

"Be careful, Mama!"

"Just wait here," Alona said.

Nina stood there scared, waiting for her mother.

"Sweetie, I opened the window. It's just rusted." Alona came down, wanting to let Nina go first. "You can go up to the rooftop now. I'll come after you."

"Mama, don't worry," Nina said.

"Sweetie, climb up, step by step. When you reach the rooftop, stay there to wait for Mama."

"Okay, Mama," Nina climbed up on the wooden ladder again. Alona watched her daughter, step by step, going up to the rooftop.

But Nina was unable to climb onto the rooftop from the last step of the ladder by herself. After all, she was only eight years old, and her arms were not strong enough. "Mama," Nina called.

"Sweetie, I am here," Alona said. "I will say one, two, three, then push you up. We will use all our power together to get on the roof."

"Okay, Mama," Nina replied.

"One, two, three, go!" Alona pushed Nina up out of the attic window and onto the roof.

Nina fell on the roof on her hands and knees.

"Mama," she called her mother.

"I am coming up," Alona said.

"I am on the cold cement floor on the rooftop," Nina reported.

"Sweetie, don't move, stay there, wait for me," Alona used her calm voice to reassure Nina again.

It seemed a long time Nina had to wait before she saw her mother's head appear through the attic opening. As soon as Alona got on the roof floor, Nina grabbed her mother and held on tight, with a cheerful heart.

"Sweetie, you are a strong girl," Alona knelt down and hugged her daughter.

Alona felt a light breeze blowing on the top of the building and into her neck. She thought she detected something scorched in the air, but she did not know what it was and from where.

CHAPTER THREE

November 10, 1938
Berlin, Germany

The air was cold on the rooftop. Nina could hear the dogs barking and the people shouting or crying down in the street.

"Mama, I smell something burning," Nina said.

"There must be a fire somewhere," Mama said.

Mama could see one building on fire in the distance. But unfortunately, it was too dark to identify which building was on fire. All she could see were many rooftops and different-sized chimneys in front of her.

"Mama, I heard someone talking below the attic," Nina's voice trembled.

"Sweetie, we have to move forward now. Follow me," Mama squatted down to hold Nina.

"Okay, Mama," Nina nodded and bit her lower lip.

She followed her mother step by step on the cold rooftop. She could feel herself quivering. Walking was difficult on the rough surface. It was dark, and there was debris scattered around. It became more challenging to walk on the rooftop. Her mother trod carefully, making a path in the dim night light.

"Can you see the footsteps, Sweetie?" Mama asked.

"Yes, Mama," Nina spurred to move even more quickly when she heard the furious howling of the men in the street. The SS men are right down there, she thought.

Nina and her mother moved on the rooftop in silence. They passed several chimneys. Nina tried to follow closely in her Mama's footsteps, believing she would not be so scared if she kept close to her Mama.

A twisted rusty construction metal bar blocked their way. Mama turned to Nina, "Sweetie, let me help you go over this bar."

Nina used her two small hands to grab the cold metal bar and got over it with her mother's help.

"You are good," Mama embraced Nina.

Getting through that hurtle gave Nina more courage, and she was proud of her achievement. After that, Nina moved forward a little faster.

All of a sudden, there was a large gap between the roofs. It was too wide for Nina to jump across. She stopped, paralyzed with fear. Mama bent down and picked Nina up. They leaped over the gap together.

Safe on the other side, Nina nestled her face against her mother's neck. She could feel the warmth of her mother's skin. She snuggled against her mother like a baby.

"Sweetie, we have to be very careful. One slip and we could have fallen to the ground, six floors below," Mama warned.

"Yes, Mama," Nina promised.

"Let's have a rest," They were exhausted.

"Look, a big fire," Nina almost called out, pointing toward the nearby building. There was considerable smoke rising from the building. A brilliant crimson fire blazed in the middle of the thick smoke, growing more prominent in midnight's darkness.

"It is our synagogue," Mama murmured sadly.

"Mama," Nina thought of the SS's brutality in attacking her home. She was sure that the SS had set fire to their synagogue.

"Those bastards," Mama whispered again. The colossal cloud of smoke and the raging fire fueled Mama's anger.

Nina and her mother had a panoramic view of the disaster from the rooftop. They watched the smoke traveling like a snake against the black night sky, the blood-red flame accompanying the thick black smoke along the sharp roof of their synagogue. The smoke was thicker than a dense dark thunder cloud, drifting over the different shapes of Berlin's buildings.

Nina covered her mouth with her hand to calm her shock. The terrifying sight of the fire was augmented by the horrible noises in the street.

"Mama," Nina grabbed onto her mother's coat. They stood together silently, watching the blazing fire destroy their beloved synagogue. A chilly breeze blew Nina's hair, and she shivered with cold and fear. But Nina's eyes shone brilliantly with her anger.

Nina followed her mother. They walk in silence. Despite the aching in her little legs and the fear in her heart, she kept moving. She wondered how much further they had to go and if she could keep going.

"Mama, are we there yet?" Nina asked. She was so exhausted.

"Sweetie, we are almost near Aunt Esther's street," Alona said.

The thought of being with her favorite Aunt motivated Nina to push 'forward.

"I've missed my Aunt Esther," Nina said.

"I've missed her too. She has loved you very much from the day you were born," Mama said.

Finally, Nina and her mother found a place to crawl down from the roof. It was a challenging climb. Nina's legs were still trembling, her breathing was heavy and fast, and her mouth was parched and tasted bitter. Once she realized they were on solid ground and had escaped the SS, Nina burst into tears. She hugged her Mama tightly.

"Sweetie, you are a very good girl," Mama gave thumbs up to Nina, who gave thumbs up right back at her mother. Nina laughed with her Mama, remembering her grandmother, who had taught her this gesture of approval.

Nina was stunned to see so many broken store windows as they walked along. Shards of broken glasses were scattered all over the street. The gloomy light from the streetlamps reflected off the broken glass, creating an eerie feeling as if they were in another world.

Nina thought the hundreds and thousands of glass fragments looked like twinkling crystals on the black cobblestone street in the darkness. When she stepped on the broken glass, it gave a high-pitched squeaking sound, which made Nina nearly jump out of her skin.

In fact, that night, most of the synagogue windows in Berlin, even in Germany, were broken. Similarly, the windows of Jewish houses were smashed. The windows of Jewish commercial buildings were shattered. Almost every Jewish store had been damaged.

Nina could imagine the SS waving their iron sticks, smashing all the windows. She had heard the terrible cracking and explosive sounds from the rooftop as they fled. Broken glass was everywhere. Large glass panes from shop display windows and doors were shattered. Nina could see broken glass, hear broken glass, and even feel broken glass under her feet. All of the fractured glass seemed to make her heart bleed. She felt the painful loss in her heart.

Berlin felt like a ghost town to Nina and her mother as they walked through the destruction. Nina was startled by the ghost-like townscape of her city.

As they walked and turned a corner, Nina saw smoke drifting from the burning synagogues, filling the air. The smoke hung in the trees like fog in the dawn light. Nina took a breath wanting the crisp early morning air to calm her. But instead, the smoke-filled air choked her.

"Mama," Nina held onto her mother's arm for security.

"Sweetie, should we take a look at our store first? I am afraid they may have broken our store windows too," Mama worried about all the musical instruments in the store.

"Yes, Mama," Nina bit her bottom lip as she answered.

When Nina and Mama arrived at their musical instrument store, it was much worse than they could ever imagine.

"Oh, God," Mama put her hand over her heart.

"Mama," Nina held onto her mother in shock.

The store's door had been smashed, and all the windows were broken. The fragments of broken glass were all over the sidewalk. It had splintered into thousands of pieces. Some shards of glass were still stuck on the window frames, looking like a shark jaw, gaping horribly.

When Nina peeked through the broken window, she saw all the damage that had been done. Everything had been destroyed. The musical instruments had been smashed and thrown around the store. It was a horrible mess.

Nina saw the flute, her favorite musical instrument, had been thrown on the floor, broken into two pieces. There were piccolos, clarinets, oboes, recorders, and bassoons all over the place. She found one violin on the ground, another torn off the wall and smashed. The cello and bass had fallen from their stands, lying like corpses on the floor. Guitar, ukulele, banjo, and mandolin had all been pushed into the corner.

In the other area of the store, shining pieces of the brass instruments were thrown. The trumpet, trombone, tuba, and French horn were all crushed as if stepped on by heavy boots. The harp's strings had been broken and hung miserably from the frame. Papa's favorite saxophone lay there as if weeping with unbearable grief.

Nina stood there, paralyzed. Tears were streaming down her cheeks. She felt confused by what she saw. How could anyone be so destructive?

"Mama, they ruined everything," Nina cried in despair.

"Those bastards," Mama's hands trembled.

"Mama, somebody is coming up this way."

"Sweetie, we need to leave here now," Mama tried to lower her voice.

"Okay, Mama," Nina hurried with her mother, aware of the squeaking sound of the broken glass beneath her feet.

They left the ruined family musical store reluctantly. Both of them disappeared into the early morning mist of Berlin.

Before the sun rose, they trudged through the enclosed network of streets. There was evidence of the disturbance in the night everywhere. When they found a quiet place, Nina asked her mother, "Where is Papa? Where did they take Papa?"

"He will be okay because he is smart," Mama tried to reassure Nina as well as herself.

CHAPTER FOUR

November 10, 1938
Berlin, Germany

Albert was pushed into a truck parked on the street corner after two SS men dragged him out of his home.

There were already several other Jewish men in the truck. Many Jews were arrested that night. The truck rumbled along the dark streets, the sound of broken glass beneath its wheels.

Albert saw the shattered glass all over the Berlin streets. The SS shouted obscenities at Jews on the street as they vandalised their properties. He saw three SS men use a telephone pole to crush a Jewish store's front door. Another man in black was carrying sledgehammers to smash store windows. The noise of broken glass filled Albert with emotion, mostly anger but sadness too. SS men ransacked the stores all the way. It seemed their goal was to destroy all the properties belonging to Jews.

Albert witnessed several SS grabbing an elderly rabbi. First, they used scissors to cut his long beard to humiliate him. A young SS had frivolously burst into a ridiculous laugh on the rabbi's face. Then two other Nazis tied the rabbi's arms and dragged him away.

"Do you know where they are taking us?" Albert asked the man with a long beard next to him.

"I don't know." He shook his head.

"Maybe Oranienburg," Another man wearing glasses said.

"Oh, that is about fifty kilometers north of Berlin," Albert recalled that location.

"What do they exactly want from us?" The bearded man's voice was agitated.

"They want to drive us out of Germany. Hitler has wanted to destroy us for years," the man with glasses said.

"Tonight is the end of Jews in Germany. I think we should try to leave this country," Albert said.

"Similar things had happened before in our long Jewish history. So let's wait and see," The bearded man disagreed with Albert.

Albert believed the bearded man was naïve, like some other Jews, holding out hope for an unlikely occurrence from the Nazis. Albert thought about how things had gotten worse since the "Nuremberg Law" passed by the Nazi government around three years ago. Most Jews had been excluded from German society by the Nazis.

Albert always thought of himself as German. He made friends with his non-Jewish neighbors and business owners, such as the barber Werner from the corner barbershop and Josef from the butcher shop. Unfortunately, some of them joined the Nazi party, like the butcher, Josef. After that, he looked the other way to avoid eye contact with Albert when he passed Albert's musical store. It was not only a friendship lost, but there was a new hostility between them. From then on, Albert's social life involved only other Jews and their relatives, such as Albert's brother, Allen, and Alona's sister, Esther. They sometimes met each other at Allen's home near Duisburburg Strasse.

The truck-load of Jews continued over the dark Berlin streets. Albert wondered what triggered the Nazis' vicious attack on Jews on this particular night.

Suddenly, the truck driver braked, throwing Albert and his peers off-balance, banging their heads, sending arms and legs flying. All the Jewish men on the truck moaned in pain.

The truck stopped in the Old Town area of Spandau, located in the center of Berlin. Albert witnessed SS men preparing to light a fire on the famous Spandau Synagogue at 12 Lindenufer Road.

A few young Nazi men rushed to the synagogue, carrying large gasoline bottles. They splashed the petrol onto the synagogue's wooden structure and set it alight. A vast flame rose from the synagogue building with a massive balloon of black smoke. Albert could smell gasoline from a distance. It only took moments, and a bright flash of explosion erupted from the blazing synagogue. The wooden frames of the synagogue flew into the air. The sound of the flame was roaring. As the synagogue burned, the Nazi SS laughed and shouted as if it was a celebration.

"This synagogue was built in 1894, a precious and ancient Jewish property," the bearded man stated.

Albert felt enormous sadness. "That is the end of this most eminent synagogue," Albert sighed.

All the Jewish men on the truck watched the fire of the Spandau Synagogue in disbelief. Explosions continued as the flames licked the walls. Finally, they saw one whole side of the synagogue ablaze. Thick, tar-black smoke belched from the windows. Then, suddenly, an orange fireball with black smoke rose into the sky. The roof crumbled. Minutes later, the synagogue collapsed into a mass of burning embers.

It shocked Albert to see firefighters from the Nazi government do nothing to fight the fire. They were standing idle, besides the flaming building, with the fire engine parked nearby. They did nothing to extinguish the fire. Instead, they just watched the synagogue burn to the ground. Gusts of wind blew on the fire, making the blaze burn more aggressively.

"The whole city seems to be on fire tonight." The man with glasses observed.

Their truck moved again. When the truck passed the famous Nathan Israel Department Store, the largest department store owned by a Jewish family in Berlin, Albert saw that its buildings had been vandalised by the SS. Albert remembered that this store had been boycotted by the Nazi SS brown shirts when the Nazi Party first came to power.

When Adolf Hitler grabbed power on April 1, 1933, he ordered his men to boycott all Jewish businesses. Many Nazi members stood in front of Jewish businesses and pushed all the customers away. They would not allow any customers to go into the Jewish stores. The brownshirts stood outside their stores carrying placards with the words, "Don't Buy from Jews."

It was happened the same at Albert's own musical instrument store, which severely suffered from the notorious "boycott." Albert vividly recalled that three Nazi SS stood in front of his store and expelled all German customers. They wouldn't allow them to enter the store to buy musical instruments. It was actually the beginning of the Nazi government's policy to drive Jewish businesses out of the German economy. This was the prelude to the destruction of the Jewish people's lives in the country. From then on, the living conditions of their families became worse and worse.

Albert and his Jewish fellows suffered nearly a whole night on the road. Then, finally, they arrived at the town of Oranienburg, where the Nazis had established the Sachsenhausen concentration camp.

Albert saw this slogan on the front entrance gates of Sachsenhausen concentration camp. "Arbeit Macht Frei" (In German: Work Makes You Free)

"They may just want us to work for them," the bearded fellow said when he read the slogan.

"I don't think so," the gentleman with glasses said.

"Maybe something worse," Albert said pessimistically.

They heard an SS bark, "All lined up for registration."

Albert and the other Jewish men stood in the chilly wind to register before entering the camp. They looked disheveled after the night's experience.

When Albert noticed a machine gun posted at the entrance gate, he realized that this place would be a nightmare. In fact, his assumption soon became a harsh reality.

On that first night in the camp barracks, Albert told everyone about what terrible things he had seen on the street. He touched his high-bridged nose when a fellow asked Albert about his injured nose. Then, he told of his fight with two SS men.

"I remember being terrified by all the noise. When I walked over to my aunt's house to see if they were alright, I saw the damage to our synagogue. There was lots of shattered glass under my feet. I got stopped by the SS on the next street. They put me on a truck and brought me here, "one of the Jewish fellows said.

"I found a mound of ashes on the window frame. They were from our prayer books and our synagogue's Torah," another inmate said.

Albert thought tonight's events were a harbinger of harsher times for Jews in this country. He believed he and his family really have to leave Germany.

Albert worried about his musical instrument store in downtown Berlin. He was desperately concerned about the safety of his daughter and wife. He could not imagine how they would deal with the mess at home.

The next morning, hundreds of prisoners come out from their barracks. The Nazi guards lined them up for roll call. The prisoners stood around in a semi-circular on the campgrounds. It was evident to Albert they had been subject to cruel treatment.

Albert was forced to do hard labor during his first week in the Sachsenhausen concentration camp. He suffered unbearable starvation and thirst. The hunger was like a gnawing animal, nibbling at his stomach, making growling sounds like a howling wolf. His mouth was so dry it was like a burning fire. Albert kept asking the camp warders for water and food, but he only got abuse from the Nazi guards. Some prisoners were so hungry they fainted.

Albert and the other prisoners had been repeatedly beaten in the following weeks, sometimes even cruelly tortured. The injuries and wounds appeared on their faces, eyes, arms, legs, and all over their bodies. The camp guards were merciless. They needed no provocations for their brutality, just a look or a word, and the prisoner would feel the guards' wrath.

Albert saw one SS point a handgun straight at a prisoner's forehead and shoot him in cold blood. While he was incarcerated in the Sachsenhausen concentration camp, Albert saw, with his own eyes, at least four Jews being beaten to death.

At night in the camp barracks, Albert and his fellows discussed whether they had a future in Germany.

"All of a sudden, there's no safe place for Jews anywhere in Germany. That's why so many Jews were hurrying to find a way out of this country," one man said.

"But how can we get out of this Nazi Germany?" another fellow was frustrated by the Nazis' strict border control.

"They said you need an immigration visa to leave this country. It is tough to get a visa from a foreign country," one man stated.

"It almost impossible to get immigration visa for us." The man waved his hand.

"So where can we go?" Albert puzzled over this serious dilemma.

CHAPTER FIVE

December10, 1938
Berlin, Germany

Alona and Nina slept at Aunt Esther's home after a whole night of running. Alona woke after a short nap, but her daughter fell into a deep sleep. Staring at Nina's beautiful face and thinking about how brave she was last night on the run, Alona recalled the difficult time she had to conceive this child eight years ago.

Alona never thought she would have such a big challenge of becoming pregnant. After marrying Albert for four years, she wasn't pregnant even once. She sought the help of a few doctors for about three years, trying to conceive, but everything failed. After that, Alona and Albert had even considered adopting a child.

That year, Alona and Albert went back to Cologne to visit her parents and take a holiday. Cologne actually is Alona's hometown, the city by the Rhine River. It was there that she got pregnant. They were so happy with this unexpected joy. Alona always believed it was the Rhine River bringing her luck. Her mother suggested she stay in Cologne for the sake of the unborn child.

Alona suffered terrible morning sickness and vomiting every time she ate during her pregnancy. Although she experienced severe nausea, Alona still felt blessed because she would have her own child.

When Alona felt her labor pain starting a few weeks early, she knew the baby might be arriving a little too soon.

"Your daughter's weight is only 1.9 kilograms because she is premature," the doctor said. "She will need special care."

When Alona first held her baby daughter in her arms, she was filled with joyful excitement. She touched her two little hands, which were so soft, and Alona felt a solid connection to her baby. That instant bond has lasted all these years.

Inspecting her new baby, Alona was shocked to find her daughter had slightly yellow skin all over her body. Her torso was petite. Her cry was weak and frail. Her skin was wrinkled like an old woman's, and her light blonde hair was thin and wispy. Although Alona was delighted and proud to be a mother, she was frightened by the enormous challenge of caring for this premature baby.

Albert rushed to Cologne from Berlin, overjoyed with the happiness. They decided to call their baby girl Nina, meaning 'God was gracious, God has shown favor' in Hebrew.

"Nina is full of grace. Nina is my sweetie." The moment Alona looked at her baby she fell in love with her instantly. Holding the tiny infant, she couldn't help but burst into happy tears. Alona was full of joy.

"I wish Nina will have a life with lots of happiness," Albert hugged his daughter with a hopeful smile.

Grandma stared at her little granddaughter's beautiful face. She said Nina had gorgeous light blue eyes, just like her mother's.

Nina's grandmother was so happy for her granddaughter, although she required a lot of care because she was so tiny and so fragile. All the family did their best to support the new parents with their care, regardless there were many difficulties. Nina's aunt, Esther, loved her the most. She often came to hold and feed baby Nina. In addition, it was Aunt Esther who baked the special honey cake for Nina's birth, which was a Jewish tradition. The sweet-to-celebrating cake was supposed to ensure a sweet life for her.

Everybody in the family loved baby Nina. They couldn't hold her enough, even though they were apprehensive about the newborn at the beginning. So they put Nina in a lovely cradle, covered with a warm cotton blanket to keep her warm. Even though they had a difficult time in the first months, this beautiful girl brought unspeakable happiness to the couple and her family.

Feeding was the most significant concern at the beginning. Alona suffered tremendously when baby Nina had difficulty eating and needed a nasal tube. Alona's heart ached when she saw her baby struggling. Two months after, Nina was strong enough to feed without the nasal tube.

Alona was exhausted but proud of their success. She also appreciated Nina's natural life power since her baby girl seemed to become cooperative during the late stage of tube feeding. Although she was so tiny, Nina showed her natural toughness at that time already. Her cry grew louder and stronger with each passing day. Sometimes you could hear Nina's giggling, which thrilled her mother and father. Nina grew slowly under her parents' and grandparents' extensive care.

Nina showed everybody that she was a true survivor. She grew and thrived in a short time. Her jaundice disappeared, she gained weight, her cheeks plumped up like cherries, and her hair shone in the sun. After her parents' hard work, this baby girl quickly demonstrated her vitality.

From the beginning, the doctor thought it would be a challenge for Nina to survive because she was premature. But Nina showed signs of a potent life force and unique energy inside her body. Her health flourished despite all the difficulties. Every day she grew stronger. When Nina reached her one-year birthday, her weight was an astounding fifteen kilograms. With her parents and family's love and constant care, Nina proved that she had an extraordinary internal power to survive.

When Nina grew up to be an adorable two years old, Alona taught her to speak both German and Hebrew. Nina called her grandmother "Oma." Oma loved to rock Nina gently in her lap and sing a song about pigeons. It was the coziest time in Nina's life. Oma also made Nina a cloth doll named "Mini." Nina loved her doll "Mini," hugging her on her chest and taking her to bed with her.

Alona and her mother brought Nina to play in the Rheinpark along the Rhine River bank. Alona was pleased to see Nina running and laughing with her Oma on the green lawn of the park. Sitting by the riverbank, watching the Rhine River flowing smoothly, was very peaceful.

These were happy memories. Alona remembered that once, Oma hid "Mini" in a bush and let Nina look for her doll. Nina searched for her doll everywhere. "Mini, Mini!" Nina was exhilarated when she found her doll in the green bush. Alona thought that her mother might want to teach Nina to look for something meaningful at the beginning of her life. The three of them shared many hours of happiness near the Rhine River together. Alona always hoped her mother would continue to influence her daughter's life.

Alona and her mother held on to Nina's tiny hand. Then, they took Nina to Cologne Street for shopping. That was a warm and lovely moment. Nina enjoyed the tulips on the road, yellow, red, and pink. The beautiful flower petals were sparkling in the wind under the morning sunlight on Cologne Street.

When Alona brought Nina to Berlin, she was nearly three years old. Alona knew Nina's favorite thing was to sit at her father's store window and let the sunlight shine on her face and warm her skin. Nina loved to watch the pedestrians walking by her father's musical instrument store.

Nina sometimes stuck her head outside the store door, walking on tippy toes and taking in all the good smells in the street. She told Alona that she just wanted to smell the bakery's fragrance from a few doors away. What a pleasant aroma! Alona also loved to taste the freshly baked loaves. She often bought new bakery products for Nina and her husband. Nina was also fascinated by the continuous spinning of the white and red swirling pole from the barbershop on the other side of the street.

Albert's musical instrument store was near the famous Prussian Academy of the Arts of Berlin. Many students from the Academy and some teachers came to the store to buy musical instruments. Sometimes they just wandered around the store, trying out the piano, violin, or saxophone.

When Nina reached six years old, she was ready to go to school. Alona had made beautiful clothes for her. She wore a matching hat and coat, a skirt, cute socks, pretty leather shoes, and a unique school bag. Alona was happy to see how stunning her daughter looked. Nina was delighted to go to school every day.

Alona walked Nina to school every morning. They talked about all kinds of different things, sometimes joking around. Nina was curious about the world around her. Alona took advantage of the walks to teach her daughter, pointing out the exciting things or events on the way to school.

Alona enjoyed walking to school with her little daughter every morning. Sometimes they pretended to be the horse, running as fast as possible if they thought they would be late for school. But they never were. Nina enjoyed this playfulness as much as her mother. Nina could easily beat her mother in this race to school. Nina would watch her mother get out of her breath, and they both laughed with exhilaration.

Once on one of their excursions to Berlin downtown, Nina asked her mother, "Is this river also called the Rhine?"

"No, this river is called the Spree River," Alona replied. Mama told her the story about the Spree, the river on which the original city of Berlin was built. Then, Mama took her across the Spree to see the museums. The renowned Museum Island was in the center of the Spree. The most impressive museum on the island was the Bode Museum. They loved looking at the art in the museum just as much as they loved watching the river, with the birds flying over the rippling currents.

As Nina grew up, Alona and Albert worried about their daughter's future. Adolf Hitler, the new ruling Nazi Party leader, advocated the removal of Jews from German society. They were uncertain and afraid of what that would mean for their lives.

"Mama, why do they not allow us to go inside the ice cream parlor?" Nina asked her mother one day.

"Why do you ask that?"

"Because I saw the signs saying 'No Dogs, No Jews' on the ice cream store's window near my school."

"Don't worry. We could get ice cream some other place," Alona said.

"Mama, why do some girls roll their eyes at me?"

"Sweetie, you don't need to talk to them."

"I know all those awful things came from Hitler," Nina said to Alona.

Alona knew Nina was too young to understand what motivated the Nazi hatred and discrimination against the Jews. But on the other hand, Alona understood that Nina was smart enough to sense the animosity at school and in Berlin society. So, even though Nina couldn't quite understand the political situation, she could feel the tension, and Alona didn't know how to protect her from that.

Alona debated with her husband whether it was necessary to send her daughter abroad.

"My father was born in Germany. He fought for this country in the First World War. He is proud of Jewish contributions to Germany's achievements as a society. So why does the German government act like we are foreigners because we are Jews?" Alona expressed her frustration to Albert.

"The Nazi's ridiculous point of view is Jews have taken over German civilization. That means Jews not only contributed to the arts and science, but they have taken control, preventing Germans from participating and excelling in many enterprises," Albert explained to his wife about the current Nazis' theory and motivation to destroy Jews in Germany.

"Our contributions enriched German society. We haven't taken over anything. We haven't stolen anything. This is absolutely absurd. We are Germans too." Alona was furious.

"Hitler wants to use this theory to remove all the Jewish contributions to civilization in Germany," Albert said.

"I used to think of Germany as our home. I felt it was the land where we could live forever," Alona stated.

"Unfortunately, not anymore; Hitler and his Nazi party want us out of Germany," Albert said.

After many months of arguing and struggling to make a decision, they never decided to send Nina away because they didn't want their beautiful daughter to leave them.

***

Alona thought of all this as she watched her daughter sleeping soundly on Aunt Esther's bed. It was hard to believe Nina was already eight years old. She had inherited Alona's physical characteristics, but she had her father's personality. Nina had an enormous pair of bright, beautiful light blue eyes and a lovely mouth with very white teeth. When she smiled, two dimples on her pink cheeks made her look so sweet. Her hair was the color of chestnuts. Nina was a happy child, always smiling, always cheerful. She was a sensible and intelligent little girl.

Alona consistently questioned herself, "Should we keep our daughter with us, or should we send her away from Nazi Germany?" These two opposite ideas of abandoning or saving had deeply troubled Alona for a long time. The turmoil of the paradoxical situation caused Alona to suffer mentally and emotionally.

"How could I send Nina away?" Alona was confused and exhausted.

CHAPTER SIX

December 12, 1938
Berlin, Germany

Tap-Tap-Tap! Someone knocked on the door.
Alona was nervous as she opened the door. It was Allen, Albert's brother. He, fortunately, had escaped being arrested in the Kristallnacht one month ago.

"Any news of my brother," Allen asked.

"None at all," Alona shook her head.

"I am here for my niece." Allen came with an important message for Nina.

"What is it?" Alona asked.

"My friend found a British program called Kindertransport to help Jewish children in this country," Allen said.

"What is Kindertransport?"

"This is a program organised by the British government. It helps Jewish children go to England. They recognise it's not safe for them in Nazi Germany after the devastating events of last month. However, there is one important condition of the program. It is only for children. No parents allowed." Allen stated the details.

"That sounds very good. Thanks, Allen!" Alona shook Allen's hand.

"You need to make a decision for Nina as early as possible because the number of Jewish children for the Kindertransport program is limited," Allen urged Alona. He was anxious to get Nina's name on the Kindertransport list.

"Albert and I have discussed this issue for a long time. But, to be honest, I truly don't want Nina to leave. It is like a knife in my heart." Alona put her hand on her chest, and she tried to hold back her tears.

"Alona, I understand. But my brother said to me that Nina should go as soon as possible if there is any chance," Allen said.

"Yes, he is right. Albert once told me, 'Even when the Nazis destroyed the last piece of our properties, we still have to have a hope.' Nina is our hope," Alona knew her husband was right.

"After that horrible night last month, now the Nazis continue to humiliate us by requiring us to wear the yellow Star of David. In addition, the SS might still come to confiscate our properties," Allen said.

"Nina is so young; she doesn't understand antisemitism. So she was very anxious when the SS arrested her Jewish teachers."

"They are saying soon the Nazis will not allow Jewish children to go to public elementary schools anymore," Allen said.

"Allen, my husband is not here. Would you please help me make this tough decision?" Alona pleaded.

"Kindertransport is the best chance for Nina to leave this country. It can save the life of my beautiful niece." Allen offered all his support at this most challenging time.

Alona was grateful to Allen and made up her mind. "All right, Please make the connection through your friend immediately for Nina," She asked Allen to start the urgent escape plans to save her daughter.

After she had finalized all the arrangements for Nina to leave for London with Uncle Allen's friend, Alona told Nina the plan.

"Sweetie, come to Mama. I have something important to talk to you about," Alona stared at her daughter's face.

"What is it about, Mama?"

"Sweetie, Mama and Papa love you very much. Since the SS took Papa away and damaged our home and store, we decided to leave Germany. But it is very difficult. So, with your Uncle Allen's help, we want to send you to England first." Alona held Nina near on her lap.

"What about Papa," Nina asked.

"That is why I have to stay here, to wait for your Papa. Once he comes out of jail, we will come to London to be with you," Alona couldn't help giving her thoughtful daughter a tight hug and then kissing her forehead.

"You mean I have to go to another country by myself?" Nina became very tense.

"No. Not all alone. You need to go with Uncle Allen's friend first." Alona could feel her heart aching.

"No, I want to stay with you, Mama!" Nina reacted very fast. She grabbed her mother's sleeve.

"My Sweetie, listen to Mama. You are a brave girl. I know you are brave enough to do what I ask now." Alona tried her best to encourage her daughter, perhaps encourage herself as well. Still, she could feel her own voice trembling.

A distressed and anxious silence followed.

A somber and sorrowful violin melody drifted into the room from far away. It instantly triggered Nina's emotions.

"Mama, I miss my Papa," Nina started to cry and hugged Alona.

"Oh, sweetie, my baby," Alona cuddled Nina. Her tears fell uncontrollably and silently.

Mother and daughter cried and held onto each other for a long time.

"Do you remember your Papa always taught you to be brave?"

"Yes, Mama," Nina bit her lower lip hard and nodded her head slowly.

"Let us do your Papa's fist bump," Alona suggested. Albert used to hold his right fist to bump Nina's right fist. It was their mutual way of encouraging each other. Fist bump! This gave Nina emotional energy for future challenges.

"Okay, fist bump!" Nina raised her right fist to hit Mama's right fist, but it was a little too soft tonight.

Nina's departure day was approaching. One evening Alona, holding Nina's hand, walked along the Spree River. Again, the sky was dark red. The wind was chilly, and tiny snowflakes fell.

"When will you and Papa come for me?" Nina kept asking her mother the same challenging question.

"We are going to come as soon as we can. We are going to meet you in London. Be a good girl and listen to the people who take care of you," Alona looked into the distance when she answered Nina.

When they came back home, Alona kissed Nina's face many times, over and over. But, deep inside her heart, Alona was so worried and sad because she didn't know when they would meet again? Alona feared she and Nina may never be together again? But, at the same time, she also didn't want to show her sadness and worry. She didn't want Nina to be any more worried at this critical time.

Alona used her hands to touch Nina's face, her beautiful nose, and cute chubby cheeks. She wanted to remember Nina's face with her fingers. Alona's vision blurred as tears came, thinking Nina's departure might not be a temporary separation.

This could be goodbye forever.

It was close to the date. Nina would leave for London without saying goodbye to her father. Every time Alona thought about that, she would get more nervous.

On January 13, 1939, Alona's anxiety reached its zenith because it was the last evening Nina with her. Alona was desperate, helpless, and hopeless.

The following morning, it was time for Nina to leave at last. Alona's eyes were red because she had cried almost all night.

Nina and her mother got ready and left their home. They walked on the street hand in hand. Alona tried to look happy and pretended to smile. Nina still didn't fully understand the actual situation. She was only eight years old, after all.

Soon, Alona saw a gray car waiting on the side street, as they had arranged for Uncle Allen's friend to pick up Nina.

"It's time to go," Alona said. She crouched down, kneeling to hug Nina, kissing her little face.

"See you, Mama!" Nina's voice was low.

"We will come to you soon, be brave!" Alona felt this may be the last time she had a chance to hug her daughter. She held her daughter tight and didn't want to let her go. "I love you, Sweetie!"

"Mama, I love you too, and Papa," Nina said.

Then Uncle Allen's friend took Nina's hand, walking to the car. Nina waved her small hand to Mama. Alona tried to wave back to Nina. She tried to smile, but her face felt rigid. She gazed at Nina's little pigtail waving in the chilly wind. She tried to hold her tears back.

Nina turned and waved a hand to her Mama again, then crawled up into the car.

The moment the engine started and the car began to move, Nina panicked. "Please wait," Nina shouted.

"Stop," Allen's friend told the driver. The little girl might want to say more to her mother. He understood that these could be the last words or the last hug for her.

Alona suddenly found Nina jumping out of the car. Nina was running to her and calling out in a loud voice, "Mama, Mama!" Nina held out both her arms, running toward Alona.

"My Sweetie," Alona opened her arms wide to Nina. She felt her heart was broken and bleeding.

"Mama, please promise to come for me soon," Nina pleaded. She hugged Alona and held her tight.

"Yes, Sweetie, my baby," Alona could not speak a complete sentence because her throat was choked with tears.

Allen's friend gave Alona a look that said it was urgent that they had to leave now. Still holding Nina, she told her, "We will come for you for sure." She knew that was the only way to let her daughter go right now. If Nina asked her one more time, Alona was afraid she might change her mind and not let Nina go at all.

Alona handed over Nina's little hand to Allen's friend again. It took all her willpower to let Nina go.

Alona waved her hand to Nina, "Auf wiedersehen! Auf wieder-sehen!" (In German: Goodbye)

"Auf wiedersehen! Auf wiedersehen!" Nina waved her right hand to her mother while Allen's friend held her left hand. He led Nina to the waiting car.

Alona stood there, paralyzed. Then, as she watched her daughter climbing into the car with unwilling steps, Alona finally realized she loved her daughter more than her own life.

She called again, "Auf wiedersehen! Auf wiedersehen!"

Alona heard her own voice breaking. She felt her heartbreaking. Her lips quivered, and then her tears burst from her bleeding heart. She whimpered uncontrolledly.

Alona saw Nina's little face in the car's rear window, waving both hands. Then Nina started to punch the car window with her small fists. Alona could hear her daughter call her from inside the car, "Mama! Mama, Mama!"

Allen's friend did not let the driver stop the car this time.

Alona hobbled toward the car. She could not follow it because she was crying and shaking so much. She didn't want Nina to go away. She wished her husband was here.

Alona stared at the car. It moved slowly and then picked up its speed. She could hardly see it through her tears. The car grew smaller and smaller. Alona tried to chase the car, to catch the car, and to retrieve her daughter.

"Nina! Sweetie! Nina!" Alona called her daughter's name again and again. Her crying changed from a sad whimper into a devastating sob.

Suddenly, Alona tripped over something, and she fell down hard. Blood oozed from her palm. "My baby, my poor baby," Alona knelt down on the ground and sobbed harder. She had never felt such over-whelming sorrow before. She bit into the sleeve of her coat, trying to control her sadness.

Alona was weeping so convulsively that she did not realize her face had been smeared with the blood from her injured palm. Her face was streaked with blood and tears, and her hair was a mess from the wind. She couldn't see the gray car anymore. The vehicle had already turned the corner.

It started to rain, a light drizzle. The wind picked up. It was cold. Gray clouds darkened the sky. The rain became heavier, and the wind became colder.

After Nina left for London, Alona was very lonely. Her sorrow was intense. She missed her daughter and her husband terribly. Alona turned to Nina's picture to console herself. But she could not look at the image of her beautiful, smiling daughter for long. She turned away, looking absently out the window, even though the sound of the rain on the windowpane could not draw her attention. Raindrops hit the windowpane like bullets pounding on her fragile heart, making her tears fall.

Nina had been gone only for a week, and Alona had significantly aged. As she walked along the Berlin streets, with light snow falling, the air frosty, she looked like an old lady, shoulders slumped, head down, trodding as if she carried the weight of the world on her back.

Alona covered her head in a wool scarf to keep warm. She put her hands deep inside her pockets to avoid the chilly wind. Her breath was like white smoke in the frigid air. The street was empty except for a lonely man on a bicycle hurrying in the other direction. Everything was frozen. All the windows were closed tight against the cold. Lots of windows were broken. Alona walked with quick steps, feeling abandoned in the eerie silence of Berlin street.

Is my daughter doing well in London? How does she get along with the foster parents? Is there a lot of rain in London? Does Nina miss her Papa and me? What is the situation for Albert in the concentration camp? All the questions Alona was preoccupied with had no answers.

.

PART II

THE THAMES RIVER

CHAPTER SEVEN

December 1938
London, U.K.

Nina was very nervous when she got on the train to London. She could feel her heart jittering.

Nina saw a girl smiling at her only after the train started to move. She sat beside her on the bench in the train carriage. The girl had black hair, holding a well-dressed doll. Nina smiled back at the girl, but both kept silent. Nina was so overwhelmed about leaving for London that she didn't notice her own dresses were brand new. She knew Mama had made special preparations for her going abroad. Later, she discovered her "Mini" doll in her small back bag. Nina felt grateful for her mother's thoughtfulness but she missed her Mama even more.

On the train to London, there were many children of varying ages. Nina noticed a boy who looked similar to her age playing the violin. A group of children stood around him to listen to his marvelous playing.

The tune the boy played was so familiar to Nina. She remembered her father had played the same music on his cello before. It was called

"Song, my mother taught me." Nina wondered why this song sounded so sad, and then she thought of her Mama.

"Oh, Mama!" she sighed.

The melancholy rhythm played in her mind all the way to London, making her miss her father and mother more, and making her want to cry again.

Before Nina left Germany, her Mama gave her a small family photo in which Nina was smiling with her parents, standing beside the Rhine River. Every time Nina missed her mother or father, she'd take the picture and stare at it for a long time.

The train took Nina to the center of London, Liverpool Street Station. The train arrived in the evening. Nina looked outside but could see very little. It was drizzling miserably. Although Nina reached her destination unscathed, she felt overwhelming sadness. It felt like the rainy streets of London commiserate with her.

When she got off the train, Nina was exhausted and anxious at the same time. She missed her parents and wondered who would take care of her now. The air of Liverpool Street Station was cold and damp. However, the energy of so many children and adults looking for each other made the atmosphere somewhat warmer.

Nina was relieved to finally meet her foster father and mother, John and Mary, at the Liverpool train station. John Dowsett was a journalist, and his wife was a teacher. They participated in the Kindertransport Program after the BBC broadcasted the details of Kristallnacht in Germany and Austria.

Because the evening light was dim and her own nervousness, Nina was not able to see clearly what her foster parents looked like. Furthermore, Nina had difficulty communicating with them because her English was limited. After that, Nina was comforted when she felt a nice warm hand holding hers and taking her home to sleep.

The next morning, Nina saw from her bedroom window that London lay under a heavy fog. A gray blanket of mist rose like gas, surrounding fences and billowing into an amorphous cloud. The milky fog surrounded trees, buildings, and roadways. Everything had

THE GIRL FROM SHANGHAI GHETTO - 51

been changed from a recognizable substance into a vague shape. With bicyclists moving through the gloom, cars, trucks, buses, and taxis were inching along the damp street.

Nina had read about the London fog, but she had never seen anything like this. The fog of London made Nina miss her parents in Berlin even more.

"Rap, Rap," Two knocks on the door brought Nina back to reality. She opened the door. Mary stood outside with a bright smile. She was a medium-sized woman with a round face. Her voice sounded gentle, "Good morning!"

"Guten morgen," Nina answered in her German shyly. "I cannot speak English," Nina explained. Mama taught her this sentence before she left Berlin. Nina wished she could speak English instead of German and Hebrew.

"Don't worry, Nina. You will learn English quickly here," Mary said, "Come, let us have breakfast."

"Good morning, Nina," Nina met her foster father, John, at the breakfast table. Nina remembered he didn't talk much, driving the car home from Liverpool Station last night. John was a tall gentleman like Nina's father. He had a cheerful face and low-pitch voice and a friendly smile. He directed Nina to sit at the table.

"Good morgen," Nina echoed back to John with half English and half German.

"You are brilliant to say that," Mary praised Nina.

Nina knew she had to learn English because people didn't understand German here. Moreover, Nina knew it was the only way to learn to live with two strangers who only spoke English. Mary and John were very friendly and patient, but Nina still was nervous and timid. Everything was new and strange for her in those early days in London.

"What do you call your mother in Berlin?" Mary asked Nina.

"Eh?" Nina did not quite understand the question because of the language difference.

"You call your mother 'Mama?" John tried to explain.

"Yes," Nina nodded to confirm.

"You call your father 'Papa'?"

"Yes," Nina nodded again.

"That is good. Do you want to call him Daddy," Mary pointed to John.

"Eh?" Nina was puzzled.

"Do you want to call me Mommy?" Mary pointed her index finger toward herself and smiled at Nina.

"Yes. Mommy," Nina flushed to agree. She thought about her Mama telling her, "Be very nice to the people who care for you."

"Daddy," Nina nodded at John.

"Ah," John was pleased.

Most nights, Mary read a simple English book before bedtime to help Nina improve her English. John was a gentle soul, and he wanted to reassure Nina she was safe and welcome to be with them. So he spent time on the weekends with her, telling her short stories.

John organized for Nina to go to a local school in London. Nina was happy to go to school again. But it turned out to be more difficult than she had imagined. On the second day at the school, the trouble began.

"You are an enemy German," a freckle-faced girl in her class bullied Nina once she found out Nina could only speak German. Another pupil followed and cursed Nina too. The bullying of these kids reminded Nina of the Hitler Youth, who insulted Jewish children in Berlin.

Nina remembered coming home from school one afternoon and seeing four Hitler Youth boys hanging around on the street. They were standing there saluting each other and yelling, "Herr Hitler!" They grabbed a young Jewish man who passed by and brutally beat him. They cursed with abusive language while hitting the man. Nina did not understand why they were beating the man. The only thing she could do was take another route home to avoid encountering those boys.

Mary was very protective of Nina. She went to the school and talked about the matter with the teacher. After that, these students stopped bullying Nina.

During that time, London was under the threat of potential war with Germany. As a result, there was a shortage of household supplies.

But gratefully, there was not the rampant antisemitism in London as there was in Berlin.

Nina missed her Mama and Papa terribly. But she felt embarrassed to ask her Daddy or Mommy too many questions about her own parents. She didn't want them to feel she was not appreciative of their attention and care. Furthermore, her English was not fluent enough to communicate well.

John and Mary liked to treat their German fraulein. They brought different kinds of fruits and foods for her to choose from. They kept teaching her English by talking to her a lot. As a result, Nina learned basic English and understood some simple conversations in only two months.

Nina was delighted one day when Mary and John, each taking one of her little hands, walked along the paths in Hyde Park. Nina was always a bit nervous in a new environment, but as her English improved, she gained more confidence.

Although London's temperature in the early spring was still not warm, the sky was blue and beautiful, and the clouds were white and fluffy. The leaves were starting to bud. The Thames River drifted at a slow pace. The famous Big Ben stood solid by the Thames in the gentle breeze.

John and Mary were happy to have Nina with them and treated her like their own daughter. On the trail in the park, Nina met two squirrels eating on the green grass, and she chased them just for fun.

The following day a squirrel came to their backyard, looking for food. Nina was fascinated by this little breathing animal with its own agenda. She thought it was very smart but wondered where its mother was and why it had to find food by itself. Nina threw a peanut to the squirrel, and it took the nut and jumped away. She loved its shiny fur and bushy tail.

John and Mary were very affectionate to Nina. They liked to take her around to see all the interesting places in London. They took her to Piccadilly Circus. She was impressed by how busy it was. They also went to a real circus. It was a lot of fun for Nina, but she still thought about her parents and wondered how long it would take before they would come to London to meet her.

Mary and John lived on Lavender Hill Road, near Clapham Junction Station. Their home was not far from Battersea Park, one of London's parks along the Thames River. Mommy often brought Nina to Battersea Park to play or just walk around. Sometimes they stood along the riverbank to watch the river flow toward London Bridge. Nina loved to play in Battersea Park. The most fascinating thing for Nina was Daddy taking her to visit the London Tower and show her Big Ben, the famous colossal clock. John was very good to Nina. He also brought toys for her to play with, after he was back from work.

Nina worried about why her parents still hadn't come to get her. It was worse at night before falling asleep. Nina feared her parents might never come because it took so long for them to come. Then, one night, there was heavy rain outside. After several months of waiting, Nina started to feel abandoned. She knew her Mama loved her dearly, so she felt guilty for this thought.

Nina remembered following her Mama to escape along the rooftop of Berlin. She understood that they were not safe in Nazi Germany because her family was Jewish. That was why she had to come to London. She thought about those horrible Nazis who took her Papa away on that crazy night. Where was he now? Was he safe? Had the Nazi arrested her Mama too? When Nina thought about her Papa and Mama, she hid under her quilt, sobbing until she fell asleep.

John and Mary noticed when Nina looked sad and worried from time to time. So to distract her, they took her to Baker Street to see the Tussaud Wax Figure Exhibition.

"Let us keep our fingers crossed," John said.

"What does that mean?" Nina asked.

"Hope for the best," Daddy smiled at Nina.

Nina learned English well and fast at school and from her Daddy and Mommy. She gradually settled down in London, and things became more familiar to her, although she never stopped missing her parents.

Eventually, Nina showed her true personality. She was an and funny little girl. She was always saying something hil innocent, and she was very inquisitive, always asking questions.

John and Mary both loved music. One night after dinner, Nina found her Daddy and Mommy playing together. John played the piano, and Mary played the flute, making a beautiful musical duet.

Nina recognized the melody as "Fur Elise" by German composer and pianist Ludwig van Beethoven. Again, Daddy and Mommy coordinated very well. Nina sat quietly, feasting her eyes on them, listening to them, and enjoying the music. Nina appreciated this flute and piano duet very much.

"Do you want to try the piano?" John asked Nina.

"Yes," Nina nodded. She went over to the piano, hesitating to play.

"One, two, three," John encouraged Nina to start.

Nina focused on "Fur Elise" notes on the music sheet and tried her best to play Beethoven's famous piece.

"Wow, fantastic playing," they clapped.

"Let us play together?" Mary suggested.

"Yes," Nina nodded.

Nina played the piano, and Mary played the flute. They played beautifully together for the first time. Mary hugged Nina to congratulate her on doing so well. It was through music that the tentative connection between the three of them became firm. In this loving environment, Nina became cheerful again.

"Do you like pigeons?" John asked Nina after seeing her watching the pigeons for a long time in Battersea Park.

"Yes. I love pigeons very much," Nina said.

"Let me bring you to a place where you can see a lot of pigeons."

"Where is it?"

"It is at Trafalgar Square, in the center of London."

That Sunday morning, they got up early and went to the tube station hand in hand. They transferred from Victoria Station to Piccadilly Circus Station. Nina was impressed by Victoria Station. It was vast and gorgeous.

"Daddy, is this a bus?" Nina pointed with her tiny index finger. She wondered if it really was a bus. It had two stories. She had never seen anything like it before.

"Yes, it is a bus. It's called a double-decker bus," John explained.

It took some time before they arrived at Trafalgar Square. Although Londoners were worried about the potential of war in Europe, many people were still in Trafalgar Square sightseeing. They wanted to feed the birds and enjoy their lives while they could despite the threat of war.

The magnificent sound of the bells ringing from the nearby enormous church astonished Nina. She knew that many people still went to church, praying for blessings in their lives. Nina prayed for her parents in Germany. She watched the pigeons flying over the church up into the blue sky.

Nina looked at a young girl with her boyfriend feeding the birds. They looked very happy. They would laugh and hug and kiss each other. Watching their happiness influenced Nina's mood. She felt happy too. Nina took some food from John's hand and fed the pigeons. After a while, a small group of white pigeons landed on the sidewalk. Nina smiled at John and stepped up closer to the birds. She was very curious. They let her get quite close. Another little girl started chasing one of the white birds. Everyone laughed.

The church's bell rang again, resonating around the city center of London. The pigeons responded by suddenly flying up into the blue sky into white clouds. What a beautiful and peaceful scene!

Nina had a wonderful time at Trafalgar Square. She nodded at her Daddy and Mommy with an appreciative smile.

On the way back home, John taught Nina about the different kinds of birds, "Wild rock doves are pale gray with two black bars on each wing."

"What about the white pigeons?" Nina asked curiously.

"Londoners called white pigeons, doves," John told Nina.

After Nina observed the pigeons at Trafalgar Square, she loved those cute birds even more. Nina liked to play with and make friends with the birds near their home. Sometimes, she fed the pigeons some food and even talked to them. They became friends with this lovely little girl. She confided her secret wishes to them, asking them if they would come true. Everything about them interested her. Nina paid close attention to them. She noticed what time they were gone and when they returned and how they played.

Nina noticed one of the white pigeons sitting in a nest for three days without moving. Soon after, she discovered three pigeon eggs lying in the nest.

Nina was excited when the baby pigeons hatched a few weeks later. The chicks were so tiny with a soft, feathery down. The baby pigeons chirped continuously, demanding food from their parents.

When she watched the baby pigeons being cared for by their parents, Nina thought about her own mother and grandma. Because she had been so small and frail, they had to take care of her and feed her just like the pigeons were doing now. Nina was grateful and appreciated John and Mary for their lovely care too.

One night, Nina overheard her Daddy and Mommy talking about Germany in the kitchen. By nature, she listened attentively.

"Mr. Churchill told the British Parliament to prepare for the possibility of war. The German air force could attack London," John said.

"How can we protect our Nina?" Mary asked.

"The British government plans to evacuate a few million children and women from urban areas, including London if the Nazi air force bombards us," John said.

"Evacuation?" Mary was surprised.

"That means we may have to move and to avoid the devastation of a bombing raid on London," John answered.

"Where can we go?" Mary asked and thought about it. "Oxford may be a possible choice. Plus, my brother is there." Mary's older brother was a professor of physics at the University of Oxford.

"Sure. I certainly agree with you. Oxford is a beautiful and peaceful city. The town is only 100 kilometers away from London."

Nina did not understand why Germany would attack England. Her only hope was to be reunited with her parents. Did this war with

Germany mean she could not be with her parents again? She never thought she would be separated from her parents for such a long time. Because of the love of Daddy and Mommy, Nina had made a relatively smooth adjustment to her new life in London. However, she still missed her Papa and Mama terribly.

After living in London for two months, Nina developed a skin rash, predominantly on her legs. It was itchy every day, worse at night. Her little hands would be bloody, with bleeding scratches on her legs.

Mary worried when she found blood on Nina's sheets. "Nina, how is your leg?" she asked.

"Sorry Mommy. I am so itchy at night," Nina said.

Mary and John were worried about her skin condition. They had gone to three clinics to see doctors. Nina was diagnosed with severe eczema. Some people suggested it might be because she was not used to the humidity in London. The dermatologists gave her various topical ointments and creams, but without noticeable improvement after applying them for weeks.

One morning, Mary talked about Nina's skin disease with her neighbor, Lisa. She was a Malaysian lady. Lisa suggested that Mary should try herbal medicine if the hormonal cream was not working. She told Mary to bring Nina to Chinatown, in the Soho area in central London. They would find an herbalist there. Lisa said her relative had received herbal treatment for his problematic skin condition and got excellent results.

Mommy and Daddy decided to take Nina to Soho Chinatown. When the underground tube train passed by Charing Cross Station, Nina remembered her visit to Trafalgar Square, where people loved to feed the pigeons. At Leicester Square Station, they got off the train and walked into Soho.

Nina found Soho was a fantastic area. So many fascinating shops, supermarkets, souvenir stores, and restaurants were on the narrow streets. The smell from the bakery reminded Nina of Berlin and that fragrant bakery close to her Papa's store.

After walking through crowded streets, they found the herbalist. A female herbal doctor checked Nina's legs and her tongue.

"Although it is a skin problem, the actual reason is internal toxin accumulation, mainly from pathological dampness," the doctor said.

"What is pathological dampness?" John was puzzled. "What does that mean?"

"This little girl has too much toxic dampness in her body," the doctor replied, "The dampness is the root of her skin problem. The herbs will get rid of that toxic dampness, and then eczema will clear up."

"Oh!" John was still not convinced, but he was willing to try. So they took the herbal formula the doctor prescribed for Nina.

Although Nina was only nine years old, she was already a very sensible girl. She knew the bitter-tasting herbal tea could be helpful. So she always finished it to the last drop without any complaints.

After Nina used the teas for only two weeks, her skin was dramatically better. She no longer had itching at night, and there were no new skin rashes. After four weeks of herbal treatment, Nina's eczema completely disappeared.

John was convinced
of the benefit of the herbal remedy. Mary was very pleased with the outcome.

She knocked on Lisa's door, "Thank you very much for your recommendation!"

"How is your daughter's condition?" Lisa asked.

"She is completely healed by the herbs. We are grateful for your suggestion," Mary said.

Meanwhile, as Nina got the treatment for her illness in London, her Mama, Alona, in Berlin, tried her best to obtain exit visas, rescue her Papa, and get out of Germany.

CHAPTER EIGHT

April 1939
Berlin, Germany

On the afternoon of April 19, 1939, Alona started out to visit her sister, Esther. On the way, she planned to look at their store, which had been ruined last November.

Alona was surprised to see so many people crowded on the street. The red and black Nazi flag was everywhere. Loudspeakers were announcing someone's birthday. Alona learned from the talk among the crowd that the next day was Adolf Hitler's fiftieth birthday. The Nazi government was formally celebrating it as a national holiday. Someone told Alona that Hitler would ride in the leading car of a motorcade of fifty white limousines on the boulevard for his birthday celebration. Alona was disgusted with this idea of a national holiday. She abhorred Hitler, having experienced firsthand his antisemitic madness.

The Nazi swastika was prominent. It was on flags, even on balloons. Alona was angry about the Nazi appropriation of an ancient symbol. Albert told her the historical fact that Adolf Hitler had twisted the swastika 45 degrees to change it from a benign symbol of Asian culture into a symbol of terror and evil.

Regrettably, the music from the great musician, Sebastian Bach, was used to celebrate the Nazi dictator's birthday. It was ridiculous that Bach's music, which was lauded for its spirituality, would be used by this cruel leader. Alona was broken-hearted by the travesty.

Although many people ran towards the Brandenburg Gate to view the parade, Alona went in the opposite direction. She walked as quickly as possible to avoid contact with the Nazi's chaos on Berlin streets.

All of a sudden, over her head, the sky roared. Alona saw many planes flying low and fast. The Nazi air forces, the so-called Luftwaffe, were showing off their military power. One of the reasons for Hitler's birthday celebrations was to make a massive demonstration to the world of Nazi Germany's military capabilities. The Nazis' intention was to warn the western countries, like the UK, France, and the United States, that they were something to fear.

As the airplanes flew through the Berlin sky, Alona could easily see that twisted swastika on the planes' tails, the symbol she loathed. She hurried to the other side of the city, avoiding all the crowds which sickened her because they were part of the craziness Hitler had brought to Germany. But unfortunately, they didn't see the danger to them at all.

The roar of the planes and the noise of the loudspeakers gave Alona a headache. She tried to hurry but felt dizzy and lightheaded. She felt weak and frightened.

Alona tried the smaller streets to avoid people. She wanted to go to her sister Esther's home to explore whether it was possible to get a visa to leave Germany. Alona needed to get her husband out of Germany, away from the humiliation they faced under the Nazi government. Alona was anxious to get to her sister's home. It was her only hope of finding a way to save Albert and protect her family. Alona's future was so unknown she could not imagine what it would be like.

Alona decided her only hope was to get an exit visa out of Germany. Even though they had been born in Germany, lived their whole lives here, and thought of them as German, it was no longer safe for them.

They had to leave. The Nazis had already destroyed their business and their home. Alona didn't care where their family would go. She just knew they had to get out of Germany fast. Although she was anxious and depressed, it became her responsibility to make every effort to leave the country as soon as possible. When Alona found out her sister was not at home, she felt very lonely. She was missing her husband and her daughter terribly.

Alona spent most of her day trekking from one foreign consulate to the next, trying to secure exit visas for her family. She tried the United States, Australia, Britain, and France, all of which refused to take more Jewish immigrants. Finally, someone told her that thirty-seven European countries had recently signed an Agreement to prevent more Jews from entering their countries. They said that Germany's 500,000 Jews far exceeded any country's visa quotas. It seemed no government was willing to increase quotas to accept more Jewish people as immigrants even when it was becoming clearer every day that they were in danger in Germany.

Alona was informed by the SS that no one could leave the concentration camp unless they had an exit visa. Jews must have proof that they would leave Germany upon release. The Nazis just wanted to push all the Jews out of Germany at the early stage of their crackdown on Jews. The Nazi government still allowed a few Jews to leave the concentration camp in early 1939 with a precondition of an exit visa.

Alona had hunted for the elusive exit visas for more than a month without any results. She was exhausted and almost lost her hope.

Later, Esther suggested Alona go to visit her mother for advice. So Alona traveled back to Cologne from Berlin. When she passed over the Hohenzollern Bridge in her home city, she found the ripples on the Rhine River looked like dark red blood in the sunset, making her feel more unsettled and afraid.

"Mama," Alona hugged her mother when she entered the door.

"Where is Nina?" Alona's mother cared very much for her granddaughter.

Alona cried as she told her mother what happened to Albert in Berlin and that Nina was sent to London.

"Oh, my poor Nina," Grandma could not hold back her tears.

While in Cologne, Alona met her cousin, Evelyn. Alona told Evelyn of her desperate search for exit visas to escape from Germany. Evelyn told her about Dr. Feng Shan Ho, the consul general in the Chinese embassy in Vienna, Austria. Alona was very excited when she heard his story. It meant there was a possibility of getting an exit visa from the Chinese embassy in Vienna.

Evelyn told an anecdote about one Jewish gentleman. He failed to get any exit visa from different consulates of ten countries. Finally, he obtained visas for his entire family from Dr. Ho, the Chinese consul. The news that Dr. Ho was issuing "Shanghai Visas" created a buzz among Vienna's Jewish community. These Shanghai visas were like manna from heaven for the desperate Jews needing to escape the Nazis.

Vienna is the capital city of Austria. It was Evelyn's hometown. Alona beseeched Evelyn to accompany her to Vienna to seek the extraordinarily attractive Shanghai visas. But Evelyn could not go with her because her husband was jailed in the Dachau concentration camp after Kristallnacht. And she still had two young children to take care of in Cologne. But Evelyn offered alternative help. She wrote a letter to her cousin, Ilsa, asking her to help Alona when she arrives in Vienna.

Alona rushed to Vienna and found Evelyn's cousin. Ilsa had kind-looking eyes, dressed in a gray trench coat and a dark fedora. She held Alona's hand and asked about Evelyn's situation. She understood they all suffered from Nazi cruelty. Then Ilsa told her more stories about Dr. Feng Shan Ho.

"While other countries refuse to issue visas in fear of aggravating the Nazi government, Dr. Ho provides support to our people," Ilsa said.

"Dr. Ho is our hero," Alona said.

"They said his boss ordered Dr. Ho to stop issuing visas. But Dr. Ho continued to sign many visas for Jewish people in direct defiance of his superior's order," Ilsa continued.

"What a personality!" Alona expressed her admiration.

"The visas Dr. Ho gave out were unique. They were only for Shang-hai, an open port city with no immigration controls because Shanghai had been occupied by the Japanese army. In fact, the Shanghai port did not need any kind of document to enter it at this time. So the city of Shanghai earned its own reputation as a safe haven," Ilsa said.

"Why did Dr. Ho issue visas to a place that doesn't require one in the first place?" Alona asked with a puzzle.

"Here was where Dr. Ho's sophistication shines through. Although Jews did not need a visa to get into Shanghai, they definitely needed a visa to get out of their own country. Thus, the holders of Ho's visas were able to escape from Nazi's control," Ilsa said.

"That's an excellent idea. Thanks for Dr. Ho!"

The next morning, Ilsa accompanied Alona to the Chinese Consu-late in Vienna. There were already a lot of Jewish people in front of the consulate. They were all waiting in line for Dr. Feng Shan Ho and his precious Shanghai Visa. Alona and Ilsa joined the queue with happy anticipation.

All of a sudden, four black-uniformed Nazi SS men rushed into the consulate. Alona and the others sensed something very wrong. Shortly, one SS man came out of the building. He announced, "The Nazi government has confiscated this Chinese Consulate because this building is owned by a Jew."

Everybody waiting outside the Consulate was shocked.

"Everyone must leave now!" The SS waved his hand to the Jewish people.

Alona was so frustrated she didn't know what to do. She lost her last hope for an exit visa. She felt desperate.

The day before she planned to leave Vienna, Alona wanted to say goodbye to Ilsa. But first, she walked by the Chinese Consulate. It was where her last hope land on. She wanted to say farewell to Dr. Ho, who had given her the last hope even though it had been crushed.

To her tremendous surprise, a small group of people stood in front of a tiny house next to the original Chinese Consulate. She hurried up to it.

"What are you waiting for?" Alona asked one lady.

"We are waiting for Dr. Ho to get the Shanghai visa."

The answer surprised Alona. She immediately joined the queue with unspeakable excitement.

A young, thin-faced gentleman looking only seventeen or eighteen years old, in a gray coat, was in front of Alona. He gave her an innocent smile, and she smiled back at him.

"I brought the passports of my entire family to get the Shanghai visas," the young man told Alona with a secretive voice. He seemed very proud of himself.

"Really, could they issue so many visas at a single time?" Alona asked, disbelieving the possibility of getting them.

"Yes. You know I had been to fifteen foreign consulates in this city for the exit visas, and they turned me down time after time," the young man said.

"Me too," Alona agreed with him, but she did not reveal she was talking about Berlin's foreign embassies.

"I came to this Chinese Consulate yesterday. Someone told me they used to work over there," He pointed out the nearby building, "They said the Chinese Consulate had been closed by the SS men a few days ago," the young man continued.

"I know about it." Alona actually experienced it.

"Dr. Ho opened a new office in a nearby building by himself. He paid for the rent out of his own pocket when his Chinese boss in Berlin cut off the official money. Dr. Ho has kept issuing visas and continues to rescue us," the young man whispered.

Alona nodded to the young man and told him what exactly happened at the Chinese Consulate here a few days ago.

The young man looked around with alert eyes and continued in a low voice, "I came to this Consulate yesterday. The reception was friendly. The Consul General, Dr. Feng Shan Ho, had an amiable smile for me. He said I could come back today and bring as many passports as I want. He promises me he will stamp them all."

"That was why so many people talk about Dr. Ho's Shanghai visas," Alona said with excitement.

"To be honest, I don't even know where Shanghai is. Is it far?" the young man asked.

"Yes, Shanghai is very far from here. I guess it is more than 8000 kilometers away," Alona assented. In fact, China was a strange and distant land to her as well.

"I guess that is why I never thought to come to this consulate to try for a visa until my aunt mentioned it to me yesterday."

"Have all the Jewish men from here been sent to the concentration camp?" Alona asked nervously.

"All our men have been jailed in the Dachau concentration camp. After the Anschluss of our country by Hitler on March 13, we have all suffered a lot. I am only a seventeen-year-old kid," the young man said,

"Oh," Alona's face flushed with anger. She immediately thought about her husband, Albert, who was still in a concentration camp near Berlin. Alona went to the camp many times. The Nazi officer there always said they could only release a person who had proof of permission to leave the country. Thus, obtaining an exit visa was urgent and vital. It was the only way to rescue her husband from the concentration camp and save her family from Hitler's destruction.

"I brought eighteen passports for my whole family, including my parents, aunts, uncles, and cousins." The young man looked around, and then he opened his bag and showed her all the passports inside.

Alona was amazed and excited. She immediately thought about her mother, brother, cousin, and Evelyn's family. Perhaps she should have brought their passports with her to Vienna. But she didn't know this could be a possibility. Her excitement was tinged with regret.

As Alona watched the young man going into the Chinese Consulate, she felt some anxiety for him and maybe for herself as well. Would this young man get his visa from Dr. Ho? Finally, after only a brief time, the young man came out of the Consulate. Alona realized right away he had succeeded. His step was light and quick, and his expression was glowing. He gave a quick smile and nodded to Alona, and hurried away. Alona understood completely. This was not the place to linger, even to celebrate such splendid news.

Then it was Alona's turn to go inside. The room where Dr. Ho waited was spotless. He sat behind a simple table. He was a gentleman of medium build, about forty years old, with kind eyes and a gentle voice. He smiled at Alona.

"Good morning, Madam," Dr. Ho said, "Please gives your passports to me. Let me stamp the visas for you." He spoke fluent German.

Immediately Alona handed the three passports to Dr. Ho.

"Shanghai will welcome you and your family," Dr. Ho said while he stamped the passports. He didn't ask Alona any questions.

"Thank you very much, Dr. Ho! You have saved my family," Alona expressed her sincere gratitude.

"I hope all the best for your family!" Dr. Ho handed over the passports with the visas. That was all. It seemed so easy. Alona could hardly believe she had the precious exit visas for her family. She thanked Dr. Ho again before she left.

Alona was very emotional. After all her struggles, trying to rescue Albert from the concentration camp, and her worry she would never see Nina again, now she had the exit visas. She and her family could leave Germany. But her emotions were mixed. It broke her heart to say goodbye to others in her family who would stay behind, especially her mother.

"Mama, keep well!" Alona cried as she hugged her mother for the last time the next day. They held on tight to each other, not wanting to let go.

"Take care of yourself! Tell Nina I will always love her." Her mother was full of tears.

Alona also said goodbye to Ilsa and thanked her for her generous support before returning to Berlin.

Although the bank accounts of Jews were frozen, they could still withdraw some of their own money for household expenses. Alona bought ocean liner tickets for Shanghai. She booked on an Italian ocean liner, which would sail from the Port of Genoa in Italy to Shanghai in China.

Alona then rushed to the Sachsenhausen concentration camp and showed the SS guard her husband's exit visa and steamship ticket. According to what they had said previously, Alona expected they would release her husband right away.

"I have recorded the information you have given to me. I will report to my boss. Only the boss can decide if he will release your husband," the Nazi guard said carelessly.

"What?" Alona was so disappointed and angry. She expected Albert to be released that day if he had the necessary documents. Obviously, that was not going to happen, but she did not want to leave the camp office without her husband or at least a promise of his release.

"Go home and wait for the approval." The guard yelled at Alona when he saw she was not leaving.

Alona left the Sachsenhausen concentration camp reluctantly. She was frustrated, afraid, exhausted, and angry. She watched the dark clouds over the town of Oranienburg. There was nothing more she could do. She had to go home and wait for her husband to be set free.

Alona could not sleep. It was midnight, and she was wide awake. She got up and looked at the bright stars in the sky. The late quarter moon was insubstantial and pale. Suddenly the doorbell rang. Alona opened the door with trepidation.

There before her stood a ragged man in a black coat. His face was so covered with grim, it was hard to see his facial features. He hung his head low. Yet, as he lifted his face to her, Alona could recognise his hawk-like nose, high cheekbones, and receding chin.

It was Albert.

Alona's lips were quivered, and tears streamed down her cheeks. Her husband looked so haggard and feeble. Alona held both his hands and helped him step into the home.

"I had to send Nina to London," She buried her head in Albert's arms and cried.

"I missed you. I missed Nina more," Albert's voice was low.

"Oh, my baby," Alona and Albert wept together.

They hugged each other for a long time.

Albert was exhausted. He suffered a lot in the concentration camp from the Nazis' abuse. The SS guards forced him to do hard labor, and they often beat him for no reason. He was weak in mind and body after the mistreatment there.

Alona let Albert sit at the table and drink some warm water.

They talked for a long time. Alona told him about Kindertransport and how she had to send Nina away so their girl would be safe. All he could say was, "We will find a way to see our daughter again."

"But why are we going to Shanghai, China?" Albert asked. He was confused by this unusual plan to go to a place he knew nothing about and had never imagined.

"Shanghai was the only city willing to accept Jews in this dreadful time," Alona told Albert all about the visa application process, how challenging it was, how afraid she had been she would fail, and how they were saved by Dr. Ho with the Shanghai visas.

"You did quite right, my dear," Albert hugged his wife and said, "Although our family knows nothing about Shanghai, it is better than staying in Nazi Germany. We could even end up dying in a concentration camp."

"The only place opened to Jews is Shanghai," Alona spoke of the harsh reality for German Jews under Hitler.

"In my wildest dreams, I never imagined my family's fate would be to go to the Huangpu River in Shanghai," Albert sighed with emotion.

CHAPTER NINE

August 1939
Genoa, Italy

On August 28th of 1939, just before the Second World War erupted, Albert and Alona had everything organized to travel to Shanghai, China, via the port of Genoa, Italy. The most crucial thing Albert worried about was whether they could meet Nina there as planned. He had urged his brother Allen to contact his friend in London to arrange the meeting with Nina in Genoa.

Albert and Alona were going to travel to Genoa from Berlin by train. There, they would transfer to the ocean liner. Albert knew that they would absolutely need valid visas to cross the Germany-Italian border. The SS troopers were ruthless at those checkpoints. They particularly scrutinized the documents of Jews. Albert felt confident in the Shanghai visas given by Dr. Ho.

The hardest part about leaving Germany for Albert was saying good-bye to his mother. They were both heartbroken. He reasonably assumed that it may be the last time they would see each other. His mother was elderly with some health problems, and the situation in Germany was difficult for even young people because of extreme antisemitism. His mother was dignified when they parted, holding back her tears. She extended her right hand to them when they left her apartment. Albert never forgot the tragedy of leaving her, how she moaned softly but held herself erect. He also thought about Alona's mother in Cologne. He believed this was a "parting forever," and his heart ached with unbearable sadness.

Albert and Alona walked in silence through the Potsdamer Platz in Berlin. They saw lots of young, uniformed soldiers laughing and shouting. Those young boys probably would be sent to the battlefront soon. Albert felt a little sympathy for them because they would likely never return to Germany.

The train would go from Berlin to Genoa. Albert's brother Allen insisted on accompanying them to the Anhalter Bahnhof train station. Like the other Jewish passengers, they had only a small piece of luggage. The Nazi government did not allow them to take anything out of the country. The only permitted money was ten Rach Marks.

Albert and his wife arrived at the Anhalter Bahnhof train station in the center of Berlin. A few groups of Jewish people were on the platform awaiting the train already. But all of them lowered their heads and tried to attract as little attention as possible. So there was no recognition among them, not even a slight smile to the others.

"You take care of your family and send me a letter when you arrive in Shanghai. I particularly want to know about Nina. I miss my beautiful niece very much," Allen said.

"Yes, for sure. You and your wife need to make a decision quickly about leaving Germany too. Do not delay." Albert held his brother's hand. "Take care of our mother!"

Before they boarded the train, Albert hugged his brother tightly one more time, holding back his tears, hoping this would not be the last time they would be brothers together.

When the train started, Albert stood at the window watching his brother standing on the platform, waving goodbye. Albert's eyes were full of tears when the train left the Anhalter Bahnhof station.

Once the train was close to the German-Italian border, the SS troopers wearing their distinctive black uniform and boots came onto the train to check passports and visas. Albert cautioned Alona to keep silent until they finished the inspection. "Don't ask for anything, don't say a word, don't look up, and don't move."

The SS stopped the train precisely on the border of Germany and Italy. Then, they ordered all the travelers off the train. The SS yelled instructions to the Jewish travelers to go to one side of the station platform while letting other German travelers go back on the train.

The SS shouted orders at the Jews. First, they were ordered to line their suitcases up on the cement floor of the platform and open them. Then the SS brought two huge German shepherd dogs to sniff around the luggage.

Albert watched as the SS took two Jewish women out of the line. The SS said their visas were not valid. So they were not allowed to go through the border. Albert wondered if they would be sent back to Germany or perhaps to one of the concentration camps.

When the SS double-checked Alona's passport and visa, with the German shepherd sniffing close by, she was so worried and nervous she had to clutch both hands under her coat. Albert couldn't look at the SS's actions. Instead, he stared across the train tracks, trying to look disinterested. Puffs of white smoke from the locomotive spewed into the gray sky. He recalled the skill of his colleagues in the concentration camp. They remained expressionless, showing no emotion, no fear or anger, no matter what the Nazis were doing. Albert did just that at the checkpoint on the border. It was important not to draw attention to yourself. Most Jewish travelers knew that instinctively. So they kept a terrible silence in the face of the SS troopers' yelling and the occasional dog barking on the platform.

Albert and Alona did pass through the callous checkpoint safely. The moment they crossed the border into Italy, they felt massive relief. They were finally beyond the Nazis' vicious grasp. When they confirmed they had crossed the border, everyone cheered and clapped. However, their joy was diminished by the sadness of being forced to leave the country they had regarded as their home and by the anxiety of the unknowable future ahead of them. They feared for those they left behind, although they could never imagine what horrible fate awaited them during the war.

* * *

In the meantime, the nine-year-old Nina was traveling to Genoa from London by train. John accompanied her without Mary to save the train ticket expense. At the London train station, Nina cried intensively when she said goodbye to Mary. She was so young, yet this was the second time she had to leave someone she loved. But Nina was consoled because she was eager to be with her own parents again.

Before Nina left London, she especially wanted to go to Battersea Park to say goodbye to her pigeon friends. A group of white pigeons circled around near the Thames River, and Nina felt they were saying farewell to her. Seeing the doves triggered an even more tremendous sadness in Nina about leaving London.

Nina and John arrived in the port of Genoa a bit early. They waited to meet Nina's Papa and Mama here. Nina could sniff the stinky oil from the ships floating in the port air. The port was very busy with people running around, full of noise. They were loading and unloading heavy cargo from the ships. The water in the harbor was dirty brown. There was a castle-like building near the water edge, and the image of the mountain was blurred in the far distance. The seagulls were flying over the water in the harbor and singing a melancholy song.

Nina had always feared deep in her heart that she would never see her parents ever again. So now she was searching for her Papa and Mama among the throng at the port.

Suddenly, Nina saw her mother and father moving through the crowd of travelers at the harbor. They were carrying suitcases and looking around, searching for her.

Nina nudged John to look in their direction and screamed, "Mama! Papa!" But her voice was not loud enough, and it got lost in the noisy environment in the harbor.

"Papa, Mama!" Nina made a trumpet with her hands around her mouth and cried out towards her parents.

Alona was the first to hear her daughter's call. Then she saw Nina running towards her. Alona dropped her suitcase and staggered towards Nina. She opened her mouth to speak but had no voice. She dropped her knees to the ground on the cobblestones.

"Mama," Nina cried out louder and rushed to her mother.

"Baby, my baby," Alona opened her arms to hug her daughter firmly. She just could not stop her tears.

"Mama, Mama!" Nina felt the profound love of her mother.

"Sweetie," Albert stroked Nina and hugged the two of them with his eyes full of tears.

"Papa," Nina could not stop her crying.

Then, Albert hurried to John.

"Thank you very much! Thank you to Mary!" Albert held John's two hands.

"We were glad to have Nina. She is a wonderful girl," John said to Albert.

"Nina, come over here. Please say 'Thank You' again!" Albert called Nina over.

"I love you, Daddy," Nina came over and gave a big hug to John.

"We appreciate your caring for Nina! You and Mary saved her life!" Alona shook John's hands.

"Mary also wanted to say, we are delighted you could get out of Nazi Germany at this critical time. We wish you all the best in Shanghai," John shook Alona's hand as well.

"I hope you take care of yourself! We will have a chance to meet again," Albert said.

"Sure," John said, "Goodbye, Nina!" John waved his hand to Nina and her parents.

"Goodbye, John!" the three of them said in unison.

Later Nina thought about this farewell. She realized a life truth. We should treat every goodbye as a scary event. Pay attention and say all the important things that need saying. Look earnestly at each other. It may be the last time to see each other. There may never be another chance.

Maybe life is a journey full of farewells.

* * *

Nina reunited with her parents and boarded the Italian ocean liner, The SS Conte Rosso. This ship would take them to Shanghai, China.

Nina enjoyed almost every moment on the ocean liner as a nine-year-old girl. Most importantly, she was together with her Papa and Mama after being away from them for about a year in London.

The luxury ocean liner was like a pleasure cruise, even with a small orchestra. Although their parents and other grown-ups were soberer, the younger people on the ship had a great time, forgetting the terror they were fleeing. Nina even made friends with a Jewish girl who was the same age.

"I am so happy to be with you and Mama again," Nina leaned on Albert and looked into the far distance over the sea, "But I also missed Daddy and Mommy in London."

"Good girl," Albert touched Nina's head. He told her, "Sometimes we may experience situations that we are helpless to change, but don't panic. We have to learn to adapt to unfamiliar circumstances."

"Yes, Papa," Nina nodded, though she didn't fully understand her father's words. She understood that her family and the other Jews on the ship would have some language difficulties in Shanghai. This was like her first few weeks in London. From speaking German to speaking English had been an awkward transition. Nina told her father that she was aware of the struggle to learn a foreign language.

"The Nazis forced us to bid farewell to our family and friends in Germany. Now we are going somewhere we have never been. Shanghai is the only place accepting us," Albert tried his best to tell Nina some of his life lessons. "All these difficult things will teach us how unpredictable life is."

During the voyage to Shanghai, Nina kept asking her father about the ports they passed by or docked at overnight. Her father knew almost every place. However, the most exciting place was between Port Said and Port Suez. This was the Suez Canal. Their ship was sailing on the river instead of on the sea. Nina was eager to listen to her father telling the story about the Canal's ancient history.

Once their ship went from the Mediterranean Sea into the Suez Canal, a few young Jews jumped off the ship. Nina did not understand why they did that so risky. Those young men, in fact, wanted to make their way to Palestine. Her father explained to Nina.

After the Suez Canal, the ship passed the Gulf of Suez and entered the famous Red Sea. Albert told Nina this was the exact place where the most famous biblical miracle took place. The Jews, under the leadership of Moses, were fleeing enslavement by the Egyptians. When they came to the Red Sea, there was a terrible storm, and they could not cross. Moses appealed to God to save his people, and the Red Sea parted, and the Jews walked to freedom.

Nina remembered the famous story. "Why is the water not red? How did the wind get such magical power?" Nina kept asking questions of her father. She was excited and leaned on the ship's rail, watching the waves rolling in from a distance.

"These stories are myths and legends. But now they are real for us. We are in exile from our homeland, going to an ancient country we have never seen." Papa laughed and patted Nina's head softly.

Albert's eyes followed the Red Sea into the distance. Albert was full of emotions he didn't expect standing on the ocean liner's deck. He was in turmoil, like the waves he watched. He was still shocked from his experience so far and nervous about what would happen next. Because his daughter was returned to them, he felt joy. But on the other hand, he was in exile, going to an unknown country.

The trip from Italy to China was very long, passing many exotic places along the way: the port of Aden in Yemen, Bombay in India,

Colombo in Sri Lanka, then Singapore and Hong Kong. Finally, they approached the port of Shanghai, China, after twenty-four days.

Nina kept looking along the craggy riverbank and the strange cliffs with an insatiable curiosity as their ocean liner passed through the South China Sea, going to the Chinese mainland.

"We are running for our lives. But, perhaps, everyone is running for their lives. It is the epitome of life for the Jewish people, maybe even for the entire human race. We left our country, Germany, with next to nothing. But we were happy," Papa said.

"Why?" Nina asked.

"Because we took our lives with us," Papa answered with a smile.

"Because our family is together, and we have hope in front of us," Mama added.

Although Nina had imagined that they would have a better life and a better future in Shanghai, the reality that awaited her family in Shanghai was beyond anything she could have imagined.

PART III

THE HUANGPU RIVER

CHAPTER TEN

September 1939
Shanghai, China

S hanghai was already the fifth-largest city in the world in 1939, but it was occupied by the Japanese army. The city was situated on the bank of the Huangpu River. The Huangpu was a vast river with yellow water rolling in waves. There were many different kinds of boats on the river. However, most of them were small and shabby.

Nina noticed how slovenly and poorly dressed the men who had maneuvered the small boats on the Huangpu River were. There was lots of trash and debris floating on the river. A small brownish boat crawled up on the river, trailing strips of black smoke behind it. Occasionally, a large ship sailed toward the shore. A pair of gulls flew above the water, bobbing on the horizon.

"Why is the river yellow?" Nina looked at the tawny water and frowned.

"It's the silt from the riverbank that turns the water yellow. The river sweeps over the soil on its 5000 km journey. That's why it is called

Huangpu River. Huang is yellow in Chinese pronunciation. It means a river which is yellow in color," Papa stroked Nina's shoulder.

"Oh," Nina nodded.

Everyone on the ocean liner watched the Shanghai port, their destination, with exciting eyes.

"See over there. It looks very busy," Mama pointed into the distance at the port.

"People called the waterfront of Huangpu River, The Bund," Papa said.

Nina watched the boats on the yellow water of the Huangpu River. The flickering lights from the water reminded her of the Thames River, and she started to miss her English Daddy and Mommy in London.

Nina and her parents stepped off the ocean liner and walked into the port of Shanghai. Many other refugees disembarked as well. Lots of the other ships also carried Jews fleeing Nazi oppression. They arrived at the Bund in the middle of a hot, humid, muggy season, full of hopes and expectations.

The newcomers were confused when they stood by the bank of the Huangpu River. Papa learned more details of Shanghai's current port situation after they arrived. Papa explained to Mama it was because Shanghai was an open port with no diplomatic controls that it had become a safe haven for Jews. As a result, hundreds of Jewish people were fleeing the horrors of Germany and Austria, seeking refuge in Shanghai.

Although passport control was not in anyone's hands, the Japanese army controlled the Shanghai Harbor after 1937. Despite their alliance with Germany, they let the Jewish refugees come into Shanghai. Japanese flags with the big red circle on a white background were flying everywhere in Shanghai, except in the International Settlement and French Concession areas.

Like most refugees, Nina's family had no means to support themselves on their arrival. Fortunately, there was a Jewish Refugee Committee in Shanghai. First, they met Nina's family and others at the Bund. Then, they took all the refugees by truck to a place called "Refugee

Kitchen," a temporary shelter converted from a school. Nina had her first meal in Shanghai there.

The Jewish Refugee Committee, established in 1938, was responsible for resettling the refugees. The committee was organized by two groups of Jewish immigrants in Shanghai. The first group came from Iraq many years ago. The second one consisted of Russian Jews. The Refugee Committee created four refugee centers in the Hongkew area near the Huangpu River. They provided two meals a day, including soup with meat. But unfortunately, the condition in the shelter was not good.

After the first dinner in Shanghai, Papa suggested walking around the local area. They passed by the Ohel Moshe Synagogue at Ward Road (Changyang Road). Next, they went by Wayside Road (Huoshan Road). Finally, the three of them walked towards the shore of the Huangpu River.

Nina found that the streets of Shanghai were narrow and crowded. She had never seen so many people on the road. It seemed like thousands, running around in such a confined space. She discovered the smells and the noise very strange. Most of the buildings were old, and the stores had interesting Chinese characters on their street fronts.

Nina saw a rickshaw on the Wayside Road for the first time, moving through narrow and crowded lanes. Cars horns blasted, rickshaw workers and passengers were calling out, traders were shouting, and everyone chatting in a distincted language. Papa told Nina that the dialect spoken in Shanghai was called Shanghainese. She was amazed at how fast and loud the people spoke.

When Nina looked by the river, she saw gorgeous buildings lining up on the riverbank. Most of them were western-style. She wished to take a closer look at these buildings because they looked like ones she knew in London or Berlin.

"Papa, why does that building look like Berlin?" Nina asked, pointing to one of those magnificent structures.

"It is a luxurious hotel on the Bund, called Cathy Hotel. It was built by a Jewish man," Papa said.

"What a comparison between the rich and the poor," Mama noticed the extravagance of the western-style buildings along the Bund compared to the small boats on the Huangpu River.

"That is true," Papa agreed with Mama.

"Our family perhaps belongs to the poorest of the poor right now in this city," Mama said sadly.

"Maybe, considering we used to have a middle-class lifestyle in Berlin before the Nazis," Papa sounded a little depressed. He did not know the poor and the rich were everywhere in Shanghai.

"Look, lots of pigeons," Nina pointed to the sky.

"Oh, they look different from the ones in Berlin," Mama said.

"We should walk back now," Papa patted Nina's shoulder.

"Wait, listen, someone is playing a musical instrument," Nina was always sensitive to any music.

They heard a flute-like melody flowing towards them from the southwest of the riverbank. The notes moved up and down, fast and slow, but Nina could not identify which kind of musical instrument.

"It must be a piece of classical Chinese music," Papa guessed.

"Can we go close to take a look?" Nina asked her father.

"Sure," Papa agreed with Nina on almost everything. So the family walked on, getting close to where the music came from.

They found a boy sitting on a rock near the Huangpu River at the end of the street, where there were not too many people. He was playing a flute-like musical instrument, facing the red sunset.

Nina admired the boy's playing. It was stunning. But she was disappointed she could only see the boy's back, not his face.

"Let's go back. It is getting late," Papa said.

"Okay," Nina was interested in the tone and rhythm of this strange new music. It was a good introduction to things Chinese. She was interested in all the new things she saw. Nina was not yet worried about their new life in exile.

"What is the name of this instrument, Papa?"

"Most likely, it is a Chinese bamboo flute. Chinese people call it dizi," Papa continued walking forward, swaying his big hands.

"Oh, dizi, why do you think it is made of bamboo?" Nina tried to catch up with her father's steps.

"Bamboo is everywhere in this area. The dizi is simple to make and easy to carry, so it may be a popular instrument among the Chinese people," Papa replied.

"But it sounds so beautiful." Nina was still amazed by the boy's music.

"The bamboo flute is lightweight, and it has a much quieter tone. It also has a nice resonance depending on the size and length of the flute," Papa said.

"I want to take a close look at a dizi flute if I can," Nina had an innate love of music.

"We are in Shanghai now. You will have a chance to see and play a bamboo flute for sure," Papa looked at Nina with his first sense of optimism since landing. "Call your Mama. We need to head back fast."

"Mama, let us go." Mama was looking around Shanghai streets, interested in all she saw.

On the way back to the shelter, Nina heard her Papa talk to Mama. He worried about the family's financial situation because they had to leave most of what they had in Germany. As German refugee Jews, they had been expelled to a far corner of the earth and forced to make a new beginning in Shanghai's unfamiliar surroundings. Mama frowned, understanding their situation precarious. Besides the emotional stress, she felt physically not well after all she had suffered. She lacked strength and had a slight cough from the long voyage on the sea.

On the second morning in the shelter kitchen, Papa still wore his new German suit with a hat and tie. Some of the other refugees looked at him in bewilderment. It was too hot and humid to dress like a German gentleman in Shanghai. After that day, Papa adapted to the environment and the local weather conditions, imitating his refugee peers and dressing more casually. He also advised Nina and Mama to do the same. "We have to adapt to a new environment for life," Papa said.

The Refugee Community had set up a shelter for people who had no place to go. Nina's family was grateful to be able to stay at the refuge shelter during their early days in Shanghai. It provided the essential temporary shelter they needed, as well as a bit of breakfast and lunch. Nina and her parents followed their peers every morning, joining the line at breakfast time. Everyone, the old or the young, held a tin container in hand, patiently waiting for the food the Refugee Kitchen distributed.

"Let's get in the line for some food," Papa said.

The man in the front nodded and gave a reluctant smile at Papa and Mama.

"How long have you been here?" Mama asked the man.

"Three weeks already. It seems there are more and more of our people coming here from Europe." He sounded worried.

"How do you feel about the city of Shanghai?" Papa inquired. He was interested in knowing what this man thought after three weeks.

"You should have an idea by now. Shanghai's weather is too hot and humid for our Europeans. Tell your daughter that she cannot drink the water from the tap because the sanitary conditions are poor here." He glanced at Nina and gave this important tip to her.

"Thanks for your advice." Papa nodded at him.

When they went up to the distribution table and got some porridge, Nina looked at her father's face, trying to read his thoughts because she was surprised by how little food she got in her container.

"Let's sit down over there and eat," Papa padded her shoulder, understanding her feelings.

Nina's family had plenty of food to eat on the ocean liner coming to Shanghai. This was the first time Nina tasted lousy food, but she did not know that was just the beginning of their struggles as refugees in Shanghai.

Papa tried to sit close to the man they chatted with a few moments ago.

"The place can only provide the most basic food and a space to sleep," the man said.

"Are there any work opportunities?" Papa asked.

"First, you need to speak good English or French," the man declared in German.

"I can speak reasonable English," Papa said with confidence.

"Maybe you could understand the local language?" the man joked.

"You mean Shanghainese? Not at all," Papa responded.

Everyone had lowered their heads to eat the porridge, but they all were thinking about their own private matters. Nina thought about school, friends, and music. She guessed Papa might think about finding a job, and Mama might think about the food.

Nina felt that living in the shelter was worse than living on the ocean liner at sea. As the days went on, the food supplied in the shelter kitchen became less and less.

"Ms. Margolis, why is the food supply getting less this week?" Mama asked the shelter director two weeks later. Ms. Laura Margolis was a lovely woman from the United States.

"As you can see, our shelter has more refugees from Europe, but we have less money from our supporters. Our staff is trying their best to accommodate everybody." The shelter director smiled at Mama but also indicated her frustration.

Papa warned Nina several times that she should not drink the water from the tap here. Otherwise, she would get sick. They had to get boiled water for drinking. The sanitary conditions in the shelter were inadequate. There were lots of bugs crawling around. Nina even saw a bug crawling on the infested clothes of some children.

Papa reinforced that their time in the shelter was only temporary. Nina's family never expected to stay in Shanghai as refugees for a long time.

CHAPTER ELEVEN

October 1939
Shanghai, China

T he weather in Shanghai in the autumn was even more humid, which was difficult for the Europeans, making them short of breath. Nina's family was no exception.

Albert learned from a friend that Nazi Germany had invaded Poland by launching a blitzkrieg attack on September 1, 1939. On September 3, Britain and France were forced to declare war on Germany. The Second World War had started. More bad news followed. By early 1940, the Nazi army invaded and took control of Denmark and Norway, then the Netherlands, Belgium, and northern France. When Hitler's Nazis occupied most European countries, the persecution of Jews escalated. The Jews in Europe were devastated by the situation. By the end of 1940, more than three million Jews had fallen into the hands of the Nazis. Hitler had sent most of them into the concentration camps.

Albert felt lucky they fled to Shanghai, barely escaping the Nazis in the last moment.

But in this city, the Jewish refugees scrambled to find jobs to sustain themselves, despite not knowing the local language. Albert wanted to be a music teacher, but without the language ability, that was impossible. He went to the city center to look for work in the Chinese companies, but he did not find any. Albert decided to try working for the Jewish shop owners in the city. He hoped to make friends as well as find work there. Finally, he got a job as a bartender in Jewish small cafeteria. He struggled to survive as a complete stranger in an unknown city. His wife, Alona, sold her knitted items to make a little money to support the family.

In an ordinary Wednesday evening, Albert found a square box one of the customers left under the bar table. He picked it up and ran out of the bar to chase that customer. The man's name was Charles Zhou, a Chinese businessman. Charles was doing business with a British company. He had an office on Wayside Road in the area. Charles spoke good English. They had a pleasant conversation and later became friends. Charles suggested Albert should think about to open a small business in the area like other Jewish people.

"Once you start a business, there are infinite possibilities, good or bad," Charles told Albert. "You need to not only work hard but also work smart. Shanghai is a city for smart, hard-working people."

"I am smart and hard-working." Albert smiled at Charles as he answered.

"Then you can do it," Charles encouraged him.

The support from Charles was like a miracle that appeared at the beginning of Albert's life in Shanghai. He set up a small fruit jam business near Wayside Road in the city with Charles's help. There were other Jewish-run businesses nearby, such as bakeries, cafes, restaurants, bars, and candy stores. A few months later, Albert's jam business was running smoothly.

After some time, Albert managed to rent a room for his family, located on one of the small lanes. The room was clean, even though still too small for his family. There was nothing like flush toilets at all. There was a shared bathroom but no kitchen facilities. But they at least could leave the crowded refugee shelter and live by themselves.

Albert and his wife sent Nina to the local Jewish school in Shanghai. It was established by the Jewish community, especially for refugee children. It was administered by two affluent Jewish families. Being a private school, you had to pay tuition. However, if you could not bear the tuition, you went for free. The school followed the British school system. An British woman, Ms. Beresford, taught English at the school. Nina was happy to be able to go to school again.

* * *

The curriculum of the Shanghai Jewish school was provided by Oxford University of UK. Ms. Beresford followed the guidelines from the Oxford University professor's design exactly. The final English examination also came from that famous University. The students' examination papers were sent back to Oxford University for marking. Under such proper training, Nina studied hard and developed excellent English language ability.

Ms. Beresford was an exceptional teacher. All the students at school liked her very much. To encourage student learning, Ms. Beresford would take the best student from the class to her home for the weekend as a reward. Nina had been chosen three times by her teacher. Nina was very happy every times.

Ms. Beresford was impressed by Nina's English ability. It was, of course, because she had lived a year in London, England. Nina spoke better English than other students, though with a bit of London accent. Nina took enormous pride in being singled out by her teacher's invitations. Some of her classmates were a little jealous of her. Ms. Beresford's home was in downtown Shanghai on the famous Xiafie Road (now Huaihai Road). Her house was gorgeous. For two days, Nina lived in a completely different world. This experience encouraged Nina to improve her English.

Nina made a Chinese girlfriend named Mei Lin in the community. She had two long pigtails and was always smiling. They often played together. Nina appreciated that Shanghai had accepted her family when no one else would. She thanked Mei Lin's mother, Mrs. Wong, for her hospitality. Nina often had snacks at Mei Lin's house after school. The most impressive snack was red bean soup, also called Acacia red bean soup. The Shanghainese friendship was sweet, like red bean soup. Nina loved it.

One Friday afternoon, after school, when Nina was doing her homework at home, she heard exquisite music coming from the opposite apartment's small window. She immediately recognized that music. It was the same tune she and her parents heard near the Huangpu River a year ago. The music was quite distinctive, soft, and even romantic. Nina wondered whether that flute boy had moved here.

Nina stood up from her small desk and listened. She moved near the window and leaned out, finding where the music came from.

She saw a Chinese boy holding a bamboo flute. Nina remembered her father said it is called dizi in Chinese. The boy looked about twelve years old, perhaps two years older than Nina. She was fascinated by his performance of this ancient Chinese music.

The flute music was so elegant that it touched Nina's heart. She was transported by the sounds of the flute floating towards her. She imagined she could see the boy's face. He was as beautiful as the music he played. In fact, Nina wished she could meet him.

Aware that someone was spying on him, the boy abruptly stopped playing. He turned, and they looked across the window, eyes to eyes. Nina's heart was beating a little fast. She was feeling an emotion she had never experienced before. The new sensation made her nervous but happy. She didn't know what it was. The flute boy seemed to be a little shy. He hid behind the window and stopped playing the flute for that day.

That night, Nina had her recurrent dream again. A piece of elegant flute music was flying from the Huangpu River into her dream. She followed the sound, walking towards it quietly. A teenage boy faced the sunset and played his bamboo flute with passion. He moved his upper body sideways, following the music's rhyme. The boy did not notice that Nina approached and was watching him. Nina stopped and listened to the ancient Chinese flute music on the river bank. The astonishing music sounded so beautiful that the music brought Nina back to the Rhine River in Germany. Nina saw her grandma in Rheinpark Park, smiling at her. Nina raised the hand to her grandma, but she could not touch her.

On the next day, at the same time after school, Nina looked at the apartment window opposite. She was looking for the boy, eager to hear his flute. The bamboo flute brought joy to Nina's dull life. Listening to the boy's flute was the happiest thing of her day. She found nothing to cheer her up in school and on the street. She wanted to lean against the window every day after school and hear the beautiful music from the flute boy.

One day after two weeks, the boy waved his hand to Nina after his performance. His smile was dazzling. That day, Nina saw a group of pigeons flying over the window and into the clouded sky. Her thoughts seemed to scatter with them. She couldn't say why but she felt happy. As an eleven-year-old girl, Nina was very resilient. Despite her exile from Berlin to London then to Shanghai, she thought her life was pretty good. Now, her heart was also full of strange new feelings. Nina believed today was the most beautiful day of her life in Shanghai.

The following day, on the way from school, Nina saw the flute boy also walking on Wayside Road. They eyed each other and smiled shyly.

Nina found the route the flute boy took to leave school. Although many peddlers were shouting to sell their goods on the street, and the noise of children playing on the road was very loud, Nina did not notice. Instead, she kept her attention on where the flute boy walked as he turned the corner.

Each evening, after his homework, the flute boy played his beautiful melody, and Nina always showed her appreciation with a heartfelt smile.

Nina wanted to have a chance to talk to him but didn't know if he could speak any English at all. The flute boy filled her thoughts, but she didn't know what she expected from him.

CHAPTER TWELVE

May 1941
Shanghai, China

There was a lilac tree near Nina's apartment building. The pinkish flowers were blooming and sending their sweet fragrance into the air since it was still summer. Nina loved it very much. She also loved to watch the pigeons around her home. Their color was different from the pigeons she knew in London. Their bodies were light gray. Mama pointed out the unique metallic green and gold feathers that flashed in the sunlight around their necks.

There were more and more Europeans coming to the Hongkew area in Shanghai. Most of them spoke German or Hebrew. They looked worried and anxious, facing an uncertain future in Shanghai. Some of them seemed to be sturdy, but others looked fragile.

"Why do some children cry so much?" Nina asked her father. As a young child, Nina always paid attention to her peers.

"Everyone is different. The animals and plants in nature are excellent examples. Some are strong, and some are fragile. The natural world is full of variety," Papa replied.

"Papa, sometimes I feel scared of leaving you or Mama, but I want to be a strong girl." Nina looked up to her father.

"Good girl." Papa's constant encouragement helped Nina build a strong character. Persistence was one of her most vital character traits. She inherited the strength from her family. Her resilience, particularly in critical times, allowed her to stay calm and courageous, make difficult decisions, and never retreat. Nina was also blessed by the love and encouragement of her parents.

Nina's family lived in a shabby apartment on Wayside Road. People were crowded together. Still, they helped and cooperated each other. They had a cordial relationship with the local Chinese people, who were without prejudice toward Jewish people.

A tentative friendship slowly developed between Nina and the flute boy. One day when Nina was on the way home from her school, at the intersection of Wayside Road and Zhoushan Road, the flute boy was waiting for her. The communication between two teenagers was a challenge because their native languages were German and Chinese. Fortunately, the flute boy's father spoke English well, and he learned a little English from his daddy.

"This is for you." The boy gave Nina a small object like a beach stone.

"Thanks! What is it?" Nina took the small stone.

"It is, it is a mud chicken," the boy tried to choose proper English words with some nervousness.

"It looks nice," Nina looked at the gift, holding it in her right hand. She found it was actually a clay sculpture of a rooster, painted in beautiful colors.

The flute boy glanced at Nina and moved closer. He wanted to show her how to play this sculpted toy.

"Try to blow it like a dizi," the boy put his right hand near his mouth and blew air into it as an example.

Nina looked at the clay rooster with care and found a small hole on the rooster's back. She put the clay rooster in her mouth shyly, trying to blow air into the rooster.

"Cock-a-doodle-doo!" A loud and funny sound was out from the clay rooster. Nina was surprised to hear a rooster crowing. Both of them laughed abruptly and joyfully after the crowing.

Nina used her left hand to cover her mouth, and her face flushed. She felt a little embarrassed but happy at the same time.

"I like it very much, thank you!" Nina stared at the flute boy.

"You are welcome," the boy said. His face flushed too.

"Goodbye," the boy waved his hand and left in a hurry.

Nina took her little gift and ran home very excited. She played the clay rooster, over and over, it was whistling cheerfully.

"Cock-a-doodle-doo!" The rooster's sweet sound made Nina very happy. She guessed that the little rooster's sound delighted the boy in the opposite window.

All of a sudden, Nina realized she had forgotten to ask the flute boy his name. She regretted about this deeply because she had wondered what his name was for a long time.

On the third day after Nina got the clay rooster, Papa returned home in a terrible mood. He told Nina to stop that awful noise. Papa said the whistle that Nina loved was too annoying. The real reason was that Papa thought the noise might draw attention to them and cause trouble in the neighborhood from the Japanese authorities.

Albert was very stressed recently because his business was being harassed by a Japanese officer. The officer said he was not allowed to run his business in his current location. The officer even smashed many jam bottles already. Albert felt very threatened by him. Albert relied on this small business to maintain his family's livelihood. It was very unusual for Albert to raise his voice to Nina. She was the most precious thing to him. After she had been sent to London, he had come to terms with the fact he might never see her again. Once reunited, he did not want to be harsh with her anymore. There was little to criticize her for, but he let it go without comment if there was.

Nina was an empathetic and considerate girl. However, she only understood that her Papa did not like the rooster's sound. So she stopped playing it and went to do her homework. However, she still put the clay rooster beside her pillow when she went to bed that night.

Before Papa went to bed, he always looked at his daughter as she slept, filled with love for her. He bent down to kiss her forehead. Accidentally he touched something hard near Nina's pillow. He grabbed it and found it was that noisy clay rooster.

Albert remembered the racket this clay rooster made. And he didn't want it to disturb Nina's sleep, so he took it away. Papa would not throw away his daughter's toy rooster. He just wanted to hide it. So he put it beside the sink in the kitchen without giving it much thought. But unfortunately, it dissolved over the night from contact with water beside the sink.

The following day, Nina could not find her rooster beside her pillow. She searched everywhere. Finally, she found it in the kitchen. It was just a lump of wet clay. Once she discovered her clay rooster collapsed beside the sink and became a lump of mud, Nina's heart melted down. She felt broken-hearted. Nina was distraught, thinking about the precious gift from the flute boy, now ruined. She started to cry. Tears streamed down her face. Nina cried every time she thought of her favorite little gift.

"Why did you make my clay rooster melt into a lump of mud?" Nina asked her Papa.

"I wanted to hide it there for a short time. How could I know this toy would melt near the sink? Sorry, I didn't mean for it to happen." Albert tried his best to explain to his angry daughter.

Disregarding her father's words of apology, Nina cried for two days. Then, she ignored her father, not wanting to talk to him because he had ruined the flute boy's special gift. Nina's sullen mood lasted a few days.

Mama explained to Nina that it was becoming more challenging to live in Shanghai. They needed to be very cautious, not make any trouble. She also described her father's stress because the Japanese officer kept harassing him. Nina could not understand all these things. She didn't understand the world of the adult business.

Nina was just a teenage girl, after all. She had a different emotional and social experience in Shanghai. She made friends with Chinese children, and they played games together. Nina still played with her Chinese girlfriend, Mei Lin, after school frequently.

Nina did recognize one thing she was happy about in Shanghai. There was no antisemitism among the Chinese people. They accepted Jewish people naturally. They did not have any hatred for them, and they did not look down on them. Both people had a friendly relationship with each other. Nina never saw any sign of antisemitism in the local Chinese neighborhood even once. Jewish children played with local Chinese children easily.

In the meantime, Nina gradually increased her acquaintance with the flute boy. She eventually knew his name was Hason. Hason had dark black hair and a broad forehead. His dark brown eyes were always smiling. He showed his white teeth when he smiled. Although his English was not good, his voice was unique, with an extraordinarily appealing resonance.

Their communication was awkward at first. Nina taught Hason English and some German, such as "Guten Morgen," which means "good morning." Hason taught Nina some of the Shanghainese dialects, such as "Nong Hao Fa?" which means "How are you?" "A La" means "We," and "Huang Bao Che" means "rickshaw."

Hason gave Nina a bamboo flute after learning the clay rooster had melted. Hason also taught Nina how to whistle by curling her lip. In addition, she learned her first Mandarin words from Hason, "Ni Hao" (How are you) and "Xie Xie" (Thank you).

Hason taught Nina to play her bamboo flute, so they could play together, which made Nina love music even more. They became best friends through music.

* * *

The following summer in Shanghai was scorching hot. Nina's family lived in a no-window apartment with inadequate ventilation, so the home was boiling hot. Some days, the oppressive humidity made it even worse. The hot daytime sunlight accumulated a lot of heat in their apartment. The heat could not escape in the night, so it was hard to sleep.

Nina and her parents sweated constantly. Papa and Mama had to use a hand fan to cool down. Mosquito bites were an additional annoyance. Papa kept waving his bamboo fan, not only to make a slight breeze but to repel mosquitoes. Mama learned from him, doing the same with her fan. The constant "Ba, Ba, Ba!" noises of the fans' waving added to Nina's discomfort during the summer night.

In late September of 1941, the humidity and heat were the same as July. Most of China was occupied by the Japanese army, and the whole country was in a state of war. The Japanese military had controlled Shanghai for some time by then. Because of the war, the economic situation was getting worse in China. As a result, life in Shanghai became much tougher, too. Although Jewish refugees' conditions were impoverished in Shanghai, they were still better off than in the surrounding areas. The Chinese people were hard-working but suffered more.

A lovely Chinese middle-aged farmer came by Nina's home with a bamboo stick on his shoulder, with two little baskets hanging on each end. Mama became a regular customer of his mobile vegetable shop. The farmer came by twice a week. He used to call at the front door downstairs, "Lady Alona!" He always brought vegetables, eggs, and fish for the family.

The evidence of hardship was everywhere. Nina saw the piles of debris on the roadside. Chinese workers carried bulky goods on their shoulders that were so heavy they staggered. Nina was distressed to see some sweaty rickshaw workers with bare feet. They wore straw hats to protect them from the intense sun, and their shirts were made from dozens of old and tattered patches. Nina often saw some workers without clothing, with a bare upper body, carrying heavy cargo, and working extremely hard. Nina's father mentioned Nina that those workers in the street made very little money each day.

It was an incredibly arduous job for rickshaw workers in the run-up to the famous Garden Bridge near the Huangpu River. They had to jump off their rickshaws to pull with their arm and leg muscles for those people who sat on the rickshaws. Someone said Garden Bridge was the border between the rich and the poor in the city. Nina felt deeply pity for the rickshaw workers.

Nina noticed that various people were riding on the rickshaws, but they were mostly well off. They were wealthy people, such as fat, well-dressed women or rich teenagers riding on rickshaws. She saw a businessman with a big cigar in his hand, wearing a white hat, an expensive suit, leather shoes, and pairs of dark sunglasses. Most rickshaw workers wore shabby shirts and pedaled the three-wheeled rickshaws, working like hell in the street.

One day as Nina held onto her father's arm and walked on Wayside Road, she noticed two rickshaws were moving in different directions. The breeze was blowing, and Nina's hair fluttered in the soft wind.

"Why do some Chinese men in Shanghai have such empty expressions?" Nina asked her Papa.

"Because some Chinese men are using a drug called opium. It is addictive like alcohol."

"Opium," Nina had never heard of it before.

"Opium was brought here from Europe nearly 100 years ago in the Opium War. The Shanghai French Concession we see now is related to this war. You may learn that history in school," Papa fondled Nina's shoulder.

Albert told Nina briefly about the two Opium Wars. The First Opium War was triggered by the Chinese Qing dynasty against the British merchants. They sold opium in China from 1839 to 1842. The Second Opium War was between the Chinese and the United Kingdom and France from 1856 to 1860. The European's modern weapons led to an easy victory over the Chinese forces in these two wars. The significant consequence of the Opium Wars was the Treaty of Nanking. According to the Treaty, the English people had created a section of Shanghai city called the international settlement. Later, the French people established their own settlement called the French Concession in Shanghai's west area. The western army used weapons to make Shanghai a tremendously wealthy city and a miserably poor one after the Opium Wars. The city became the commercial center of China in the meantime. Some referred to Shanghai's French Concession as the Paris of the east and Shanghai's International Settlement as the orient's New York.

At that moment, a Japanese army motorcycle flew past Nina and her father. It made a harsh noise, which made Nina grip her father's arm for security. She recalled the Nazi motorcycles in Berlin.

"Let's go fast." Papa put his arm around Nina.

"Okay!"

"Papa, why are some people nice, but others are mean?" Nina asked her father when they turned into a small lane.

Albert took the opportunity to teach his daughter by watching the variety of people and their behavior on the streets of Shanghai. He offered this pearl of wisdom from his own life experience.

"People are born with their essence, either merciful or merciless," Papa said.

"What do you mean born with?" Nina was perplexed.

"It means it is essentially who you are, even at birth. You are kind or cruel. You cannot teach this essence. People rarely change. At least in my experience, I don't know anyone who has changed. Therefore I don't believe anyone can change their essential character," Papa emphasized.

"Wow, why is that?" Nina asked.

"Because kindness or meanness is inside a person's blood and bone from birth, I call it a personal essence," Papa continued.

"Why is this personal essence so important?" Nina asked her father.

"Because it is the fundamental criteria you should use when considering whether to make friends with a person or stay away from him." Papa stared at Nina's eyes, pointing his index finger to his forehead as an expression of seriousness.

"A classic Chinese proverb says if you plant melon, you get melon. If you plant beans, you get beans. That means when you give love, you get love in return. If you spread hatred, you will get hatred," Papa told Nina.

Nina learned from her father that an essential thing in life is to be kind and be conscience. If you do something good for other people, you will be rewarded well. But, on the other hand, if you are cruel, the consequence will be felt in your life as hardship and strife.

* * *

It was the early winter of 1941. The chilly wind started to whip into the city from the Huangpu River more often than ever.

One night Papa brought home a radio. He also somehow got some warm air into the house. Nina loved to listen to the radio and snuggled with her Papa or Mama. Mama often joined them to listen to the news after tidying up everything after the dinner.

"Why did the gentlemen give the radio to you?" Mama asked Papa.

"Maybe because I referred a friend to his business," Papa always had nice friends.

"I like to listen to the Voice of America radio station," Nina said to Mama.

"Why?" Mama was curious.

"Because that station broadcasts news about the war, even though all the news they report is forbidden by the Japanese," Nina said to her mother mysteriously. In fact, Nina's family got the most critical information from that precious radio.

They learned by listening to their little radio about the Japanese air force attack on the American military port, Pearl Harbor, on December 7, 1941. The next day American president Mr. Roosevelt made a formal declaration of war on the Empire of Japan. Three days later, on December 11, Germany and Italy declared war on the United States. Papa told Nina that something would happen to them in Shanghai after all these declarations of war.

The Japanese military took over the international settlement in Shanghai immediately after the Pearl Harbor Attack. The British and the Americans became enemies of Japan. The Japanese imprisoned some of them in internment camps on Shanghai's outskirts. Germany and Japan were allies, having the same fascist mentality. As a result, the Nazi government became involved with the affairs of the Jewish refugees in Shanghai. Jewish refugees in Shanghai were regarded as prisoners of war.

That weekend, Nina and Hason went over the Garden Bridge to the city. This Bridge divided the International Settlement and Hongkew District, one of the most impoverished areas of war-torn Shanghai. They were surprised by how crowded the people were in the Bund area. They stepped closer, fed by their curiosity. Nina and Hason saw many Japanese soldiers yelling with red faces. Some of them wore a white band on their foreheads. Nina did not understand the red Japanese word "Warrior" in the band. Hason said this word meant "soldier" in Chinese characters. Later, Nina realized that the Japanese were celebrating the attack on Pearl Harbor. After the Japanese navy's surprise attack on US land, Japanese soldiers in Shanghai marched to the Bund to show their military power.

* * *

Time passed, and Nina continued to grow up in Shanghai. It was the late spring of 1942. The furry flower sepals held many beautiful pieces of white magnolia petals. Several fluffy flower buds were waiting for the warmer days, so they could all bloom together. Against the blue sky, the pure white petals reflected a little pinkish color. The soft sunlight made the flower petals transparent. Again, Nina felt a sensation of spring warmth.

A large cluster of flowers opened up together. The distinctive fragrance spread over the green leaves and flew head-on into Nina's face. After a light breeze, several petals danced and floated to the ground like white butterflies. White magnolia petals fell on the verdant green grass, which provided Nina with a sense of serenity in the area that morning.

Nina watched some teenage boys and girls holding hands as they passed by where she was sitting. It reminded her of the first time she held Hason's hand. She was barely twelve years old, but she remembered it was an exciting experience.

A few soft white clouds were floating in the indigo sky. Yellow flowers were all over the Huangpu River bank, and the air was balmy with a breeze.

"What is the name of this flower?" Nina asked Hason one day. She was curious about everything in the world.

Hason told her that the small yellow flowers were called dandelions. His father taught him dandelion could be a medicinal herb for infection.

Hason picked up a piece of flat stone and threw it into the nearby pond. The stone skipped on the water's surface like a fish, making many tiny splashes of water, which connected like a series of beautiful flower petals.

Nina counted as many as twelve splashes on the water, the same number as her age. Nina was genuinely amazed about it, and she insisted Hason teach her to do the same. "How do you do that?"

"You have to try first," Hason grinned at her.

She tried several times, with no success at all. In the end, Hason had to hold her hand to teach her the skills. Finally, she got three splashes. Nina was very pleased with herself and the three lovely splashes.

When Nina walked home, she stopped her steps to think about the way Hason had guided her hand with his. She felt her heart galloping. Nina could not stop thinking about Hason. She could feel his hands still holding her hand. His touch was sensitive and gentle. Her heart was full of a new excitement she never had known before.

Nina was surprised when she thought maybe this new feeling was love. She was immediately embarrassed, her face flushing hot and red. She believed she was too young to think about being in love.

CHAPTER THIRTEEN

February 1943
Shanghai, China

On February 18, 1943, Albert and his Jewish friends found a bulletin posted on the wall by Japanese soldiers. The Japanese Army's commander in Shanghai ordered all Jewish refugees who came to Shanghai after 1937 to move their businesses and residences into a designated area in Hongkew. The Japanese authority created this "Restricted Sector for Stateless Refugees," which later was called the Shanghai ghetto.

The occupying Japanese military authority stated that all the Jewish refugees had to follow "The Proclamation Concerning Restriction of Residence and Business of Stateless Refugees." The proclamation was signed by commander-in-chief of the Imperial Japanese Army, general Yasuji Okamura. The designated restriction area was bordered on the west by Dent Road, east by Soochow Creek near Yangtzepoo Road, south by Wayside Road, and north by the boundary of the International Settlement.

In the following weeks, Albert discussed the situation with his Jewish fellows seriously. They analyzed the Japanese army's proclamation order for moving into the Hongkew area and concluded that Nazi Germany influenced the Japanese army's decision.

In fact, the Nazi's influence became much stronger after the Pearl Harbor Attack. The Japanese put all the Americans and the British into internment camps. At the same time, Jewish refugees were moved into the Shanghai ghetto. It was located on the northern bank of the Huangpu River, which was only about one square mile of the southern Hongkew district. Nearly 23,000 Jewish refugees were relocated to that area.

"After the attack on Pearl Harbor, I had predicted that something like this would happen to our refugees in Shanghai." Albert's friend, Mr. Cohen, talked to a group of Jewish peers.

"In fact, our luck changed after the German delegation came to Shanghai," Albert said.

"The problem is we don't know the actual Japanese plans and motivation of this announcement," Mr. Cohen proposed the question to everybody who gathered around the bulletin wall.

"Why have the Japanese put the stateless refugees in such a small area in Hongkew?" One Jewish man with a black hat sighed powerlessly.

"I worry that the Japanese will also want to establish a concentration camp for us in Shanghai," Albert suggested a scarier scenario to his refugee peers.

"I have no doubt the Restricted Hongkew District will have a serious effect on all of us. We must not panic. We must keep calm and deal with it together." Mr. Cohen's comments were consistently rational.

"We have already been through worse times in Berlin and Vienna under the Nazis. So I am sure we will get over this huddle." Albert tried to encourage everybody and embrave himself as well.

Albert and Mr. Cohen later heard a horrible rumor. The rumor said the Nazi SS representative, Josef Meisinger, had come from Berlin with an order from his boss. The Nazi's goal was to make Europe "Judenfrei" (In German: Jew-free). SS Meisinger's mission was to convince the

Japanese Imperial Army to do the same in Shanghai with the exiled Jews in the city.

Josef Meisinger tried to convince the Japanese leader to send all the Shanghai Jews to a small island called "Chong Ming Island." It lay just at the mouth of Huangpu River. He wanted the Japanese to establish a Jewish concentration camp similar to Europe on that island.

The Nazis were determined to annihilate all the Jews exiled in Shanghai. They even provided the equipment to make a gas chamber. Controversially, the Japanese commander did not have any interest in doing so. Instead, he sent a senior officer to Chong Ming Island with SS Meisinger. It was more of a social outing than anything else. The Japanese leader did not accept the Nazi's plan to set up the concentration camp there. The reason is not known. However, the Japanese military forced the Jewish refugees to move their residences and businesses into the Hongkew area. Thus, the Shanghai Jewish ghetto was officially created amidst the chaos of WWII.

Compared to Jewish ghettos established by the Nazis in Europe, the Shanghai ghetto had no walls, barbed wire, or other barriers. Although the Shanghai ghetto was different from the European ghettos, it was patrolled, and a curfew was enforced by the Japanese military. Jewish refugees all needed passes to enter or leave the ghetto. Their food was rationed. This area was still one of Shanghai's poorest and most crowded areas. With the increasing restrictions, the living conditions and business environment became worse. Most refugees lost their jobs or businesses after being pushed to the restricted Hongkew area. The relocation brought severe financial problems and disrupted their daily life terribly.

The Hongkew area was one of Shanghai's poorest sections, made worse by the war with the Japanese destruction. The place was filthy and crowded. The Hongkew area was home to the poorest Chinese as well as Jewish refugees. No one had any money or resources, certainly not enough to support them own. The boiling hot and humid weather made everything even worse.

Albert's business took a plunge, and his income was significantly reduced. Nina's family had to move to an apartment crowded with five other families. They only rented an attic, in which Albert could not stand up straight. They had to share a small dark kitchen, where they took turns cooking their meals. There was no private bath and only one outside cold water tap. Although their quality of life had dropped considerably, the Jewish refugees were still a little better off than most of their Chinese neighbors.

"Most of the Chinese people's lives are very hard," Albert told Mr. Cohen, "Just look at the poor rickshaw workers and you will understand what I am talking about."

"Yes, you are right," Mr. Cohen said, "I have never seen this small wagon with two wheels called a rickshaw in Berlin. I have seen the veins popping like earthworms on the legs of those rickshaw workers. I have never seen legs like that before. How does that happen?" He was bewildered by this phenomenon.

"Look, you can imagine how hard it is for the worker to pull the rickshaw, carrying fat rich people and running on the streets all day long, day after day."

"Sure." Mr. Cohen nodded his head.

"I am worried about my son getting a serious illness," Another man said. He mentioned that a boy from his neighborhood contracted polio. The living conditions were so crowded so that he was anxious for his child.

"Well," Albert said, "We will be in the Hongkew area for some time, and things are getting worse. My earnings can't buy enough food for my family. Even if my wife works, we are still hungry most of the time. So I don't know what to do?"

"Everyone is in the same situation in the ghetto. There is no work, and we are starving," another Jewish man said.

"My daughter is in her adolescence. She needs decent food to nourish her growth. Look at her, so thin the wind could blow her over," another man said sadly.

After Albert's family moved into the Shanghai ghetto in Hongkew, their life became more difficult. Essential foods were scarce, and the food prices escalated unreasonably.

Alona tried to make hats to earn a little money for their livelihood. One evening, Nina saw her mother washing the dishes and noticed that she licked the last bit of food off the plate. She realized her mother was depriving herself by giving as much food as she could to her. Nina was touched by her mother's effort.

Nina and her parents struggled because the food was scarce. Moreover, the food available was of inferior quality, often causing diarrhea. Nina's face was drawn and looked like she was suffering from malnutrition. Mama knew that they needed more food, especially for their growing daughter.

One day, Nina saw a shabby little Chinese boy running on the street, chasing a car that carried bulging sacks. The boy used a small knife to cut a hole in one of the sacks when the vehicle was stopped. Suddenly potatoes fell on the street and into the gutter on the roadside. The boy's partner swept them up into their own containers and ran away. Later these boys would sell the potatoes to people, including Nina's mother, at a meager price.

That night, Nina sat with her mother under the gas lamp to clean the cheap potatoes. She found lots of debris, tiny stones, broken glass, and a rusty nail. At least, the family got some extra food. Later on, Nina had to deliver newspapers on the street to make some money for food.

Many refugees were dying of disease or starvation because there was so little food in the Shanghai ghetto. Nina's family and other Jewish refugees lived in extreme poverty. They suffered not only from being stateless and forsaken by the world but also starvation and illness.

The winter was especially harsh for refugees in the ghetto. There were no heating devices in the apartments in the Shanghai area. Albert often found someone frozen to death on the street in the early morning. He saw that the corpse had been wrapped up in the straw mattress to be taken away by the garbage truck.

During the worst time in the Shanghai ghetto, beside the severe food shortage, there was a shortage of everything, even suitable clothing. Some Jewish children were no longer going to school because they lacked appropriate shoes and clothes. Albert knew one of the refugees who lost his wife and daughter because of illness, and he lived alone without a job. His neighbor said he didn't change his underwear for weeks. Finally, when lice were everywhere in his home, he had to burn all his infested clothes. The neighbors could now see him wandering around ghetto streets in garments made from old jute bags. People understood that he suffered so much that he had been pushed into profound psychological distress. He had lost his self-respect.

Once the Shanghai ghetto was established in the Hongkew area, every Jewish person was restricted in their freedom to travel outside the ghetto. The Japanese authority announced that the refugees could not leave the ghetto without special permission. Furthermore, refugees' passes to leave the ghetto were only temporary. The Japanese declared that anyone who violated these rules would be severely punished. As a result, even though the Chinese had always been more disadvantaged than the Jewish refugees, at least they could go out and come into the area as they wished.

To go to school or work, every Jewish refugee had to get an exit pass from a Japanese officer. He was in charge of all the matters in the ghetto.

Mr. Goya was one of the most notorious Japanese officers in the Shanghai ghetto. He was a short, fat man with bulging eyes and a densely veiny nose. He also had a pinch of typical toothbrush-style mustache, making him look as cruel as Adolf Hitler. That toothbrush mustache scared many Jewish refugees in the Shanghai ghetto. Goya frequently touched his ridiculous mustache. He often bragged about the power of his Imperial Army. Goya had a huge belly, most likely because he had an enormous appetite. He spoke with a brusque and booming voice. He was the only Japanese soldier who could speak a little English, which allowed him to become the Japanese officer with authority in the Jewish ghetto.

Goya was unpredictable. He could be kind to the Jewish children, giving them some candies. He also played music with some Jewish children occasionally, although he was a lousy musician. But most of the time, Goya acted like a devil from hell, who was so capricious that it made the ghetto Jews miserable. Albert's friends told him that Goya was a Japanese evil. He was treacherous. He seemed to enjoy humiliating the Jews in the Shanghai ghetto. Goya caused a lot of trouble for them. Everyone was terrified of him.

For Albert, the feeling of imprisonment inside the Shanghai ghetto was not a big deal. The worst thing was the awful routine of applying for a pass from the Japanese officer. Albert did not like Goya, but he kept silent. Goya tried to antagonize Albert, often wagging his index finger at him.

Goya had a short man complex, and he took it out on anyone taller than he was, unfortunately, that included Albert. When Albert wanted to apply for a pass, Goya often made things difficult for him. One day, Albert was fed up with Goya's bullying.

"Just give me the pass," Albert snapped.

"I am the king of the Shanghai ghetto," Goya said. His voice was sonorous and harsh. He punched the table and yelled at Albert. Then Goya jumped on the table and slapped Albert hard across his face. Albert's nose was bleeding. Albert staggered back a couple of steps, out of Goya's reach. Finally, Albert staggered home with his bloody nose and bruised face.

"Papa, what happened to you? Papa," Nina rushed to her father when she saw him trudging back home in the terrible shape.

***

Even though Nina's family faced threats and bullying by the Japanese officer and lived in overcrowded and unsanitary rooms, her Papa managed to re-establish his business. He rebuilt his jam business in the ghetto. Papa made the business thrive despite all the challenges.

Papa encouraged other refugees to do the same as he did. He said, "We can be self-sufficient if we are willing to do anything that works." Nina often heard her father talking about this. His positive spirit inspired her at difficult times.

Despite their hardship, the Jewish refugees were undefeated. They developed small businesses in the ghetto and established schools and music facilities. They organized several theater groups, an orchestra, and sports teams such as soccer and table tennis. Refugee journalists and editors produced ten German publications circulated in the Shanghai ghetto.

Even with so many disadvantages in the ghetto, the Jewish refugees created a viable cultural life. They published their own incredible newspaper weekly. One person gave their outdated newspapers to others to read. The Jewish refugees brought some of their German lifestyles to Shanghai and created a new environment. Bakery and coffeehouses were a standard in Berlin or Vienna. Now they also were in Shanghai.

In a nearby coffee house, anyone could taste the authentic German cakes. The owner of the hairdresser spoke German with her customers. Even though they suffered bitterly in Shanghai, most Jewish refugees were grateful to the city because it allowed them to carry on living. The Wayside Road became known as "Little Berlin" for its cafes, shops, and nightclubs. It had the appearance of a German or Austrian city. Jewish refugees were well organized, preparing a dormitory to accommodate the Jewish refugees who lived in the Peace Building on Wayside Road. Someone also said that Wayside Road was becoming the "Broadway" of the Jewish ghetto. Another called it "little Vienna" because there was always a musical show in the area.

Music was an important aspect of Little Berlin. Nina played the bamboo flute to perform a classic Chinese piece that Hason had taught her. Hason was invited to see her performance. He was impressed by the enthusiastic atmosphere they created. He also appreciated the music shown by the Jewish refugees. Despite all the hardships in the reality of their lives in Shanghai, everyone was uplifted by the music.

Once in a while, Albert brought Nina and Alona to a small restaurant. Nina always felt fabulous there. It made her feel like she was back in Berlin somehow.

CHAPTER FOURTEEN

July 1943
Shanghai, China

A lthough life in the Shanghai ghetto could be distressing, Nina developed her own interests. She loved to observe the pigeons just like she had done in London. Her observation skills were improved, so she was even better than when she was in England.

Nina found the pigeons inspired her life here. She watched a flock of pigeons flying up into the sky and diving down, then swooping near the chimney, and at last landing on the roof gently and calmly. All the actions of the pigeons were in perfect unison. Nina wondered how these birds could fly together with such excellent coordination. She was also curious to know how the pigeons communicated with each other when they moved so fast.

Nina guessed that something might exist inside their brains that enabled them to communicate without words, just like what happened between Hason and herself. But she didn't know what it was. She wondered if it could be chemistry.

One day, Hason invited Nina to his home for a snack. Hason's mother gave Nina a bowl of sweet potato soup.

"Wow, this soup tastes sweet. Aunt, what is the name of this vegetable?" Nina asked Hason's mother.

"It's called red potato, Nina. I hope you like it," Hason's mother answered.

"I like it very much, thank you, Aunt!"

"The flavor of red potatoes is sweet and tasty, whether they were raw and cooked," Hason said.

"I will try raw red potato next time. Have you eaten a raw one before?"

"The uncooked red potato tastes better because it is full of sweet juices. Wow, it is juicy and tasty," Hason closed his eyes for a minute; it looked like he was biting into the raw red potato and tasting the juicy sweetness.

"Stop it," Nina giggled. She liked Hason's sense of humor.

On the way home, Nina wondered how she could be so connected with and interested in someone who doesn't even speak her language. She was surprised by the strength of her feelings for Hason.

***

Living in a big city like Shanghai and being naturally curious, Nina observed how the Chinese people lived.

One day, walking home with her Papa, Nina saw many Chinese workers on the street, running vigorously with their heavy rickshaws. Despite how hard the work was, the men did not show any stress on their faces. Nina was puzzled as to why so many poor Chinese people were suffering from hunger on the streets of Shanghai.

"Papa, did you see the legs of the rickshaw workers?" Nina asked her father.

"What did you see?" Albert asked her.

"So many big veins on their legs," Nina said.

"This is because their bodies were so overworked that their internal veins were distended and visible on the skin. This phenomenon is called varicose veins," Albert said.

"How can these people suffer so much, but their faces did not have any painful expression?"

"You must understand that the suffering person has no opportunity to feel sorry for himself," Albert patted Nina's head.

"Why is that?" Nina was more puzzled.

"Because once a person gives in to self-pity, he would lose the courage to face the grim reality of his life. Without the strong mental power to withstand his suffering, he would be swallowed up by all that suffering," Albert said.

"Oh!" Nina nodded.

"It is the same with us, becoming refugees from Berlin to Shanghai. we have had to learn to endure all kinds of hardships. We can't succumb to these difficulties. We must insist on our integrity and develop various ways to overcome all the hardships and be proud of our efforts." Papa continued to explain.

"You mean I have to overcome my fears and go through the Japanese guards every day with bravery?" Nina asked with a timid voice.

"Sure, that is what you should do," Papa, once again, touched Nina's head to encourage her.

That evening, Nina told her father she was so scared when she almost fell off the rooftop in Berlin with Mama during Kristallnacht. Then, she turned her head and stared at her father, "Papa, I wonder how you could fight with those two SS men without fear?"

"That is because I love you and your Mama so much. If any-one threatens your life, Papa will fight with my full strength for both of you."

"Papa," Nina called, leaning her head on Papa's shoulder.

"Sweetie, listen to me. You can be brave too. You have already shown that. You need to look around immediately when you are under a life-threatening attack. Find something, anything that you can use as a weapon to defend yourself. Even a piece of rock or a glass of water, anything could become a good weapon as long as you are ready to fight back, whether the attack is from humans or animals."

"Okay," Nina nodded.

* * *

One weekend in the early summer, Hason suggested that Nina go to the nearby Shanghai suburb for a stroll near the Huangpu River bank.

"What is the name of the song you played near the river that evening?" Nina asked Hason.

"Ah, It is called Jasmine Flower," Hason said.

"Oh, Jasmine Flower, it is beautiful. I like it very much," Nina said.

"I can show you more pretty flowers in the nearby suburbs if you like. Would you like to see the flowers and vegetables that grow in the countryside?" Hason asked.

"Sure, I'd love to," Nina agreed without hesitation.

Nina wore a black skirt with many tiny white flowers, and Hason wore ordinary white clothes. They walked for less than one hour. After they turned the corner of a big building, there before Nina was a sea of golden flowers. They spread out before her, a gorgeous sight with a distinctive fragrance fascinated Nina.

"What a smell!" Nina lifted her head and closed her eyes, "It is so fresh, and the scent is beautiful."

"Enjoy the gifts of nature," Hason said and opened his arms to the air.

Nina heard the bees buzzing on the flowers. She walked a few steps into the field to get a closer look at the bees. All the bees were busy and concentrating on collecting pollen from the flowers.

"Look at them," Nina said. First, she got excited seeing so many bees hard at work. Then, she pointed them out to Hason. "Are they working to make honey?"

"Certainly," Hason smiled.

"This yellow sea of flowers is so beautiful. What are they called?"

"This plant is called You-Cai," Hason said.

"What does the name mean?"

"The pronunciation of 'You' in Chinese means oil, and 'Cai' means vegetables. So this plant's name tells you exactly what it is for. It produces unique seeds to make vegetable oil," Hason said.

"Ow, I never knew that our vegetable oil comes from such beautiful flowers," Nina sighed and continued exploring.

"Is this green plant another Cai vegetable?" Nina pointed to the other side of the farmer's field.

"No, this is not a vegetable. This is wheat. We call it Mai Zi. The plants are young now, but they will be made into flour for bread and pasta."

"Really," Nina was surprised and somewhat embarrassed, "Well, I don't have too much knowledge about plants."

"That is normal for a city girl. It's easy to understand because you have lived in Berlin and London," Hason said.

"Thanks for your understanding. And thank you for teaching me about You Cai and Mai Zi," Nina said.

"Follow me, please," Hason waved his right hand to Nina.

When they went into the farmland, they walked on a narrow ridge separating two fields, one with green wheat and the other with yellow You Cai. In the far distance were the blue sky and white clouds. A thin column of smoke curled out from a low chimney of a farmer's house. The sunlight splashed on their young faces.

Hason turned around to see whether Nina had followed him. He found Nina was walking on the small ridge in the middle field of the yellow You Cai flowers and the green wheat leaves. She used her left hand to touch the wheat's tender leaves and her right hand to wave at the bees on You Cai flowers. Nina smiled happily. She enjoyed the natural beauty. She sauntered along, humming the gentle rhythm of "Scarborough Fair."

Hason was amazed by the beauty in front of him, the beautiful girl inside the amazing scene.

* * *

The following weekend, Nina wanted to see the beautiful yellow countryside field again with Hason. But he could not go because he had to work with his father. So Nina decided to go by herself. The weather was very nice. The sunshine and the warm breeze caressed her face.

Nina saw a pair of yellow birds, like finches, flying overhead and landing on a bush. They jumped around and chirped at each other. As Nina observed the little yellow birds singing and kissing, she thought about Hason and felt her face flush hot. She continued to wander around in the countryside.

All of a sudden, a strange noise came with the wind. Someone was shouting, and it sounded like a young girl. Nina stood still to listen carefully. She also heard what sounded like a man giggling and then another man chortling. An extreme fear urged Nina to escape right away. But, at the same time, she was curious too. So she hid in the dense bushes and remained silent to keep safe.

Through the tree branches and leaves, Nina saw two drunken Japanese soldiers chasing after a young Chinese girl. Nina's heart raced, and she held her breath.

The Japanese soldiers grabbed the girl and tied her up with a rope, and pushed her down to the ground. One of the soldiers ripped off the girl's shirt, and then he squeezed her breasts. The other soldier pulled off her pants. The young girl kept yelling, crying, and fighting. There was no possibility she could fight off the two madmen. They were like greedy wolves, ravishing this young girl.

Nina was so scared by what she saw. She had to cover her mouth with her hand to quiet herself. She could not keep from shaking, so she knelt down on the ground to support herself.

Then Nina saw one of the Japanese soldiers climbing on top of the girl and raping her. The girl cried out loudly. The other soldier stood there and waited for his turn. They were indeed like crazed animals. The young girl kept crying and screaming.

Nina had to close her eyes for a while to calm her nerves, but she couldn't block out the crazy sounds.

Finally, the young Chinese girl became so enraged and desperate. Somehow she managed to break loose the rope ties on her hands. She jumped on one of the soldiers. Her despairing rage turned into furious revenge. The girl bit a piece of the soldier's ear off.

The blood oozed out and dripped down on that soldier's ugly face.

"Baka, Baka!" (In Japanese: Idiot, Idiot!) The soldier covered his bleeding ear and cursed the girl. Now he was hurt badly and full of rage. He took out his bayonet from his trousers and stabbed it into the young girl's belly like a insane man. Fresh red blood splashed out from the girl's body.

Nina was shocked. She used both hands to cover her mouth, to stifle her crying. Her entire body was trembling. Even though a fury blazed within Nina, she kept herself quiet. She felt an unbearable sorrow for the Chinese girl. Her revulsion and fear of the Japanese soldiers grew enormously from that moment.

The Japanese soldier continued to stab the young girl's pubic area frantically. The girl was crying out loud, and then her sounds became diminished. The other Japanese soldier was watching and smirking.

Nina could not believe what had happened in front of her eyes. But she had to keep absolutely quiet to avoid any potential catastrophe landing on her. So Nina closed her eyes, slowed her breathing, moved further inside the shrub, and hid for her life.

She did not know how much time had passed. There was no longer any sound in the woods. Instead, she sensed an unusual quiet that had never been before. But her heart was still in her throat.

She opened her eyes, and a Chinese bulbul bird landed on a tree branch above her. It started to twitter loudly, turning around its large white patched head. It made a familiar sound, "cha-ko-lee...cha-ko-lee", which Nina usually enjoyed, but now she thought it was bothersome and annoying.

Nina peeked at the body of the Chinese girl. It was covered with blood. She was terrified to look at the site. She hurried away from the place as quickly as possible in case any Japanese soldiers came back.

"Cha-ko-lee," The Chinese bulbul bird continued its chirps. Nina thought maybe the light-vented-bulbul bird was singing a lament for the Chinese girl dying at the hands of murderers. With this thought, she no longer disliked the bird or its song.

Once she got home, Nina did not want to tell her parents what she had seen because she did not want them to worry about her. She didn't tell Hason either, although she expected he would give her some comfort. Nina decided to keep the secret to herself. She did not realize she had been seriously traumatized by this terrible event. The gruesome, bloody scene and the girl's horrible sounds haunted Nina for a very long time.

Nina feared that something terrible could happen to her too. She was scared for now and for the unknown future.

CHAPTER FIFTEEN

December 1944
Shanghai, China

In the winter of 1944, most of the refugees in the Shanghai ghetto thought the war would not end soon. They tried to prepare themselves to survive the war in the long term. More and more Jewish teenagers were no longer going to school because they didn't have enough food or clothes to wear. Due to poor health and hygiene conditions, refugees were vulnerable to diseases. Some children's hair grew longer and longer, and their scalps became itchy. Everyone was always thinking about how to make money to buy food and make a living. The refugees in the ghetto struggled to survive.

Nina once drew a series of pictures to illustrate her family's life story from Berlin to Shanghai: from walking on the Rhine riverbank with her grandma to seeing their burning synagogue in Berlin with her Mama; then playing with the pigeons in London near the Thames River with Mommy and Daddy to listening to her Papa on the Italian ocean liner over the Red Sea; then playing flute with Hason by the Huangpu River; until finally helping Mama to light the coal stove in the Shanghai ghetto.

Nina always helped her Mama use a Chinese-style small coal stove for cooking food. The coal stove should first be ignited with some paper and then burned with a small black coal cake. This was used for cooking rice and warming the winter house simultaneously. Unfortunately, this coal-burning stove emitted a dark smoke with an irritating smell at the beginning. But later on, the stove released an odorless, colorless gas, which contained toxic carbon monoxide. Nina was once poisoned by that gas. She felt dizzy and sleepy because she had inhaled too much monoxide from the coal stove in her tiny room.

* * *

The time was flying faster than the rapids on the Huangpu River. In the spring of 1945, Nina was 15 years old and was already a tall and beautiful girl. Her eyes became brighter, and her body started to grow up to maturity beauty.

One day after school, Nina walked toward the Huangpu Riverbank. She promised Hason they would play a particular piece of flute music together that day. Nina was thinking about her best friend, Hason, and his smiling face.

Nina ambled on the Wayside Road with light steps and hummed the flute melody. When she was near the end of the road, Nina suddenly found a drunken Japanese soldier lurking at the corner. The stink of alcohol made Nina frown and cover her nose. She did not expect that a Japanese soldier would be there. Nina was afraid, and her heartbeat became fast.

Nina instantly turned around and walked away quickly. She hoped the soldier would not see her. But he did. The soldier shouted out to her, pleading, "Bishōjo, Bishōjo" (In Japanese: Beautiful girl). The Japanese followed her. Nina glanced back and saw the soldier waving his hand and yelling at her. She could tell he was drunk by his slurred words and staggering gait. Unfortunately, he did not stop chasing her.

The terrible scene of the Japanese soldiers raping and killing the Chinese girl immediately came into Nina's mind. She realized that horror could happen to her today, and she sped up her footsteps, going from walking fast to a quick trot. Then she heard heavy stomping sounds behind her. Nina moved her legs as fast as she could, starting to run.

Nina assumed that she might be attacked by this Japanese soldier and that she might be killed by him. She was terrified. She was sweating and panting, hands trembling. She just kept increasing her running speed.

The sound of running footsteps behind her continued. She checked back with a swift glimpse and saw that the short Japanese soldier was still chasing her. He mumbled something in Japanese but kept chasing her with his drunken steps.

Suddenly, the Japanese soldier ran up fast, and he grabbed Nina's shirt at her shoulder. Nina screamed and struggled away. The soldier had ripped off a piece of fabric from her clothing, but she had gotten away. She ran as fast as she could. She was short of breath, gasping to fill her lungs. Her heartbeat was racing like an escaping rabbit.

Nina ran into a roadside field. She abruptly tumbled over a stone. She fell and, in her panic, almost could not get up. Nina bit down her lower lip and stood up, and kept running.

In front of Nina, a broken ruined wall blocked her way. Even though that wall was only waist-high, Nina found it challenging to crawl over it. She had just gotten up from a sudden fall, and she was exhausted from running. Nevertheless, Nina knew she must hurry and get over this ruined wall before the drunken Japanese caught up to her.

At that moment, Nina had just heaved her right leg up on the wall when she felt someone grab her left hip. The sensation was horrible.

"Bishōjo," the drunken man yelled form her back.

Nina was terrified.

Nina was screeching out vehemently. She struggled along the rough brick wall, shaking her left leg combatively and kicking her right foot ferociously on the drunken soldier's clutching hand. But the drunken man would not release his grasp.

"Help, Help!" Nina screamed.

All at once, Nina's leg was released. She heard the Japanese soldier suddenly falling down beside the wall with an enormous thud.

Nina did not understand what had happened.

"Run, Nina, Run!" Hason's voice burst out like a trumpet.

"Baka, Baka!" The drunken Japanese soldier shouted at Hason. Hason was fighting with the Japanese. They were falling to the ground together and combating with fists each other.

Nina gathered her energy to crawl over the broken wall. It took all her body's strength to heave herself over. She landed on the debris of the broken bricks on the other side. She could hear the mixed battling noises on the other side of the wall.

Nina turned around to look at Hason. She shouted out, "Hason, Hason, run!"

"Nina, you run!" Hason shouted back urgently.

"Hason, Come on!" Nina paused, waiting for Hason.

"Nina, you run! Run!" Hason shouted again.

Nina ran into the field with some reluctance. She paused again. She was still a little distance from the small woods in front of her.

The drunken soldier got up from the ground. He was still searching for Nina. His arms leaned on the ruined wall, and his red eyes watched her running into the woods.

Hason jumped up and grabbed the soldier's arms from behind. Hason forcefully pressed the Japanese soldier's two arms on the broken wall. The soldier could not move at all except to yell a barrage of Japanese curses. He howled and struggled to free himself but was too drunk to succeed. Because Hason was able to restrain the soldier, Nina had enough time to run into the woods.

"Baka, Baka," the drunken soldier cursed and struggled.

Hason watched Nina run beyond the soldier's view and disappear into the woods. It was only then that Hason saw a bayonet swinging from around the soldier's light yellow army trousers. This knife could be a huge risk for him if the Japanese soldier take it off. He released the Japanese arms and ran away in the other direction.

Nina's breath still was coming in gasps, and her heartbeat was frantic. She kept looking back for Hason at the edge of the woods. She was so worried about him.

The second day after Hason rescued Nina, his family moved away from the Shanghai ghetto area. They disappeared with no chance to say farewell to Nina. She didn't know where they had gone. They might be moved to the rural area of nearby Zhejiang Province in the south of Shanghai because Hason once mentioned to Nina he had relatives there. Nina was so sorry that Hason didn't even have the chance to say goodbye to her.

That night, Nina could not fall asleep, and she cried under the quilt for a long time. She longed for another day like the one when she and Hason played their flutes near the Huangpu River. Nina remembered she dreamed of dancing with Hason, but she never did. She always regretted that.

Nina dreamed of Hason that night. They danced and danced together. It seemed to be her lucky day, and it was exhilarating to dance with Hason in a white cloud. She was a fantastic dancer in her dream, skillfully spinning around to the music. Nina and Hason danced and jumped, even flying beside the riverbank, even above the Huangpu River. Nina took Hason's hand in a farmer's field, running joyfully. Then all of a sudden, she lost hold of his hand. Hason was going further and further away. She could not catch up with him even though she could fly like a bird. She was flying fast and then started to cry. Nina didn't wake up until her tears soaked the pillow. After that, Nina remembered her bitter-sweet dream, full of sadness and happiness.

The following day, Nina walked down the Dent Road in the ghetto area. She missed Hason a lot, primarily because of the dream the night before. She saw so many people walking and moving in front of her, but there was no one like Hason at all. Nina's tears blurred her eyes and then fell into her wavy hair. All the way through the street, along the river, and over the bridge, she immersed herself in the memory of last night's dream. She repeated his name in her head, "Hason, Hason!"

At the intersection of Dent Road and Yougtzepoo Road, someone called out, "Hason!" Nina thought Hason had come back. She could feel the rapid beats of her heart, and she felt excited and happy. She sensed her face getting red and hot.

Nina sped up her pace, looking around for Hason. She searched and searched at the intersection, but there was no Hason. She began to get anxious. Finally, she couldn't help but shout out on the street, "Hason!"

To her huge surprise, a bearded old man turned back and looked at her with wide-open eyes. Nina flushed when she found the old man staring at her with such a bewildering look. Nina was embarrassed and rapidly turned around and hurried back home.

Nina almost right away realized that this old gentleman's name was probably Hason too. Hason was a common Chinese first name. She was embarrassed by her mistake, but it was because she missed her friend so much.

Three weeks later, after school, Nina ignored her father's warning about not going to near the Huangpu River. On the way to the river-bank, Nina heard the frogs croaking from the field as if they were singing an aloud sorrowful song. The unceasing cicadas' chirpings made Nina a bit light-headed. A warm wet breeze blew on her unhappy face. She saw the petals of blooming magnolia flying around and dropping to the ground with sadness and grief.

Nina sat on a gigantic rock near the water and watched the waves hurrying by meaninglessly. Then, finally, the squawking of a group of seagulls broke the evening silence on the Huangpu River. The sunset was a burgundy red with thick dark gray clouds in the background.

Nina looked vacantly into the far distances of the Huangpu River. The breeze from the river was blowing her hair. She felt anxious and worried. She focused on a ship drifting away over the river. Her eyes filled with tears again. She imagined that the distant ship was carrying Hason away from her.

A particular sense of loss made Nina heartache. Sometimes it was as sharp as a stab. Nina did not understand these feelings because she was so young. Why did Hason's leaving make her so miserable? Why did his disappearance make her so sad? Why did she miss him so much? Finally, Nina admitted to herself that the sound of Hason's bamboo flute would never be heard here again. Nina realized that her sadness would last for a long time.

After that, Nina would spend much more time practicing her own bamboo flute. Sometimes, she would cry when she played some piece of music that Hason used to play.

Nina thought about Hason all the time, with or without tears. Hason had been willing to sacrifice his own life to save her when she was threatened. She believed there was a superlative friendship. Nina wondered how a particular moment in a person's life could be crucial to that person's fate. But Nina was sure that Hason's name was engraved in her heart for the rest of her life.

Spring had come to Shanghai quietly. Nina passed by a magnolia tree with white flowers, which was a common sight. An old Chinese lady told Nina that the white magnolia was a bitter flower because it was in blossom without green leaves to serve as partners. Nina thought the white magnolia flowers looked lonely and sorrowful in the chilly spring wind. Nina realized that she might never see the flowers of this tree ever again if she left Shanghai. Once she thought this, she also thought she might never ever see Hason again. She burst into tears. She could not take her eyes off that magnificent magnolia tree and thought she would surely miss its flowering next year and the year after.

Nina went to the Huangpu River on a windy day with a particular purpose. She wrote a sad and romantic lyric poem for Hason. She wanted to let her dreams and feelings fly over the Huangpu River, just like the pigeons flew up into the sky. Nina stood upon a huge rock, the rive waves lapping at her feet. She took out her poem from her chest pocket and lifted the paper up high in the air. She closed her eyes and then let her poetry fly over the river in the wind, flying up even higher than the birds.

"Please tell me!

Blue sky in the far distance

Please tell me why my heart is so fluttery?
White cloud on the move
Please tell me why my mind is so blurry?
Flying gulls above the river
Please tell me if you could carry my feelings to the one I love?
A soft breeze from the river
Please tell me if you could let me know where he is?
Please tell me!
Please tell me!"

CHAPTER SIXTEEN

July 1945
Shanghai, China

One of Papa's friends, Ivan, who worked for a Russian-Jewish club in the Shanghai ghetto, got unofficial news about a planned bombing of the ghetto on July 17, 1945. The Allied Air Forces commander believed the Japanese Army had a large oil warehouse hidden in the Hongkew area near the Jewish ghetto. Because oil was an essential resource for the Japanese Army, the bombardment was a major strategy to defeat the Japanese Army and end the war.

Ivan said that was why the Allied Air Forces bombed the Hongkew area during the daytime. They did hit a Japanese oil warehouse, killing some Japanese soldiers. Sadly, thirty-eight Jewish refugees and hundreds of Chinese lost their lives in that bombing.

Nina was on the way to see her girlfriend Mei Lin. She experienced the horrible bombing and saw her friend's building had been bombed with her own eyes. She never forgotten the fears of being bombed under her table at home when the Japanese oil tanks explored by the air raid. That afternoon, Nina and her Mama went out to take a look at the bombed streets. They saw destruction everywhere. Where houses had been bombed, there were piles of rubbles. They could see abandoned clothes covered with blood on the street. Nina knew she would never see her girlfriend Mei Lin and her mother ever again because their home was destroyed. It was a terrible disaster for Nina. She could not fall asleep for a month because of nightmares of the bombing.

Information was piecemeal, coming through different channels during the war into the ghetto. Nina's family and the other Jews in the ghetto were largely isolated from the rest of the world. As a result, they could not get much reliable information about the war. They learned from different sources that Hitler's Nazis had been defeated gradually in the spring of 1945. Still, the news was spotty and ambiguous about the Japanese inland.

"The defeat of Japan was only a matter of time," Papa told Mama.

"Why?" Mama puzzled.

"Since the military activities around Shanghai have visibly increased," Papa said.

Albert analyzed the situation for his wife. He paid more attention to the Japanese Army's maneuvers in the area these days. Nina listened to her parents as she was older and could understand the situation now. After the Allied air raids on the Hongkew area, the tension in the ghetto was acute. Everyone was on alert.

Ivan brought more news about who was victorious in the war. The most fantastic information was the German Army's defeat and its withdrawal from Russia. He said that the mainland of the Japanese empire was under attack by American air forces. Then comes the shocking news about the atomic bombs that destroyed Hiroshima and Nagasaki on August 6 and 9, 1945.

All Nina knew was that they were super bombs that almost wiped out two big cities entirely in Japan. They said that thousands of people in Hiroshima and Nagasaki had been killed. Nina imagined the whistle of those great bombs. Even though Nina hated the Japanese soldiers, she was sympathetic to the Japanese civilians who died.

It was a terrible fear for Jewish refugees in the Shanghai ghetto because Shanghai was indeed a Japanese military deployed and already became a bombing target. It could be a super bomb target too.

"How do we know they will not drop the superbomb on Shanghai?" Papa and his Jewish peers worried that this horror could come to them.

During this time, Nina was working. She delivered bread in the mornings that summer. In one early morning, Nina discovered that the Japanese soldiers had disappeared. They were supposed to guard the Shanghai ghetto, but they were gone without any notification. It only for a week when Jewish refuges worried about the superbomb.

It was on August 15, 1945, that the first rumors of Japan's surrender swept through the ghetto like wildfire. Because it came with dramatic suddenness, most refugees thought that the news was too good to be true. So they kept silent at first. But gradually, Nina and her parents confirmed that all Japanese soldiers had disappeared from the streets. Finally, they got the official information. The Japanese government announced that it would surrender without condition.

The war was over.

The Jewish refugees would regain their freedom and think of their families back home. Soon it would be time for them to go home too. Everyone was excited and anticipating the day they could leave. People were laughing, talking, and planning. Everyone was thrilled.

"It is true. Japan has surrendered, the war is over. We are free," Papa told Nina and Mama.

The Japanese Army left Shanghai. All the soldiers left the Hongkew area. Goya escaped the refugee ghetto. There was no more horrible ghetto king.

What a wonderful time!

Nina never forgot the date, September 3, 1945, when the Shanghai ghetto, at last, disbanded officially.

During this time, the United Nations and Jewish relief organizations' representatives came to assist Jewish refugees. Nina recognized many American soldiers and navy sailors walking and laughing around the

Shanghai streets. She felt excited and happy when the United Nations distributed canned foods, clothes, and medicines. The city was full of hope for Jewish refugees.

Soon their attention and thoughts turned to the fate of those left behind in Germany, their parents, siblings, and loved ones. All the time, they had wondered what was happening inside Germany during the war. They worried about their family members and relatives under Nazi's ruling. They were sure their families also wanted to know about their lives in Shanghai.

After the war was over, the Red Cross posted the list of survivors on the bulletin board in the Hongkew area. All the refugees rushed out to see who had survived in their families. The news was devastating.

Albert and Alona joined the anxious crowds in the Hongkew area almost every day, gathering around the United Nations list that showed the names of the few found alive. They never imagined the extent of the horror of the gas chambers and Hitler's machinery of death. They anxiously searched for the names of parents, siblings, and other loved ones. Only a small handful of friends and relatives had survived the Holocaust in Germany.

Virtually everyone was gone from the European ghettos.

Only then did they realize that what was always thought of as the misery of the Shanghai ghetto was a paradise compared to the European ghettos under the Nazis. The hardships of life in Shanghai were minimal compared to the death of so many of their relatives in Nazi Germany.

Nina's family was devastated after learning about the tragedy. The indescribable sadness almost crushed everybody. The horrible news of the deaths in Germany came in terrible waves.

Nina and her parents could hardly bear the reality of what they were learning. Their dear parents and siblings had been murdered by the Nazis. Nina had so many loving memories of her grandma and her aunts and uncles. She was full of tears. Her parents also felt terrible sorrow for their parents and brothers, and sisters.

When Nina thought about her uncles and aunts, especially the vivid memories of her grandma, she cried sadly. It was hard to believe she had no aunts and uncles anymore. Nina felt guilt when she heard about Uncle Allen because she had survived, and he had not. The feeling of losing her loved ones broke her heart, piece by piece, in endless grieving.

One of Albert's friends, Robert, had survived the Sachsenhausen concentration camp. Albert knew the Sachsenhausen camp because it was where he had been jailed right after Kristallnacht. Robert said it was estimated that 30,000 people had been killed by the Nazis in that concentration camp alone.

Robert also brought some detailed information about Allen's family. One of Allen's friends passed a message to Allen about the last chance they could have to leave Germany. There was a passage on the Trans-Siberian Railway to Shanghai. But Allen had to take care of his ill mother-in-law. Plus, it was an exceedingly long journey from Berlin to Shanghai by train. Allen could not know his family had already lost the opportunity to escape from Nazi Germany. His entire family received deportation order a week later. Everybody in Allen's family was sent to a concentration camp, and no one in that family ever came out alive.

Albert's cousin, Rose, sailed on the MS St. Louis on May 13, 1939, and went to Havana, Cuba. But she could not enter Cuba. The United States refused to let the ship enter their ports. Canada ejected the immigrants as well. Finally, they returned to Europe. Rose landed in France. Unfortunately, Nazi Germany invaded France in June 1940, and Rose was not immune to the disaster. She was a victim of the Nazi's massacre of French Jews. The Nazi SS murdered Rose in one of their concentration camps.

Albert still remembered saying goodbye to Rose in Berlin before she left. Papa told Nina, with tears, that each goodbye could be the last one, particularly during the war.

Nina had so many family members who stayed in Germany. Almost all of their relatives, friends, classmates, companions, and neighbors had been murdered by the Nazis.

Now, Nina's family never wanted to step on German soil again because they could not bear the immense grief from their enormous loss. Germany could no longer be their home.

Nina's parents were grateful they had the good fortune to stay in Shanghai.

"Although the Japanese ghettoized the Shanghai Jews, at least they did not agree with the Nazis to exterminate us," Papa said.

Nina understood they had at least good possibilities for their lives and their children's lives. They were alive, so there was a possibility for future growth, development, love, and new generations.

In September 1945, the city of Shanghai confirmed its liberation from the Japanese army and the war was over. However, because the United States and British still did not accept Jews at that time, Nina's father and mother decided to stay in Shanghai. They were sure they did not want to return to Germany.

Nina had serious insomnia for many nights because of all the sadness. Finally, one Friday afternoon, when she returned home from her school, she complained, "Mama, I've got a severe headache, and I feel exhausted today."

"Sweetie, go to bed and get some sleep," Mama said, not even lifting her head. Instead, she sat in front of her sewing machine and paddled it with the consistent "da-da-da" sounds. She was awfully busy that day because she had a large order from an affluent customer.

"Okay, Mama," Nina went directly to bed. A few minutes after lying down, she felt severe cramps in her stomach. Soon she started to vomit.

Alona rushed over to her daughter and asked, "Sweetie, what happened?" When she touched Nina's forehead, she cried out, "Oh gosh! Your head is so hot."

"My stomach hurts, Mama!"

"Let me get you some water and check your temperature, Sweetie!"

"Sweetie, come on. Drink some water first, "Mama said. She held Nina's back and fed her some water. Alona could feel the fever in Nina's body when she hugged her daughter.

Nina's temperature was 40-degree Celsius. That was much higher than Alona expected. "We need to see a doctor right now," Mama said with a firm tone.

"Should we wait for Papa to come back home?" Nina asked her mother, "I feel so exhausted, Mama."

"Your Papa sometimes comes home very late. We better go now and see the Jewish doctor on Wayside Road before he goes home," Mama insisted. She hurried to take Nina to the nearby clinic.

After the check-up, the doctor's diagnosis was serious, "Nina has typhoid fever, a dangerous disease caused by bacteria."

"Has she got bacteria?" Alona asked.

"The infecting bacteria are called Salmonella. She most likely contacted some contaminated food or waters somewhere a few days or weeks ago."

"Typhoid fever is dangerous to a child, isn't it?" Alona became more anxious, and she hugged her daughter tightly as if Nina could slip away from her. "Doctor, are you sure?"

"I am sure. My diagnosis depends completely on the symptoms and the area you live in. Madam, you should understand that other diagnostic techniques such as bacteria culture are not available at all. We are in Shanghai now, not in Berlin. If not treated on time, the risk is high."

"Doctor, please save my daughter," Alona tried to control her panic.

"Here is the prescription for an antibiotic, which is good to treat this disease," the doctor said. He handed the prescription to Alona.

"Thank you very much, doctor!" Alona hurried to leave with Nina.

"Wait for a minute, Madam," the doctor said, "There are three things I have to mention to you. First, let your daughter drink lots of water and have a good rest. Second, once you get the antibiotic, bring it here; I'll inject the medicine for you. Third, because this disease is contagious, you want to keep her away from your other family members."

Alona appreciated the doctor's instructions and left the clinic. After she brought Nina back home, she ran to Albert's workplace.

When Albert saw his wife rush into his store, panting and sweating, he knew something was wrong.

"Nina has typhoid fever," Alona gave the prescription to her husband.

"Is it medicine for Nina?" Albert asked.

"It is antibiotics for this illness. It may cost a lot of money," Alona said.

"Honey, don't worry. I will definitely get it, even though antibiotics are difficult to find in the Shanghai market," Albert knew the scarcity of medicine because of the war.

"The medicine must be expensive," Alona said.

"I will find a way to get it for Nina," Albert promised.

Ultimately, Albert sold his watch to buy antibiotics to save Nina's life.

When Nina got the injection, it was a harrowing experience. She tried not to cry when she got the shots of antibiotics. The doctor emphasized good hygienic habits like frequent hand-washing for Nina as well as her parents. Nina recovered from the illness reasonably well.

* * *

The next few years passed quickly. Shanghai became a home Nina was reluctant to leave, even on the eve of a new war. Nina's family had to look for a chance to leave Shanghai because the domestic war in China was becoming intense. But which country should they go to? England should be the first choice.

"Let's go to England," Nina suggested. She missed her Daddy and Mommy a lot. But she did not know that Britain's immigration policy still restricted the number of stateless Jewish refugees. Nina was looking forward to a fresh beginning since she had lost all hope of ever seeing Hason in Shanghai again after such a long time.

Until 1949, Israeli diplomats came to Shanghai. After that, lots of Jews from all over the world immigrated to Israel. Nina's parents decided to start their new life in a new city and a new country, Tel Aviv, Israel.

The Israeli government had chartered three Greek ships to carry Shanghai Jewish refugees to the newly established country. Once on-board one of these ships, sailing on the Yangtze River, Nina realized her family was finally headed to their new home, Israel.

Before leaving Shanghai, Nina walked along the humid, deserted Huangpu riverbank. The seagulls flew in silence as if they were numbed in a flash by something. Nina let the cold morning wind blow on her cheek, stinging her eyes as if the pain could make her heartache less.

Nina waved her hand and shouted to the Huangpu River,

"Goodbye, Shanghai! Thank you!"

"Goodbye, Hason! Thank you!"

PART IV

THE JORDAN RIVER

CHAPTER SEVENTEEN

August 1949
Tel Aviv, Israel

I t was a sunny day in the late summer of 1949. Nina already had her nineteenth birthday.

Nina heard a piece of familiar, rousing music that touched her heart when their ship sailed into Tel Aviv, Israel. It indeed was Antonín Dvořák's Number Ninth Symphony, the "New World Symphony." It was the perfect music to welcome her family to their new life in a new country. Nina had played the same tune over in her mind many times on the way from Shanghai to Tel Aviv. As she heard the melody, an anthem for their "New World" became more vital and more brilliant as the Israeli shoreline emerged. Nina's face flushed with inspiration, and her eyes glistened.

Nina thought of all her previous hardships when she had almost given up hope. She remembered the day she and Mama crawled onto the rooftops in Berlin, where she lost her balance and almost fell from the roof, and then she went to London and Shanghai. Now she realized she must be patient in life. Nina reminded herself she must never give up. She must continue to have hope because God will take care of her.

Nina had reached her new home. Finally, she could build up a new life. The powerful symphonic music expressed the joy she felt. Her eyes were full of joyful tears.

"We are coming, Israel," Someone beside her cried out.

"We are coming, Israel," Then almost everybody cried out.

"We are coming, Israel," Nina cried out without holding back her excitement, accompanied by the glorious climax of the "New World Symphony." The sonorous musical cadences became a proper celebration of their arrival.

But, even more, important than their starting a new life in Israel was that their life in exile was over.

Nina's Mama jumped from the boat into the water at the seaside in Tel Aviv. She held an Israeli flag and walked to her new homeland in the water. Nina followed her Mama, jumped into the water, and walked to the shore. Her face was full of excitement, and her heart was filled with joy. They, at last, had their own home, where there were no any anti-Jewish activities, not at all.

Nina's family started their hectic new life with a joyful spirit. They began to build their life in a kibbutz. The word kibbutz means "gathering." At the beginning of the country, the kibbutz was an agricultural settlement in Israel, a unique community the Jewish pioneers created. The kibbutz residents shared everything and worked as members of a collective. Their lives were hard in the early days in the kibbutz.

Nevertheless, everyone worked together to create and enjoy life. Everything was shared, and kibbutz members participated in all aspects of the community, working in the fields or kitchen and kindergarten. In addition, all members eat meals in the kibbutz dining hall.

Nina not only worked hard in the kibbutz, but she also made some good friends. She did various jobs, cooking, planting trees, organizing younger kids, and playing musical instruments with other young people. Everyone liked her.

* * *

Nina lived on the kibbutz for six years, growing into a mature, beautiful young woman. Eventually, however, she wanted a new experience outside of the kibbutz, in the city of Tel Aviv.

"I want to do something else other than agricultural work, Papa," Nina said.

"The sense of community in the kibbutz is great. You could not find that anywhere else." Albert was a devout kibbutzim.

"I know that, but I am 25 already, and I want to see more of the world outside, Papa!" Nina did not want to argue with her father. Instead, she felt sorry to disagree with her father's belief.

"Kibbutz is the root of our country. Look, Israel's first Prime Minister moved into a kibbutz recently." Albert was proud of his kibbutznik colleagues, who became members of Israel's parliament.

Nina gave in to her father at that time, although she did not wholly agree with his ideas.

In the meantime, Nina's Mama developed a chronic cough and became weak. Nina was worried about her mother's health. Then, one evening, Mama called Nina to her bedside. She clenched her daughter's hand, "Sweetie, you have grown up to be a beautiful girl. You are charming. You have a good heart. I am blessed to have you."

"Mama," Nina called. She knelt beside her mother and sensed something strange in her tone.

"At last, we have made a better life here than we could have in Berlin or Shanghai. Now it is time for you to find a good husband to build your future. I know a suitable man is not easy to find," Mama said.

"Mama, I know."

"I have to go to a hospital to treat my illness within a few days. The hospital will isolate me from everybody, including your Papa and you," Mama continued.

"Why?" Nina realized it may be her illness that made her mother talk this way. She worried about how serious the disease was.

"Doctor said I may have tuberculosis in my lung. So it would be better to admit me to the hospital and prevent it from spreading to anybody else. But before I enter the hospital, I want to give you the most important advice for your life." Mama squeezed Nina's hand gently.

"Mama, I am listening carefully," Nina said. Her heart was heavy.

"There are many good men in the world, healthy, good-looking, talented, and maybe even wealthy. But not everyone will be good for you." Mama took a deep breath.

"Mama, don't worry about my future husband. I don't even have a boyfriend yet," Nina said. She tried to ease the atmosphere for a moment.

"I am serious, Nina," Mama continued, "You have to find a man who is good to you and is suitable for you. That means he really cares about you. He has done good things for you. He can accept your strengths and weaknesses. At the same time, you will accept his strengths and weaknesses. Sweetie, you must remember my words."

"Yes, Mama, that is exactly the boyfriend I am looking for." Nina nodded.

Mama smiled and was satisfied.

After that talk, Nina knew what kind of boy to look for. But unfortunately, most of the boys she met were either not the type of boy she was looking for or didn't meet her lofty standards.

A few months later, Nina met David Feldstein. They were in a musical seminar in Tel Aviv City Center. David was tall and handsome and brilliant. He could play the violin skillfully. They sat together at the workshop by chance and had a pleasant chat about musical instruments. Later on, David helped Nina improve her Hebrew.

When David finally asked her out, Nina hesitated. "Why do you like me?" she asked.

"I like you for no logical reason," David said. Nina's heart had been touched by his answer. From that time, she accepted him as her boyfriend. David was very thoughtful. He tried to make every situation better and more comfortable for Nina. David was always concerned about what Nina was worried about. He tried to help her whenever he could.

One significant reason Nina liked David was his smile reminded her of the Shanghai boy Hason's. But Nina kept this secret to herself. She liked that David was always smiling at her. It was so helpful when they could speak the same language, Hebrew. That made communications much more comfortable.

Little by little, step by step, David won Nina's heart. Nina fell in love at last. They got along well, enjoying each other's company. If there were some minor arguments, they could get over them without too much effort. Nina felt everything seemed hopeful.

But life always has challenges. David's parents wanted him to go to the United States for university. If he had agreed to go abroad at such an early stage of their relationship, their love story would have ended. David stubbornly resisted his parent's wish and stayed with Nina. He did not want to end their relationship like that.

They grew closer together with genuine love. Nina had her first kiss from David, and soon after, she accepted his proposal of marriage.

Right after their wedding ceremony, David had to go to the army for his compulsory military service. It was a requirement for all Israeli citizens to serve their country. That night, before David went to the front line, they lay on the bed and kissed each other for a long time. When David hugged her so tightly and entered her, Nina felt a slight ache at the beginning, then a bit of tickling. Then, at last, like a bird's pecking, she woke up hundreds and thousands of birds flying off into the beautiful sky. All these sensations happened at the same time. Nina felt thrilled and pleased.

David went to the front at the end of October 1956. She was told the battlefield was near the Suez Canal. Nina recalled vividly her father's narrating the story of Moses when they went through the Suez Canal about twenty years ago when her family was in exile at that time.

Nina wondered how cyclical life was.

Nina was married for only one month in November 1956, when she got the unbelievable news. Time was spinning so fast that Nina felt dizzy, as if in a dream.

It was a cloudy Thursday morning. The Lieutenant from David's platoon came to her home to deliver David's medal.

David was dead.

"David made the ultimate sacrifice in the war for his country. He is a hero," the Lieutenant said.

"Ah," Nina only mumbled, holding back the tears. Albert held on to Nina's shoulder to support her. Fortunately, Papa came to her home early in the morning.

"Thanks for coming," Albert said. "Sit down, please."

"Excuse me," Nina said to the Lieutenant and wiped her face. Then, she walked into her room with David's medal.

"David is a real hero of our platoon. Initially, he was fighting as an assistant to our machine gunner," the Lieutenant told Albert,

"Then," Albert listened to what the Lieutenant had to say about his son-in-law.

"The gunner was killed by the enemy's bombing. David immediately took over the gunner's position and continued fighting," the Lieutenant said. His face was mournful.

"One of the enemy's bullets passed through the small hole in the metal shield of the machine gun. Regretfully, it shot David in the head. The time was exactly one hour before the cease-fire was declared." the Lieutenant shook his head sadly.

"He was a good boy," Albert sighed.

"Thank you, Lieutenant!" Nina came out of her room. She had tidied up her hair by then. Nina tried to be polite to her husband's Lieutenant.

"Please accept my deepest condolences!" The Lieutenant gave Nina a military salute.

Nina lost her husband in a local war during a relatively peaceful time. As a result, her grief developed into a depression. She got lost in her deep thoughts.

David sacrificed his life in the Second Arab-Israeli War for the newly established country. But for Nina, the loss was personal. She lost the dearest man, her love, and her happiness.

When Nina walked by the riverbank, she could not figure out why war never left her alone. The nearby seagulls cried above the Jordan River. The misty fog moved in from the faraway mountains, surrounding Nina like a caress.

Mama was still in the Contagious Disease Hospital. She was despondent when she heard about her son-in-law dying on the battlefield and worried about her daughter's depression.

To make matters worse, Mama suffered from a severe relapse of tuberculosis in her lungs. She had already been isolated in the hospital for some time. However, the doctor insisted she continues the quarantine. Alona did not know where she got infected with tuberculosis. A probable cause may be her working hard and lack of sleep. The treatment for tuberculosis required a long time. Medical professionals decided that all patients with the disease needed to be isolated in a hospital, far away from their communities.

"Mama, how are you doing?" Nina called her mother often during those first few months.

"Sweetie, I am exhausted," Mama said.

"Please tell me what the doctor said."

"The doctor said my condition has deteriorated."

"Papa misses you. I miss you a lot," Nina's voice was intense and tearful.

"Sweetie, I also miss you very much. I'd love to see you and your Papa," Mama said.

"Mama, you got to take care of yourself for Papa and me," Nina said. Her tears were on the brink of falling, glistening in her eyes.

Albert was rubbing away his tears as he stood next to his daughter. Nina noticed her father looked much older recently.

"I want to see Mama," Nina said to her Papa. She was stressed because the hospital did not allow anyone to visit. They were afraid of spreading the disease.

"I also miss your mother very much, Sweetie," Albert said. His hand was trembling.

Nina's grief over David was augmented because she missed her mother so much. She kept replaying the same unforgettable memories over in her mind. Nina recalled the horrible time Mama carried her running over Berlin's rooftops. She remembered the terrible scene of the Nazi SS men burning their synagogue and destroying their musical store. She remembered the sensation of her mother holding her.

Two months later, a doctor from the hospital phoned Albert. He said the harsh reality of Alona's condition was she might never return home. Even with intensive treatment, her condition worsened. Albert knew he had to tell Nina, "Your mother may never get out of that hospital. Her pulmonary tuberculosis is not getting better after eight months in the hospital."

Once Nina realized she might never see her mother ever again, she felt a stabbing pain in her heart. She could not bear the thought of losing her.

"Mama, I must see you," Nina called her mother right away.

"Nina, Sweetie," Mama started to cry.

"Mama, Mama," Nina intuitively sensed something worse was happening to her mother because Mama seldom cried.

"Nina, my Nina," Alona cried.

"Mama, I want to see you. I want to hug you," Nina sobbed on the phone.

Then it was time to hang up the phone. Mama said in a distinct voice, "Auf wiedersehen! Auf wiedersehen!"

Nina said goodbye to her mother with immense sadness. She kept holding onto the phone aimlessly until there was only a beeping sound on the line.

CHAPTER EIGHTEEN

January 1957
Tel Aviv, Israel

M isfortune never comes alone, as the proverb says.
Nina lost the two people she loved the most. First, her beloved husband in the war, and then her dearest Mama passed away from tuberculosis in the hospital. The two of them had gone into another world almost at the same time.

Nina's grief was inconsolable because she did not get to say goodbye to either of them. Nina's sadness grew when she thought about how she didn't have a chance to see, to touch, to hug, or to kiss them before they left this world.

The deep grief she felt for her husband and her mother drained all of Nina's mental energy. She was sad, regretful, and lonely. She had no motivation to do anything in her life.

Nina felt David was sending her his love. She sensed Mama calling her with her familiar, loving voice, "Sweetie, Sweetie." Those were the moments Nina looked like a statue, sitting very still with eyes full of tears on the Jordan River bank.

Loss of life and loss of love was too harsh for Nina. It crushed her heart. She went to the Jordan River to soothe her pain. She did not know whether time would heal this enormous psychological and emotional trauma, even though Papa told her that time heals everything.

Before she fell into a severe depression, Papa encouraged Nina to pay attention to music. "We have to shore ourselves up from the grief of this irredeemable loss," Papa said.

Nina focused on the only thing that gave her comfort. She was practising her flute day and night. She gradually learned to play other instruments, even learning how to conduct. She felt as if all the music was saving her life.

In the meantime, Papa was getting older. He missed Mama. He was concerned about Nina's personal life. Sometimes he was not able to understand his daughter's situation. Nina had already survived a tough life, exiled from Germany, being sent to London on her own, living through terrible hardship in Shanghai, and the loss of family in the Holocaust. He didn't know why she could not overcome these difficulties now.

"Human beings always have distinct challenges at every stage of life, regardless of age," Papa said to Nina.

"I remember you said only time would heal," Nina sighed heavily.

Papa started to wear his kippah all the time. Even in Germany, he had researched all the Jewish religious traditions, but he did not practice them. He was either busy with his business, or it was wartime. In Shanghai, they participated only briefly in the religious activities at the Moshe synagogue. Now he wanted to teach Nina about his religion.

"Yom Kippur is the holiest day for the Jewish people," Papa told Nina, "We need to pray the whole day long."

"I have fasted before, Papa," Nina said.

"Rosh Hashanah is the Jewish New Year. It is on the first day of the seventh month," Papa continued.

"I knew that," Nina nodded.

"There are two days of celebrations at the beginning of the new year. Everyone is supposed to attend synagogue service, recite specific literature, and enjoy the festival's special meals. Eating symbolic food is a Jewish tradition, such as dipping an apple in honey, hoping to evoke a sweet New Year." In addition, Papa immersed himself deeply in religious research and activities.

Four years went by unnoticed. Then, when Nina celebrated her thirtieth year's birthday, Papa expressed his grave concern about her life.

"Sweetie, you cannot have such a lonely life anymore," Papa said.

"I am fine," Nina said, but she knew her voice was not confident.

"I believe you should look for someone to establish a family with," Papa said.

"Okay, Papa," Nina agreed if only to please her Papa.

A few months later, a music circle friend introduced Nina to a man at a concert. His name was Dan Coleman.

Initially, Nina did not know whether she would like him or not. Dan was attractive, tall, thin, and handsome. He had a high nose and bushy eyebrows. His voice had a magnetic quality, different from anyone else she knew.

Dan pursued her continually, finding every opportunities to contact and talk to her. He was persistent. Nina enjoyed listening to his voice, maybe because it reminded her of a similar sweetness in Hason's voice in Shanghai. Nina gradually accepted him, and they started to date.

Nina and Dan walked and shopped on Rothschild Boulevard in Tel Aviv. They often went to the Habima Theater and hung out on Herzl Street, and had coffee on Allenby Street. Dan took many pictures of Nina on Chen Boulevard, a beautiful tree-lined street. Nina posed and smiled at Dan for the camera. Their dating life mainly was sweet, but it had bitter moments. Dan often joked with Nina about his mischievous behavior, and then Nina would grumble to Dan afterward. Nevertheless, Nina was willing to accept being loved. She slowly fell in love with this man, who had such a soft and magnetic voice.

One weekend, Nina and Dan put up tents with ten other friends for a picnic party. Unfortunately, there was a delay in constructing the tents because Nina did not know how to install the proper nuts on the tent pieces.

"What is going on? Why are you so slow?" Dan shouted at Nina. He came to Nina and threw a few nuts at her feet.

"Ah," Nina said, mortified.

"You are useless," Dan continued. He did not notice Nina's face.

"You, you..." Nina could not speak.

"I am so sorry, Nina," Dan changed his ferocious attitude swiftly. He came up to her and embraced her, all his anger gone.

"Okay, Dan," Nina said, but she sensed something was awfully wrong. It seemed like Dan had changed his personality.

Nina let him hug her but did not return the hug. Then other friends came over to cheer them up. After that, everybody continued the picnic party in a happy mood.

Just two months later, Nina went to her father and told Papa that Dan slapped her for the first time after a minor quarrel.

Papa was outraged and distraught because this confirmed what he had thought from the beginning. Dan was not good for Nina. He warned Nina that she would pay an enormous price in her future life if she continued with this man.

"If a man uses violence on his wife once, he will definitely do it again," Papa said.

"But he apologized to me several times last night," Nina tried to reassure her father, "He promised he would never hit me again."

"Whatever he promises, he will do it again. You should not believe him because that kind of mentality will stay with him forever," Papa said in a firm voice.

Unfortunately, Nina chose not to take her father's advice. Instead, she accepted Dan's many apologies and sweet words. Dan looked so sincere and sounded very honest.

Nina married Dan three months later, ignoring her father's critical warning.

After their marriage, they decided to manage a fruit farm, although Israel's land was parched, hopeless for any agriculture business. The country had few land resources, sparse deserts, harsh environments, and limited water supplies. As a result, few types of crops could flourish in the early stages of the country's development.

Although any farm in Israel was challenging to run, it could be successful if it had water. With the help of an efficient watering system, it became possible to grow various fruits and vegetables. Dan learned about the first experimental irrigation system established in 1959 by Mr. Simcha Blass. Dan quickly obtained the unique and innovative irrigation system called the Drip Irrigation system.

Using this irrigation system, Dan was confident of a bright future. He realized he had incredible potential for his fruit farm. So he borrowed money from the bank, rented lots of farmland from local landowners, and developed a large fruit farm with new technology.

All their efforts and hard work were fruitful. Of course, the good fortune in their life was always unexpected. Still, Dan and Nina had done an outstanding job, created a successful business, and made a satisfying profit from the farm.

Dan negotiated a deal with a large supermarket store to supply fresh oranges. He presented to them with a well-prepared speech. Dan said, "An orange contains an abundance of vitamin C, which can help you prevent colds. The human body needs 60 mg to 100 mg of Vitamin C a day. So one orange has about 100 mg of Vitamin C, which is enough to meet the body's needs. Plus, the oranges from my farm are juicy, fresh, and sweet. Please, everybody, try tasting these samples." That year, Dan sold more oranges than ever.

There was a fantastic harvest of various fruits and vegetables produced on their farm in the second year. The beauty of that harvest was seen in an abundance of colors: red tomatoes, green spinach, yellow pumpkins, purple aubergines, orange carrots, white cauliflowers, and brown potatoes. There were also juicy oranges, crunchy apples, sweet watermelons, fresh grapes, and tasty strawberries. All the vegetables and fruits were packaged in boxes. Their produce was sold in the Jaffa market in Tel Aviv first. After that, it was sold in Tel Aviv's local markets and abroad. There always were several trucks waiting at the farm's gate to transport the fruits or veggies to the port for export overseas.

As a famous philosopher said, business success does not necessarily mean living a happy life. Nina did not know whether that was right or wrong, but time would tell.

CHAPTER NINETEEN

June 1963
Tel Aviv, Israel

Nina felt life was just like the Jordan River, sometimes quiet and sometimes with rough waves, or even worse.

Although Nina and Dan achieved financial stability with their hard work, they were deprived of the joy of having a child. After three years of marriage, Nina was not pregnant.

Nina had seen a lot of doctors and tried a lot of treatments for her infertility. After many hospital visits and fertility clinic appointments, nothing was successful. Finally, when Nina was approaching her thirty-sixth birthday, she discussed with Dan about the idea of adoption.

"I really would like to have a child in our home. Dan, do you think we could adopt a child, like our neighbor?" Nina asked.

"I like children too. But an adopted child is different and difficult," Dan said. In fact, he was hesitant about the adoption idea.

"Most adopted kids are very good. We could have a great family," Nina said positively.

"But you need to adopt the kid at a very young age and keep the secret forever. Can you do that?" Dan said. He challenged Nina.

"I am willing to try," Nina nodded.

"Okay, you may try," Dan finally agreed.

While Nina and her husband made plans to adopt a child, they had no idea that two little girls would enter their lives.

The moment Nina saw the two baby girls, she loved them right away. The babies were beautiful and they were real sisters. Their biological parents were students. The father was Palestinian, and the mother was Jewish. The custom in Israel was that the birth parents never have a chance to meet adoptive parents. They said that would protect the children from any turmoil that could hinder their growth.

Nina and Dan were truly delighted with these two adopted daughters. They named the older one Anna and the younger one Bela. There was only eleven months difference in ages.

As a new parents, they had a lot of struggles in caring for the new babies. Nina was awake often at night, first with one child, then the other. She experienced arduous hours taking care of the babies in the middle of the night. Anna cried for food as if she were not given enough, while Bela vomited up her food all over Nina's clothes as if she had been fed too much. Some nights, Nina did not know why Bela was cranky and cried, while Anna slept so well. Nina had to solve all these problems herself. At these times, she missed her Mama, wishing she could ask her mother's advice on how to care for her babies. The worst time was when one baby caught the flu, and she feared the other one would also get it. The sick babies' crying was a hardship for new parents, especially when it caused sleepless nights in a row.

Of course, bringing up the two daughters also gave Nina and Dan a lot of joyful times. For example, they brought them to play and swim at Tel Aviv's best beach. Traveling to the suburbs for a picnic was always the favorite time for their two daughters. Bela was always so excited. Nina found Anna was the quieter of the two. Bela was more active.

Anna and Bela brought Nina and Dan a lot of happiness, enhancing their family life and making their marriage enjoyable. But it wasn't always like that.

One day, Dan came home from work very early. "Nina, you want to hear a crazy story about my friend?"

"Sure," Nina was busy to her house work.

"My friend, Gary, is two years younger than me," Dan started.

Nina looked at Dan and paid attention to him.

When Dan was sure Nina was listening, he continued, "Gary married only two years ago. His wife is a stunning woman with many friends outside her work. Gary started to suspect that his wife may be having an affair, primarily because she often returned home very late for the last four months."

Nina felt kind of strange listening to her husband telling this story.

"Oh," Nina nodded her head and sipped a little water from a glass.

"There is some funny business going on with his wife. Every time she goes out, she wears a lot of makeup and keeps changing into new clothes," Dan added more details from Gary's observation.

"That is not strange. Many women do that," Nina looked at Dan.

"Last week, Gary found out she was cheating on him. The man's name is Seth. The son of a bitch," Dan sympathized with his friend.

"How did Gary find out?" Nina asked with surprise.

"Gary started to search surreptitiously for any connection between them. Gary found out his wife made phone calls to Seth frequently. One day when Gary was shopping, he saw his wife and Seth having coffee on the patio of a restaurant."

"He may be just a normal social friend, only drinking a cup of coffee?" Nina said.

"No, Nina. Gary saw his wife touching Seth's face several times. They even fucking kissed each other on the lips before they left the restaurant," Dan's voice became excited with the inappropriate curse word.

"Really," Nina could feel her husband's anger at Gary's situation.

"Seth looks taller and thinner than Gary, but the son of a bitch is a lazy drinker," Dan said. He realized he should not mention drinking when he noticed how Nina looked at him because Dan had a drinking problem himself.

"Dan, watch your tongue, please," Nina requested.

"After seeing them on the restaurant patio, Gary was almost sure that his wife must have slept with this man, this son of a bitch," Dan kept cursing.

"Dan, tell me the story quietly," Nina touched Dan's hand to calm him down.

Dan did not calm down, and he said, "Because Gary has been insulted by this affair, he is so angry and agitated. He even talk about to kill that guy."

"What?" Nina covered her mouth with her hand.

"Yes," Dan nodded.

"But that is a dangerous idea," Nina said.

"So what, Gary bought a gun, a revolver," Dan said.

"Oh gosh," Nina said. Her face became rigid because of Dan's friend's crazy action.

"Gary showed me the gun with bullets this afternoon," Dan said. He seemed to take pleasure from how scared Nina was.

"Do you think he is going to do it?" Nina asked.

"Gary said he was looking for a proper chance to shoot this guy," Dan said.

"He will be charged with murder if he kills someone." Nina regained her mental strength.

"You don't know, Gary even want to kill his wife." Dan opened his eyes wider, impressed by his friend's threat of violence.

"What a crazy man! You should stop your friend."

"Yes, he is a little crazy, but for a good reason," Dan defended Gary's crazy intention.

"There is no reason for murdering a person," Nina said.

"Gary and his wife have had several arguments about this affair, but nothing is resolved."

"They should sit down to talk about how to divorce peacefully," Nina suggested.

"Gary is divorcing his wife right now, by the way," Dan added.

At that moment, the telephone rang, interrupting Dan's story about Gary for that night.

The distressing story of Gary and his wife lasted a long time and was one of the topic of arguments between Nina and Dan. Finally, seven months later, Nina asked Dan about his friend Gary. He said everything was settled because Seth had moved to another city.

Because Dan's time was always taken up with the hectic work on the fruit farm, Nina and Dan had less time to communicate with each other. Although Dan has been successful in his farm business, he always had too many unconventional ideas. He wanted to try them all and stubbornly stuck with an idea until he saw if it worked or not. So Dan always stayed at his job for a long time. As a result, he did not have enough time with Nina at home.

Nina was exhausted taking care of two young girls. Dan was constantly fatigued at night. So every night, they were too tired to be intimate anymore. Their emotional life became less close.

Seven years past quickly they hardly noticed. Their rocky life had so much hustle and hassle. Nina and Dan quarreled all the time. The nice talking with each other became less and less. As time went on, the stress of life pushed them further apart, moving their marriage into a dangerous stage.

It was the year 1974. Nina was already forty-two years old when the younger daughter, Bela, was eight years old.

Nina and Dan had many disagreements about how to educate their girls. They could argue about any issue, ending without a proper resolution. The frequent quarrels eroded away their emotional attachments. Their squabbles extended into almost all aspects of their life.

Dan tended to get involved in an argument, especially after his alcohol drinking. He did not care about Nina's feeling anymore. One day, Nina had a severe toothache, and the dentist performed root canal surgery. It was painful. She was unable to eat and speak well because of the surgical wound in her gum. She did not have the energy for another useless argument.

"I just had surgery. My mouth is very painful. I can barely open it. Can we have a break from any unnecessary discussion today?" Nina asked Dan.

"I don't care," Dan grumbled and sipped his drink.

"I know you do not care about me anymore," Nina said. She held her chin because the argument made it ache even more. She looked at Dan with a disdainful expression.

"Why are you such a bitch?" Dan said. He cursed her when he saw the scorn in Nina's eyes.

Nina shut her mouth and kept utterly silent. Finally, she turned, leaving the hopeless battlefield, and closed her bedroom door. Nina knew Dan did not care about the family anymore. However, she had little sympathy for him. She blamed his alcoholism. Nina understood her relationship with Dan was in an awful state, as was her marriage.

The following afternoon, Dan had recovered from his hangover. "Why can I not find my cutting knife?" Dan complained to Nina.

"Can we have a cool-down period between us?" Nina suggested with a soft voice.

"I can't find my stuff. So what do you want?" Dan was still screaming as loud as he could. He gave Nina a contemptuous glance.

"I just want peace. Can we have a calm day?" After so many years of quarrels, Nina knew her request would be ignored by Dan.

"Peace? Peace is only in the grave," Dan screamed out of control.

Nina cleared her throat and gave Dan a withering stare. She swallowed the lump in her throat, kept her silence, and then turned away.

One night, Dan drank a lot of alcohol to cope with a big problem at work. Nina had tried to persuade him not to drink so much for his own health. They got into a major argument over his drinking, and Dan slapped Nina in the face. Nina recalled her father's warning, "One slap will never be the end." Nina remained upset for several weeks, while Dan tried to apologize to her numerous times again. Nina did not want to let Papa know about the abuse this time. She felt embarrassed regretfully.

Nina smiled bitterly because she knew this marriage was not going to last long. After such a long time of indecision and unwillingness from her heart, she knew her hopeless suffering would end. She had been afraid to end the marriage for the sake of two young daughters. But she made up her mind that she would no longer sleep with her abusive husband ever again from that day on.

Besides her difficulties with Dan, Nina had to contend with the teen-age rebellion of her daughters. Nina still remembered how cute the girls were when they were little, learning to talk. Now Bela was thirteen, and Anna was fourteen. It seemed to have happened so fast. Nina realized she was already nearly forty-seven years old.

Nina realized she had indulged both girls when they were growing up. But then, she remembered a Chinese proverb she had heard in the Shanghai ghetto. It says, "Wood-sticks make a filial child. Chopsticks make a wicked child." She asked Papa, at that time, the meaning of the saying. Nina still recalled Papa laughing when he explained it to her on the Wayside Road in the Shanghai ghetto.

Ancient Chinese people believed that if parents use a wood stick to hit a child's butt and discipline the child strictly, this child will become a decent man when he grows up and treat his parents well. On the other hand, if the parents use chopsticks to feed the child and spoil him, the child will most likely become a spoiled man who does not treat his parents well.

Nina did not really understand the true essence of the proverb even after Papa's explanation until now. Currently, her two teenage daughters cause great emotional stress and mental pressure in her life. Although the two girls were lovely and bright when they were younger, as teenagers, Nina had many challenges in educating them.

Per her own personality, Nina was strict in all aspects of life. The two children grew up with a certain amount of discipline. But when they reached thirteen and fourteen, they became so rebellious they were disobedient in almost everything. They would not listen to her anymore. Even though they would still go to school, they made friends with other rebellious teens. They are involved in premature love. They even started to take drugs.

Bela and Anna lost respect and affection for their parents when they saw them constantly fighting. They stopped listening to them. They hid in their own room most of the time and did not even talk to their parents. They made their own decisions about what they want to do and with whom. They went out at night to parties with friends. Bela even suggested she wanted to leave home.

Nina was very puzzled about her daughter's rebellion. So she went to the local library to borrow books on this topic. Nina's readings and research gave her a deeper understanding of the issues and to deal with rebellious behavior better.

Luckily, Nina made a friend at the library. Sara borrowed and read the same type of books as Nina did. Sara had dark black hair and a pair of sharp, witty eyes. She was talkative and always had a smile on her face. Sara worked as a literature teacher at Tel Aviv University.

One afternoon, Sara invited Nina for coffee. Since the coffee shop was too noisy with so many people, they went to the bank of the Jordan River. Each carried a book about teenage rebellion.

"I've found an important concept describing how the minds of teenagers work," Sara said.

"What is it?" Nina urgently wanted to learn everything, which could to help her to deal with her daughters' issues.

"The concept describes the subconscious idea, called an entitlement mentality in some children," Sara said, using a psychological term.

"Entitlement from their subconscious," Nina asked, puzzled.

"These children's values and life philosophy hold a misconception, which is that their parents are obligated to pay for them, serve them, and love them always. As a result, these rebellious children subconsciously think they are entitled to be loved by their parents," Sara said.

"But every parent loves their children unconditionally."

"The issue is that children take it for granted. They think they deserve to receive love, support, and money from their parents," Sara said.

"But the parents are willing to do anything for their kids," Nina said, not understanding these new ideas.

"The puzzling situation is that these children think their parents are indebted to them."

"All the parents indeed have an obligation to raise their children, but not necessarily owe debts to them," Nina said. "But I remembered the interesting Chinese saying, each child is a debt to their parents' previous life."

"Generally speaking, parents love their children more than children love their parents." Sara tried to summarize.

"I agree. I have to admit my parents loved me more than I loved them," Nina nodded her head with a bit of embarrassment.

"This is an essential feature of human nature. Nina, you do not need to feel guilty about your feelings for your parents, even if they loved you more than you loved them. It is natural."

"Oh," Nina thought about her parents' love for her.

"The most fascinating phenomenon is that it is the same with most animals as with humans. Parents would even sacrifice their own lives to save the next generations," Sara added.

"I knew that. I was astonished by an amazing story about older elephants who sacrificed their life and jumped into a deep pit to lift up water and save a younger one."

"Okay, once we know this human characteristic, we should not be surprised by the unequal relationship between parents and their children."

"You are right. We should not be angry with the rebellion of our children. It is natural for them to want to move away from their parents, to be able to start their own families," Nina said.

"Misunderstanding between parents and children do happen as the children struggle to be independent. The parents need to let them go but keep the lines of communication open between them," Sara explained.

"You can say that again," Nina agreed with her friend. "Thank you, Sara. You are a wonderful researcher and teacher!"

Nina told Sara that Dan rarely played with the children. He did not talk to the kids enough, keeping a distance from them. They were never close. Perhaps the girls thought he was cold to them.

"Do any of your daughters have a speech problem or isolate themselves from the family or friends?" Sara asked seriously.

"Yes, I worry because Anna is reluctant to talk, and she spends most of her time in her room," Nina answered.

"I heard that autism in children is related to a lack of warmth from the parents. But I do not think Anna has autism. She is just an introvert," Sara tried to comfort Nina.

"I hope so. I just wish my husband could give the kids more affection," Nina said.

"The loving environment at home is so important for a child's emotional health," Sara declared.

"I am happy that Anna's condition is not so bad." Nina thought about her older daughter on the way home.

***

Nina's younger daughter, Bela, grew up into a beautiful girl. She had beautiful brown hazel eyes, with a more dynamic personality. And she was a little taller than her sister, Anna.

One night, Bela had a massive argument with her father because he said she was wasting food. Then, as he got more and more wound up with his anger, he leaked the fact to girls that they had been adopted.

This was a great shock to the girls. This fact drove them to search for their biological parents. They did this covertly, not confiding in Nina and Dan.

Through the adoption network, Bela found information about their biological parents. Their birth father passed away a few years ago. Their birth mother lived in a refugee shelter. She did not want to see Bela. She had no interest or feeling for the children she had to give up because of her own miserable life. Bela could not find any connection with this woman who gave her life. She was deeply disappointed, and the rejection of her natural mother was a psychological trauma in Bela's adolescence.

Bela felt she and her sister had been abandoned by her biological parents. Although she knew Nina loved her and gave her a better life than her birth mother could, she thought Nina was too strict. Even though Bela loved Nina, she preferred to have her own life with her own independence.

While Nina focused on dealing with the issues of rebellion in the children, she did not notice a huge trouble was dangerously approaching her.

CHAPTER TWENTY

November 1976
Tel Aviv, Israel

One Saturday afternoon, Nina got a call from her girlfriend, Zilla. She wanted Nina to meet her in the park about an urgent matter. Zilla was a beautiful singer with a melodious voice. Nina hung up the phone and prepared to meet her girlfriend.

"Why are you going out again?" Dan's eyes bulged as he demanded an answer. Lately, whenever Nina went out, Dan became agitated. Dan's unwarranted jealousy was getting worse.

"I have something important to do," Nina kept her voice calm and low.

"Who do you want to meet today?"

"My girlfriend Zilla," Nina replied, and she took her coat.

"Girlfriend, really," Dan said. He sneered at Nina.

"Yes, her name is Zilla," Nina kept her voice low.

"What's so important that you have to see her now?" Dan stepped into the doorway.

"I don't know yet until she tells me," Nina snapped.

"You don't know?" Dan stood in Nina's way.

"Dan, I don't have the time or the energy to argue with you."

"Then, when do you have time to talk?" Dan asked.

"How about tonight, Zilla is waiting for me now," Nina gave Dan a reluctant smile.

Dan paused for a minute and let Nina go.

On the way to the park, Nina could smell the coming rain. She did not like the rain. When she arrived at the park, a pair of magpies flew away from the treetop. Since her childhood in the Shanghai ghetto, Nina believed the magpie meant good luck. Now she saw the magpies had flown away. It may indicate a bad omen.

Zilla ran over to Nina in great distress, grabbing her arms and crying.

"Nina, please help me! I've got a big problem," Zilla said and shook Nina's arms.

"What is it?"

"I had an affair with a married man," Zilla cried. Her face was bright red.

"A married man," Nina was surprised.

Nina asked Zilla why she wasted her emotion on a married man. Nina could never understand the reason for her infidelity.

"To be honest, I wanted to be loved," Zilla said. Then, Zilla revealed her deep love for this man, who was her best friend.

"Oh, Zilla," Nina tried to hug her.

"I also enjoy the feeling of controlling a man," Zilla added with a brief, wicked smile.

"To control a man," Nina asked, confused.

"Yes, Nina! I do not have any logical explanation for that," Zilla said, shrugging her shoulders.

"For sure, I don't see any rational reason," Nina said.

"At the beginning, I don't think it was harmful because we were just normal friends."

Nina looked at her friend and held her hands.

"When things started to get awkward, and I wanted to end it, he refused. The man threatened to come my home and tell everyone.

Then, he frightened me by suddenly grabbing my arm, which left me with some bruises," Zilla started to cry again, and she showed Nina the bruises on her arms.

"You now realize there is too much danger in this kind of game, Zilla," Nina said.

"Nina, I don't know," Zilla said with a distressful moan.

"A wise man says, almost all the extramarital affairs end up badly," Nina quoted solemnly.

"It is a hard lesson to learn," Zilla recognized.

"Anyway, let's figure out the solution for the current situation," Nina suggested.

"Nina, can you give me some idea about dealing with this man right now?"

"A Chinese proverb says, 'Give somebody a dose of his own medicine.' I learned it in Shanghai. So we will deal with this man as he deals with you, using the same method," Nina said.

"What do you mean?" Zilla asked. She was not able to think rationally because she was in too much distress.

"We are going to warn him that he needs to stay away from you. Otherwise, his wife and work colleagues will know his entire secret," Nina said. However, she felt uncomfortable with this indecent strategy herself.

"That is an excellent idea!" Zilla accepted the plan without hesitation.

After saying goodbye to Zilla, Nina thought about her own marital problems with Dan. His paranoia was getting worse. He also often exaggerated his own self-importance. Whatever he said was essential, and Nina had to obey his decisions and his orders. If she did not obey, he would become furious, get agitated, start yelling, and then become violent. When Dan raged, Nina wondered if he had a personality disorder.

In fact, Dan showed this controlling characteristic early on in their relationship. Unfortunately, Nina was too young and naïve to recognize these dangerous personality traits. Now she was living with the consequences of her own choice. Nina was saddened and confused by the turmoil in her own marriage.

Dan constantly misunderstood Nina's words and deeds. The emotional turbulence led to further separation. Misunderstandings were compounded by a lack of communication between them. Nina became sadder and more hopeless about the situation. She and Dan were walking toward separation with increasing speed. Nina concluded that the misunderstandings between them were the crucial reasons for all their marital problems.

Nina decided she would try to communicate with Dan that very night.

"You are always out of the house with excuses like seeing a girlfriend," Dan yelled at her as soon as Nina got home. He did not even lift his head to look at her. Instead, he continued to drink his alcohol at the table.

"Dan, we have to end this war, or this war will end us," Nina said desperately.

"I don't give a damn shit," Dan cursed and looked back at Nina with his usual drunken gaze. Then he drank more liquor, waving his arms aimlessly.

Nina clasped her hand over her mouth in despair. There was no possibility of communication now. She felt humiliated. Any possibility of communication was blocked by the destructive energy between them. Dan's abusive words and humiliating attitude sabotaged Nina's willingness to talk. His curses instantly turned her off.

Nina looked at the mess Dan had left on the table and was disgusted. However, she kept her mouth shut, not wanting to say a single word to him anymore.

Suddenly, Nina realized the core reason for their communication problems was emotional blockages. The use of abusive words and offensive body language caused these blockages and separated them.

Nina closed the bedroom door and opened the window. She watched the stars in the sky, trying to understand her marriage. She realized a logical, progressive sequence of behaviors led them to current situation. First, it started with abusive words, causing emotional blockages, sabotaging communication, and leading to many misunderstandings, psychological isolation, and physical separation. Nina knew the last step of this sequence was a divorce. Nina disliked the idea of divorce. She never thought she would be a divorced woman with two children.

Nina looked far into the distant sky. She sighed, and her thoughts traveled far. For sure, there were so many possible reasons to break up a marriage. Sometimes, the couple's personality differences caused them to clash.

Nina believed she was naturally more sensitive, thoughtful, and considerate than Dan. She was paying too much attention to everything Dan said or did. At least she tried her best to say nothing that could possibly hurt him. But, on the other hand, she had her own standards for how to live. There was a limit how much she could take.

In contrast, Dan did not have this sensitivity at all. There was no such thoughtful consideration when he spoke to her. He did not try to restrain the emotional pressure he placed on her. He did not care about Nina's feelings anymore.

Nina remembered someone saying the three personality traits that lead to divorce is negative complaints, harsh criticism, and humiliating ridicule. If a couple accumulated multiple misunderstandings and had no chance to communicate thoroughly, they could not understand each other. They would become emotional strangers. If one party suffered from another's malicious treatment, the psychological damage could be enormous.

Dan continued his heavy drinking. Every week there were many quarrels between them. Nina kept thinking about divorcing Dan. Finally, she could not take the constant arguing anymore. Nina thought she should warn Dan that she would leave sooner or later. She wanted to avoid any violence and to leave him peacefully.

Besides the troubles at home, the farm was hit by two natural calamities at the same time, bad weather and harmful insects. Dan lost a lot of produce, and his business lost a lot of money. He had suffered a substantial financial loss. Dan was under tremendous stress. When he came home, he was bothered by the loud voices of the two girls. "Shut up!" Dan yelled at them and slammed his keys on the floor, making a harsh, violent noise.

That night, after drinking heavily, Dan had a massive argument with Nina about disciplining the children. All of a sudden, he became very violent. He even threatened to kill Nina and the kids. When she tried to calm him down, he hit her with his fist so hard she knew she could not endure it anymore.

"I want a divorce," Nina said. Her eyes were red and full of tears.

* * *

When Dan realized that Nina would leave him, he regretted his behavior but became more irate. He thought about any other reason Nina might have to leave him other than his alcoholism. He tried to look for issues outside his own troubles.

He started following Nina to her workplace, a musical band Nina worked for now. He saw Nina talking a lot with one of her colleagues, the pianist in her band. Dan imagined Nina may have an affair with this man, so he directed all his anger toward this person. He assumed the pianist was responsible for destroying his marriage.

Dan remembered his friend Gary had bought a gun at the nearby gun shop. So he went there, but the shop demanded a gun license first.

He went to a bar to drown his sorrow. He met a friend, Joe, who was also drinking in the bar. Joe was a construction worker. They met at the bar a few weeks ago. Dan ordered a drink and sat beside Joe.

"What is going on, buddy?" Joe asked.

"I got trouble at home," Dan said. He drank a large gulp of whiskey.

"What is it?"

"My wife wants to divorce me," Dan said.

"For what," Joe asked. He sipped his drink.

"She says because I drink too much, but I think she may be having an affair with a piano player," Dan said. He drank another large gulp of alcohol.

"How do you know she is having an affair with that man?" Joe asked.

"I'm almost sure. But, unfortunately, I don't have any actual evidence," Dan said.

"Do you still love your wife?" Joe asked. He sounded like a professional.

"Sure. That is the reason I am so depressed," Dan said.

"If you love your wife, then what do you want to do?"

"I want your help, Joe."

"Me? Help? How," Joe was puzzled.

"I want you to find a way to beat that piano guy up, the son of a bitch!" Dan looked at Joe and hoped he could agree.

"Why me," Joe said. He obviously disagreed with the idea.

"Because I don't think I'm strong enough to hurt that guy. You are strong. You could hit him with one big punch," Dan waved his fist in the air.

"Sorry, Dan. I can't do that for you. It would cause me big trouble," Joe said.

"I will pay you, Joe," Dan insisted.

"I am sorry about that. But I can't help you." Joe spread out both his hands to Dan.

"Come on, buddy," Dan said. He stared at Joe with his drunken eyes, disappointed.

"Forget all these shits. Look forward. My friend," Joe patted Dan's shoulder. Then he hurried out of the bar.

Dan was frustrated by Joe's refusal to help. He stayed in the bar, drinking, watching the television, feeling increasingly lonely.

The TV show was about a hunter confronted by a massive grizzly bear in a remote forest. The hunter aimed his gun at the bear and shot it right in its chest. However, the bear was not killed. Instead, it charged at the hunter.

Dan put his glass down on the table and stood up to watch the exciting scene. He gazed at the TV with his drunken eyes.

The brown bear's attack back was quick. It was roaring, an ear-splitting howl of revenge. The hunter didn't have any time to reload his rifle. He turned and ran as fast as possible. The grizzly bear ran after him much faster. It was coming closer to the hunter. The hunter turned and threw his gun at the bear, but the bear hesitated for only a second.

Everyone in the bar stood up to watch the thrilling fight between the hunter and the bear.

After a brief pause, the bear resumed charging. The hunter hid behind a huge tree, and he took out something like an alcohol bottle from his waist. He shook the bottle and aimed it at the bear. A spume of mist shot from the bottle into the bear's face. The bear bellowed. It was a furious growl. The bear stopped and used its two front paws to rub its face and eyes like mad. Within this short moment, the hunter sneaked away and disappeared into the forest.

"What was in that bottle?" Dan asked the man beside him. He was amazed by its power.

"Oh, that is a bear spray," the man replied.

"Bear Spray," Dan repeated the name. "Thanks, man," Dan thought he found something that could help him better than his drinking friend, Joe.

Dan decided if the bear spray could disable such a mighty grizzly bear, then it could disable that tall piano guy. He thought this was a good idea and was encouraged.

The next day, Dan bought the bear spray. Then, he prepared to attack the piano man.

Dan constantly thought about the piano player whenever Nina practiced her flute at home. He imagined him flirting with his wife. The piano man became a serious enemy in Dan's mind. Dan spent a lot of time in the bar drinking. Mostly he drank alone. He thought about using the bear spray to disable that son-of-a-bitch. "I will beat up his pretty face until his ugly body drops down flat on the ground. He will learn a hard lesson." Dan thought about his plan and was excited, and he continued his drinking.

One evening, Dan brought up his suspicions about the piano player to Nina. She was humiliated by the accusation and became angrier. Because Dan and Nina were estranged from each other, he put all the blame for his relationship problems on the piano player. He thought about him all the time. He became so agitated that he gradually developed an idea of killing him, not just hitting him.

When Nina told Dan that her work was planning a music party on the first Friday of next month, Dan felt his chance appeared and he prepared his revenge on the pianist.

Dan followed someone's suggestion and gave up the bear spray idea. He purchased a pistol and a box of ammunition in the black market in downtown Tel Aviv. No gun license was needed. Then he joined a hunting club to train himself to shoot.

On that Friday night, Dan wore a black hoodie, and put his gun in his pocket. He walked beside the bushes of the building where they had the musical party. He hid in the dark bushes and stalked his wife and the piano player. He wanted to see them in a compromising position.

Dan's plan was that if he saw them just once in a romantic scene, confirming they indeed were having an affair, he would not hesitate to use the gun to kill that fucking piano guy. Dan was obsessed with the idea that the piano guy had destroyed his marriage.

Dan hid in the shadows of the bushes listening Nina playing her flute with the piano player inside the house. She played a flute solo called Greensleeves, accompanied by the piano.

The party lasted nearly two hours. Dan became super alert and nervous when the audience came out of the building. He was eager to identify them together.

Dan watched the audience walking out of the building until the performers came out. Dan touched the pistol in his trousers pocket but was aware he was trembling and panting. In anticipation of the upcoming shooting, he was extremely anxious. Dan focused his attention on the building's door, watching for Nina.

Finally, Dan saw Nina come out in the dim light of the lamppost near the door. He couldn't see clearly from a distance. A tall man followed her out of the door and walked beside her. He was talking to her, waving his hand as he talked.

Dan quickly pulled out the pistol. He slowly lifted it with his right hand, supported by his left hand. Dan aimed his pistol at the target man. He glared at him. Dan prepared to pull the trigger and shoot the piano man.

Suddenly, Dan's finger froze, his hands dropped, and his legs ceased shaking. He opened his eyes ever wider. His heartbeat was louder, his breath shorter.

"Oh, shit! I almost made a terrible fucking mistake," Dan mumbled to himself.

Dan now could clearly see the man who was walking and talking with Nina, as they walked closer.

He wasn't the piano player. The person beside Nina was a 70-year-old man who was the band's leader. Dan stared at them as they walked by the bushe where he hid in. Then, he realized he was most likely wrong about the assumption he had made about his wife.

Watching Nina walking away with the old gentleman, Dan felt relieved. He relaxed his right arm holding the pistol. But he also felt immensely frustrated. He almost shot and killed an old man tonight by mistake. Dan became bewildered about the situation.

He collapsed to the ground, crushing the bushes. He saw a couple of stars twinkling when a dark cloud was moved away by the wind. One thing for sure was he still loved his wife. Another thing was that he certainly would not do anything tonight. He felt tremendous relief that there would be no dangerous action or tragic events involving him this night. The psychological pressures almost crushed him to the hilt.

CHAPTER TWENTY-ONE

July 1979
Tel Aviv, Israel

As Nina walked home, the night sky was a beautiful indigo blue. There was a gentle breeze. As always, the music performances made her happy, even though she still had to face the harsh reality of her married life.

When Nina opened the door, the first thing she saw was Dan's empty alcohol bottles on the table. It looked like he had a lot to drink, as usual. Nina remembered what Dan said to her before she went to the party, "Be careful, you could regret it." Nina felt Dan was even more neurotic that night. She worried about his mental health. She expected there would be another useless argument again.

The house was quieter than usual. She knew Dan was not sleeping because he always snored loudly. But because she felt unsettled, she went to the bedroom to double-check. She wondered where Dan could be at this late hour.

Nina sat down on the chair and looked at the mess on the table. She thought about Dan. He was not only resistant to trying to communicate with her, but he was often offensive in his approach to her. His abusive language was becoming more frequent and was unprovoked. For example, when Dan saw Nina dressed up for the concert that night, he viciously attacked her.

"Do you think you are beautiful? Do you think you are smart?" Dan's words were sarcastic, and Nina felt humiliated.

Nina did not respond to him. Nothing could come of trying to talk to him except more abuse. However, Nina could not imagine how she could carry on in this marriage anymore. She needed to divorce him. Therefore, Nina searched for their marriage certificate in the closet.

Nina was astonished to find a pistol box and an ammunition case hidden under Dan's clothes. The pistol was gone, but there were many bullets left in the case.

Nina's heart was pounding. She was afraid to think why he would have secretly bought a gun and bullets. "There are only two terrible possibilities for this gun, kill me or kill himself." Nina started to panic and felt a deep sadness. She remembered that Dan had threatened to commit suicide one day. Then another day, Dan made a death threat against her during an intense argument. All their terrible wrangling had grounded away any loving feelings between them.

Nina thought about leaving Dan for a long time, but because of her two daughters, she always put off the decision to leave. But tonight, looking at the pistol box and bullets, she had been pushed to make the final decision. There was a real danger to her and maybe her daughters if she stayed. But Nina didn't know if the threat was imminent and whether she should leave with her two daughters that night.

Nina tried to call her friend Sara, who didn't answer the phone. She called Zilla instead.

"Zilla, I have an important thing to talk about with you," Nina's voice was urgent.

"What is it?" Zilla sensed Nina's nervousness.

"Dan has bought a gun and bullets!"

"What?" Zilla sounded shocked.

"I told him I want to leave him, and he is crazy with rage."

"But a gun is a danger to you and your girls," Zilla was frightened.

"Dan threatened to kill me and the children," Nina said.

"Really, When?"

"Early this evening, Dan said that he would shoot the kids and me," Nina was obviously very scared.

"If Dan made this threat and had a gun, I strongly suggest leaving home with your girls immediately," Zilla advised.

"You are right. Dan had a lot of drink tonight. I don't know what is happening to him?" Nina became more panicked, thinking about Dan's alcoholism.

"Do you want to leave your place tonight for the sake of your children?" Zilla asked.

"Yes, we have to leave. It is too risky to stay here now," Nina said.

"Okay, wake up the girls and get ready. I'll pick you up and bring you to my home," Zilla was never so decisive.

"Yes, I am going to get Anna and Bela. I'll see you shortly."

Just after Nina convinced the girls to get ready, the front door banged open. Dan stood in the door frame and stared at the three of them.

"Why are you kids not in your fucking bed?" Dan stomped into the room, grabbed a half bottle of alcohol on the table, and drank it all.

Nina noticed a bulge in Dan's pocket. "It must be the pistol with ammunition," Nina realized how unpredictable the situation was, considering Dan had a gun. They were in real danger.

"You kids go to bed. I have to talk to your mother," Dan started to control the situation as always. The two girls went into their room.

"Calm down, please," Nina said.

"How can I fucking calm down when my business fails, plus I got a huge bank debt?" Dan punched the table with his fist.

"A bank debt," Nina never knew about the amount of money Dan borrowed from the bank.

"You can't fuck help anyway." Dan was very drunk, and he roared, so the house sounded like it was full of thunder.

Dan was out of control. Nina worried that the worst thing possible could happen tonight. She needed to leave this loveless and lifeless home immediately for her children's safety.

At that crucial moment, Nina heard a car parking outside her home. "Please be quiet!" Nina warned the person outside.

"I need to go to the washroom." Dan pushed Nina aside, going straight towards the washroom, and banged the door behind him.

Nina realized this was her only chance to run away. She opened the front door and saw Zilla waving at her.

Nina let her two daughters run out of the house first. Then she closed the front door gently before she rushed into Zilla's car.

"Are you okay?" Zilla asked.

"Yes. Let's go quickly!" Nina said urgently.

Zilla started the car and drove into the darkness with Nina and her daughters.

Nina was grateful her friend was able to rescue them from a life-threatening situation. However, she knew when Dan realized they were gone, he would be furious and run after them. Nina was glad she never mentioned Zilla's address to Dan, so he couldn't follow her there.

When Nina and her two girls had just arrived at Zilla's home, Dan was already calling there. Nina didn't know how Dan got Zilla's phone number, but then she remembered she had left her notebook beside the phone.

"Is Nina there?" Dan asked.

"It's Nina. I will talk to you tomorrow. Please go to sleep," Nina said.

"Nina, can you come back home? I want to talk to you for the last time." Dan's voice sounded extremely desperate.

"You know we already have had enough arguments, enough fights. There was no way any talking could help us now. Go to bed." Nina hung up the phone.

Nina said to Zilla that Dan wanted to have a last talk with her. Zilla looked at her with suspicious eyes.

"I am scared because Dan is violent. You know he has a gun," Zilla expressed caring for her friend. Then she pointed her index finger, forming a gun with her hand.

"Dan's death threats and his having a gun really scare me," Nina was obviously frightened.

"So, Nina, you better not go home tonight," Zilla advised her.

"Thanks! Zilla! I will not take any risks tonight. It makes no sense to argue repeatedly when there is no way to solve our problems. I am not going back home for his so-called last talk," Nina convinced herself as much as Zilla, but she still felt a bit of hesitation. She was still worried about Dan's unhealthy mental state. Anyway, Nina already firmly refused Dan's request for the last conversation tonight.

The next morning, Nina woke up early. She made many phone calls home, but Dan did not pick up. Nina told Zilla she was worried about Dan's mental health. She decided to go home to check on him even though Zilla disagreed entirely.

Nina walked home in the chilly wind. Her friend Zilla accompanied her for safety. The cold wind was blowing onto her face and neck.

"Why do you insist on going home to see him today?" Zilla asked Nina, puzzled.

"Zilla, my intuition tells me Dan may have done something crazy last night," Nina was worried about what could happen to Dan.

"Don't worry, Nina, things always have a solution," Zilla tried to comfort her friend.

A black crow was chattering and squawking angrily in the tree above their heads. Nina recalled when she was in Shanghai ghetto, an old Chinese lady told her about the black crow's story. It was a harbinger of bad luck if someone heard a crow chattering at them. Nina felt the crow was a bad omen that morning, although she rarely was a superstitious person. Her anxiety became aggravated by the crow. She quickened her pace to rush home.

Nina stood in front of her home to listen for a while as a precaution, and then she knocked on the door. Zilla stood beside her, which made her feel secure. Nobody answered the door.

Nina used her own key to unlock the door. She and Zilla cautiously walked into the house. It was strangely quiet.

"Dan, Dan!" Nina called out again. No one answered.

They found the room and kitchen in a mess. There were more empty alcohol bottles and food leftovers on the table. Dan was not in the bedroom either.

At last, Nina went to check the bathroom. It was hard to see because the bathroom window was covered by a curtain. An eerie sense of dread followed Nina into the room. She stepped in and fell to the floor as she reached for the light switch.

Bang!

Zilla heard the fall from the hallway.

"Ah!" Nina screamed out involuntarily.

Zilla rushed over, carrying a wooden stick. She tried to switch on the light. She found Nina on the bathroom floor, surrounded by splashed blood. The red color was on the curtain, the wall, the sink, and the mirror. She was speechless.

"Zilla, I am fine," Nina said, struggling to get up but slipping on the gory flooring.

"Dan, Dan!" Nina called for her husband.

Zilla was in shock, leaning on the door frame, the stick still in her hand.

Nina tried to look behind the shower curtain. Her heart began pounding. She was petrified of what horror she would find there. She wasn't aware of the tears streaming down her face.

Zilla used the stick to pull open the shower curtain.

It was a horrible scene.

Dan laid sprawled face-up in the bathtub. His eyes were closed, and his head was slumped to one side, with blood trickling down from his temple to his ear and then onto his cheek. His hair was plastered with blood. There was a small bloody hole at his temple. His face was ghostly pale, with splashes of blood all over it and clotting in his nostrils. Blood was splattered all over the bathtub and the walls. The dark red color looked dreadful.

Nina almost fainted, and she felt a gush of nausea. Her heartbeat was fast, and she could not hold herself up. She bent forward and started shivering. She felt her chest tighten, and she couldn't breathe. Within a few minutes, she was screaming in horror. Her face was distorted with agony. Her tears flowed like a waterfall. Finally, she was so exhausted she whimpered like a wounded animal.

Dan had carried out the threat he had made and killed himself with his own pistol. He had chosen a very violent death.

Nina knelt beside Dan and cried. She didn't dare to touch Dan's body.

Zilla pointed to Dan's gun, lying in the corner where he had dropped it. Nina stared at that suicide weapon. She could imagine how he did it. Dan aimed the muzzle at his right temple, his eyes red full of tears, then he closed his eyes and pulled the trigger. Nina just covered her mouth, unable to stop crying.

She did not know how long she sat there crying before she realized she needed to call the police as soon as possible. And, of course, she also had to call Dan's mother.

Nina staggered to the dining room to reach the telephone. She called the police in a trembling voice, "My husband killed himself last night. Could you send someone to my home?"

"Wait there as long as you are safe. We are coming." The police took her address.

At that moment, Zilla shouted to Nina, "Nina, come and look," Zilla discovered a piece of paper on the table that could be from Dan.

Nina saw that Dan had left a suicide note. He had scribbled something on a piece of brown lunch paper. It had been pushed under a half-empty glass. It sat among four empty liquor bottles.

Dan's last words were as follows:

Nina,

I know you don't love me anymore. I understand that's because of all the terrible things happened. You refuse to accept my apologies. You even don't want to see me for the last time.

I just, I just want to say, I still love you...whatever...
Even the two kids don't want to talk to me...
I ruined the farm. The business is gone...
I have no love, no fun — only failure and debts.
I don't want my life anymore...
My head is hurting too much. It feels like my head will explode.
But this life is going nowhere. I cannot carry on with this life anymore.
I decided to end my life tonight.
I want to have a long break and a good rest.
I want to go to sleep forever. Sleep and rest forever...
I say sorry to my mom!
I say sorry to my two daughters!
I say so so sorry to you!

Dan

CHAPTER TWENTY-TWO

August 1979

Tel Aviv, Israel

Nina walked to the Jordan River and watched the murky water rushing forward. She sat on a light brown rock. A lonely pigeon flew over the river.

Nina took out Dan's suicide note to read again. Her eyes were wet again when she read the note. First, she looked at the brown river and the brown rock, then the brown paper with Dan's last words.

Nina imagined that Dan had drunk a lot of alcohol after making the phone call to her that night. He was inebriated and not thinking straight. If not, he might have felt like ending his life but been able to reconsider. Even in his distress, he wanted to leave a last message to those important to him. That was why he left the suicide note for Nina, saying sorry to his mother and daughters.

Nina went to the Jordan River many times to calm her mind. The peaceful flow of the river always soothed her. Gradually, she realized that at least Dan had loved her at one time. Even though he would rage against her and threaten her life, he never acted on it. Instead, he turned his anger on himself. Nina recognized that his apologies to her might be sincere, even though he could not free himself from the resentment he felt. The stress and disappointment he felt, fueled by alcohol abuse, increased his rage and diminished his ability to cope. The violence of his words became violence to himself.

Nina recognized that nobody knows the future of their life. At least nobody knows for sure. Because the future cannot be known, it allows for all kinds of possibilities. There will always be challenges. These challenges require compromises and goodwill, and decency. People are different in their personalities and life habits. Without compromises, how can two married people live together peacefully and happily?

Watching the river flow into the far distance, Nina felt sad about Dan, about their relationship, and about life itself. Her tears were falling down her cheeks again, and she did not want to wipe them away. So instead, she just sat and let the river wind blow on her face, blowing away her tears and her sadness.

Nina felt sorrow but was also responsible for Dan's suicide. She profoundly regretted that she did not go back to see him that night. She kept thinking if she had gone back home, things might have come out differently. Although her friends were empathetic, Nina still felt some guilt about Dan's suicide. Her thoughts were in turmoil, remembering how controlling and angry Dan was, but, on the other hand, they had shared a life for many years.

Even after the tragedy of Dan's death, Nina continued to be close to his mother. Nina needed to show her his suicide note. First, they talked about it over the phone. Then Dan's mother asked to see it.

"I think that alcohol may be the main problem. Dan drank too much just like his father did," Dan's mother said.

"You are right. Dan was a decent man most of the time, but he lost his dignity with the alcohol abuse, "Nina agreed.

"I have some horrible memories of his father. Those memories span about forty-seven years." Dan's mother looked out the window.

"Ah?" Nina was surprised Dan's mother would mention about the hidden family history.

"I don't even want to think about it," Dan's mother said, upset.

"Please don't make yourself more distressed," Nina said.

"Nina, we all have suffered because of their alcoholism. Now, you need to take care of yourself and my granddaughters," Dan's mother said after seeing Nina's tears.

"Thank you, you need to take care of yourself too," Nina touched her one more time and said, "I feel so sad that Dan ended his life so tragically."

After this long conversation with Dan's mother, Nina learned that Dan was raised in a family with lots of domestic violence. His father was violent to his mother, including name-calling, cursing, and hitting. She said her husband bullied her from the beginning of their marriage. Dan often saw those abusive behaviors, and he copied them in his relationship with Nina, unfortunately.

"I was told that most of the mental problems for adults are caused by trauma in their childhood." Dan's mother said. After these deep communications, Nina was more attentive and caring to Dan's mother. Both women also felt sorry that they had been the victims of abusers. They had a shared experience of suffering and a common language to understand it. Nina even worried that her troubled marriage may have harmed her daughters. Sadly, Nina admitted that her understanding of all this meaningful information was too late.

After Dan's suicide, Nina experienced nightmares almost every week. One night, Nina had a terrible dream. She dreamed Dan jumped into the Jordan River and drowned. The waves washed his body to the shore, churning with many yellow bubbles. His body was swollen like a balloon and had a terrible stench. His face was pale, eyes closed, and the blood flowed from his nostrils. It was horrible. Nina woke up with a scream in the middle of the night. Her body was covered with sweat, and her bedsheet was soaking wet.

Nina was scared to sleep because of the gruesome nightmares. This situation became a growing problem, affecting her life, and she couldn't take it anymore. She was developing into a crippling anxiety disorder.

Plus, there was added stress from the two children. As a result, Nina's depressed state became much more severe.

It was Papa who helped Nina through this nightmarish period in her life. Her father invited Nina to meet in the nearby park. They sat down on the bench to talk about Dan's life and his emotional and psychological issues.

"Dan lost genuine faith in his life because of what he went through with his parent's divorce. His father never visited him and never contacted him after they separated. Dan did not even know where he lived," Nina told her father.

"Poor boy," Albert said.

"Dan always felt abandoned. This haunted him so much that he initially did not want to have children," Nina said.

"You should have told me all of this earlier, Nina," Albert sighed.

"I didn't want to bother you, Papa," Nina said, "Dan thought his emotional dependence would be better once he was married."

"But he did not know how to care for the marriage," Albert argued.

"I think Dan did try, but he had too many emotional burdens," Nina said.

"Everybody knows that marriage is like planting trees. You need watering regularly," Albert said.

"Dan had lots of regrets and losses. He lost the love of his father, the respect of his community, and the same from his wife," Nina said.

"Look, Nina, we should realize something from Dan's tragic ending." Albert thought about that Nina was still immersed in the emotional turbulence of Dan's death.

"How can we understand all those losses?" Nina demanded.

"Loss is a normal part of life, just like failure is part of everyone's life," Albert said.

"Death is part of life," Nina repeated Albert's words, "How about suicide?" She asked her father an important question, which kept bothering her.

"Suicide is the worse type of death. It is a tragedy when someone takes their own life."

"I've heard there are many people who choose suicide every year. Why?"

"Most of them are because of a disease called depression," Albert said.

"I am sure Dan had severe depression," Nina said.

"I think this disease comes from anxiety and frustration. So the best way to overcome depression is to deal with that anxiety and frustration correctly," Albert said.

"Getting rid of destructive habits like drinking alcohol may also be important?" Nina suggested.

"You are right. Anything removing negativities will help, like exercising, good sleep, talking to friends, and taking medicine. But, of course, never giving up is the most important mindset," Albert emphasized.

"I guess Dan chose to give up at last," Nina said.

"Nina, we have to learn to accept the reality of Dan's death," Albert advised. "We need to accept it and deal with it. Then we can move forward for a better future." Papa encouraged Nina.

"Thanks! Papa," Nina was getting quiet. She felt calmer.

"During our lifetime, we confronted many challenges, a lot of failures, and a lot of puzzles. But, unfortunately, we couldn't resolve them in time," Albert said.

"Should we try to overcome those challenges?" Nina inquired.

"Yes and No, 'Yes' for anything you can use your wisdom and ability to resolve. 'No' for anything you don't have the sources or competence to deal with." Albert looked at Nina and gave her a big smile. "In life, we need imagination, creativity, and hard work to resolve any problems."

Nina had a long conversation with her father. They sat at a small table face to face, talking quietly while they sipped Chinese tea like in the Shanghai ghetto many years ago.

"I do not understand how a person could destroy his own life like that?" Nina asked her father.

"You know, Nina, people's lives are actually fragile and relatively short. So, therefore, we ought to be more rational when considering and dealing with the issues that challenge us," Albert said.

"Rational, yes, rational," Nina was digesting her father's words.

"Do not overextend yourself. Set limits. Never go to the extreme." Albert waved his hand twice to emphasize his point.

"Yes Papa!"

"If you are confronted by a very stressful matter, leave it or put it down when you feel overwhelmed, and deal with it later." Albert was staring at Nina with extra softness.

"I am exhausted from all the problems," Nina said.

"Never let any life dilemma exhaust you. Take care of your health," Albert said firmly.

"But the problem will chase after me," Nina said.

"Sometimes, the best way to deal with conflicts is to leave the battle-field," Albert said.

"To avoid conflict," Nina asked.

"Yes, to leave the battlefield to avoid the intensification of contra-dictions."

"You mean let time heal the inner wounds?"

"Yes, Nina. Time can cure almost everything," Albert said.

"Time, I need more time," Nina nodded.

"It is a good idea to see a qualified psychologist help you organize your thoughts," Albert said.

Two weeks later, Nina went to see her psychotherapist. Amy was a chubby lady whose voice was calm and pleasant.

Nina told Amy that after Dan died of suicide, she had suffered from insomnia. Nina not only lost her marriage and her husband, but she also felt a certain degree of guilt about the loss of Dan's life.

"Is there anything I could have done to prevent the suicide?" Nina asked Amy the question she most often thought about.

"Nina, it is not your fault. You don't need to have any feelings of guilt," Amy said.

"Ah," Nina nodded.

Amy taught Nina some simple methods to help her manage the anxiety attacks. "Nina, when you feel anxious or depressed, you can do deep breathing exercises for five minutes. For example, you can inhale, hold the air for five seconds, and exhale another ten seconds. In the meantime, you can shift your thoughts to something else, something positive and happy, away from the negative."

"I should have helped Dan do all of these things." Nina kept thinking Dan might have been saved if he could have accepted some strategies to help his emotional issues adequately.

"Nina, please try to look forward, not look backward," Amy knew that Nina needed time to heal her broken heart.

After many psychotherapy sessions, Nina realized that her marriage had been defeated by an accumulation of many significant details of daily life, not by the typical so-called third person. Those details included lack of responsibility, unreasonable expectations, and endless complaining.

Nina followed Amy's suggestions, and she went to the library every week, borrowing and reading lots of books about marriage and depression. The knowledge from those books gave her wisdom, inspiration, and strength.

Nina thought about her marriage to Dan. Some people, like Dan, have a tendency to focus on negative issues. Dan always concentrated on what he was not satisfied with or was not happy about. But, in fact, life is supposed to be the other way around. We ought to focus on something positive. We should focus on our hopes and a bright future.

Nina remembered that a famous German philosopher mentioned this crucial concept of never focusing on negativity. He had a famous saying, "If you gaze long enough into an abyss, the abyss will gaze back at you. If a person focuses on the abyss, this person will end up in that abyss." So the philosopher's message tells us that if you focus on negativity, you will end up with negativity.

You are what you eat. So if you eat positive stuff, you will end up positively. Nina only wished she could have learned all this wisdom much earlier.

Nina learned that people divorce because of the differences in their thinking patterns and emotional expectations. The accumulated misunderstandings that are harmful in a marriage are primarily due to a lack of communication. Nina felt regret because she found all the wise advice too late for her own marriage.

Nina wondered why there is always something sweet and something sour in life. She believed that perhaps that was the true meaning of life. Life lets us taste both good and bad.

Nina gradually got out of the shadow of her depression under Amy's supervision and support. Then, unfortunately, another unpredictable massive emotional storm came upon her.

CHAPTER TWENTY-THREE

April 1982

Tel Aviv, Israel

I t was a cloudy afternoon when Nina received an urgent phone call from the hospital in the town where Albert's kibbutz was located.

"Your father has been hospitalized because of vomiting with blood."

It shocked Nina.

Nina rushed to the hospital, where she saw her father lying on a bed, his face gaunt. Nina's heart shuttered. She literally felt the pain in her chest. Papa looked thin and fragile. His hand was trembling, but he tried to smile at his daughter.

"He has lost lots of weight because of stomach cancer," the nurse said softly.

"Oh, gosh," Nina covered her mouth with her hand. She felt so sorry for her father. She should have come much earlier.

Nina glanced out of the window, her thoughts twirling. There was a strong smell of disinfectant in the hospital. It increased the fear for her father and the seriousness of his illness. Nina realized how much she loved her father, regardless of any disagreements they may have had in life.

"Papa," Nina knelt down beside Papa's bed and held his hand with tears in her eyes.

Papa touched her hand with his bony fingers.

"Papa," Nina croaked.

Nina wanted to say something, but at the same time, she also did not want to say anything. She wanted to tell her father, "Oh Papa, I am sorry I didn't take your advice all these years. I'm sorry I did not meet your expectations for my life. Oh, I am so sorry!" But, instead of saying all these words to her father, Nina didn't say a word at all. She only cried. Nina thought it might be too late to say these things. Also, she had difficulty admitting maybe she had been wrong not to take his advice. All she could do was hold Papa's hand. Her tears were coming down uncontrollably.

"Sweetie, whatever happens, you need to be strong," Papa's voice was not steady.

"Yes, Papa," Nina said.

When Nina held Papa's hand and cried, she was reminded of their journey together from Genoa, Italy, to Shanghai, China.

"I will leave this world sooner or later. I'm going to see your mother in another world," Papa said.

"Papa, Papa!" Nina said gently as she tried to soothe her father.

"I am happy to have you for my daughter, Sweetie," Papa turned his head to Nina and looked at her with exceptional love. Nina could hardly bear to keep her father's gaze.

Papa held Nina's hand. He had a lot to say that night. Eventually, he told her the truth about her foster parents in London. Papa said he did not reveal this information for so long because he got the news when Nina lost her newly-married husband and her mother at the same time. He did not want to give more sorrow to her.

Papa told Nina how her foster parents, John and Mary, died in London from Hitler's bombardment, the so-called Blitz, in 1941.

One of Papa's old friends brought the information about them from England.

Nina stood up without crying when she got the news about her foster parents. She walked out of the hospital and sat down on a giant rock near the Jordan River. Nina closed her eyes. She could hear John calling her "Little Princess."

She could not hold back her sorrow any longer, crying out loudly, "Daddy, Daddy!" Nina put both hands on her face and called, "Mommy, Mommy!"

Many times in the past, Nina had asked Papa to search for any news about her foster parents, although she knew she only had a slim chance of ever seeing them again. She felt her heart aching when she got this sad news. Nina didn't want to think of them perishing in the Nazis' bombing of London. They had gone to heaven. She would never forget them," Daddy, Mommy!"

Nina remembered vividly when John and Mary took her hands and went to Hyde Park in central London to see the beautiful cherry blossoms. It was a meaningful memory. Nina remembered her Mommy's warm hugs and her Daddy's encouraging voice. They were lovely, kind, and selfless. They had given so much love to her. Nina believed John and Mary planted, in her young heart, a beautiful seed of a good conscience, which might be the essence of life's existence.

The doctor in the hospital indicated that Papa's cancer had already metastasized into other parts of his body. So they had to give him some strong medications. Thanks to the medical treatment, Papa did not feel too much pain.

Nina thought about Papa's life. She reviewed her life with him. It was like watching a movie. It started in Cologne and then Berlin, then from Genoa to Shanghai, and finally here, in Tel Aviv.

Nina found a bench to sit on in the hospital's corridor and held her face with her palms. The vast sadness crushed into her broken heart. She started crying, unstoppable. She was immersed in an unbelievable pain.

When she was calmer, Nina went into her Papa's room. Papa had fallen asleep again, so she quietly left. The walls of the hospital ward were all white. There was a powerful antiseptic smell in the atmosphere, which gave her the sensation of illness and death. Nina felt her chest being pressed. She was short of breath as she walked out of the hospital.

Outside the hospital, the Jordan River flowed calmly. A mist covered the water's surface in the late morning. A pigeon was landing on a tree stump to rest near the riverbank. The pigeon turned around, looking at Nina steadily. It looked like it wanted to talk to her.

Nina's eyes were still burning from all her crying. She could not look straight into the pigeon's eyes. Instead, she looked away toward the Jordan River, where the water rippled towards the seaside of Tel Aviv. She found that the Jordan River had become a little murky over the years. It was no longer as clear as it once was.

The Jordan River seemed just like a person's life, from a pure baby to a naive toddler, from hopeful youth to a complicated adult. Nina took an involuntary gulp of air near the river. She moistened her colorless lips and thought about Papa and how he was exhausted because he carried too many thoughts and memories in his mind.

Nina went back home with a restless heart. She was worried and fearful.

A few days later, the doctor called Nina, "Your father is in a critical condition as a coma."

Nina immediately felt devastated because she knew she had lost the last chance to say goodbye to her Papa. She rushed to the hospital. She wanted to speak to him. But unfortunately, when Nina reached the hospital, Papa had already passed away quietly. Nina cried. She almost fainted in the hospital.

The kibbutz community paid great respect to Albert. They held a solemn funeral. The members gathered in the hall. The head of the kibbutz gave a formal speech about Albert's contribution to the kibbutz. He mentioned that Albert oversaw children's education. He taught all the Jewish kids about zionism, the idea of Jewish people returning to Israel to survive and develop a prosperous life. Albert's granddaughters, Anna and Bela, attended the funeral. They felt the loss of their grandfather.

Nina made a solemn speech about her father at the funeral. She revealed that her father had written an impressive memoir about his whole family. It took him almost ten years to complete. It traced back to their earliest ancestors, coming out of Egypt, going to Europe, and settling down in Germany. How they were run out of Germany by the Nazi party. He described the life they were in Shanghai ghetto during the war. He wrote about how many of his family members had been murdered by the Nazis. More recently, he had recorded the incredible achievements of the kibbutz in the land of Israel.

Papa's funeral was ceremonious and dignified.

Nina was uncommonly resilient at her father's funeral. She showed an unusual calmness. It was only after she came back home that she found her Papa's hat and held it. That hat triggered Nina's enormous sorrow, and she dissolved into tears.

"Papa, Papa!" Nina sobbed uncontrollably. The most profound sorrow crushed her heart into pieces. Nina could not stop weeping. Nobody could soothe her. Nobody could stop her. Nina had fallen apart completely, holding her father's hat.

The following day, Nina sorted out the things in the house. At the bottom of one wooden box, she found a picture of her Papa with her. Papa looked happy with his hand on her shoulder beside the Jordan River in the early days. Nina remembered that it was that year when her father had opposed her decision to marry Dan. Regrettably, she did not listen to him at that time.

Nina also remembered another occasion when they disagreed. They came back from Jerusalem, where Papa joined his friends to visit the castle in the old town. After a meal, Nina and Papa become involved in a debate about educating children. Papa got exhausted. They had to stop the conversation unfinished. Later, they never found a suitable time to continue. Nina's heart was full of regrets.

Nina stared at her father's pictures. She felt the terrible sensation of losing him. She cinematically remembered all the way her father showed his love for her, from her birth to walking her to school in Berlin, sailing on the ship from Genoa to Shanghai, saving her from the severe typhoid disease with expensive antibiotics in Shanghai, then struggling to settle in Israel. Later on, Papa was not so involved in Nina's life. When she was younger, he was a strict disciplinarian with lots of ideas about how she should live. Papa let her do whatever she wanted as an adult, but there always was a profound love for her deep in his heart. Even though Papa did not always speak of his love for her, she knew it was strong because of his actions, and Nina always has had room in her heart for the love for her Papa.

Nina gazed at her father's photo and burst into tears. Nina felt sorry and remorseful that she didn't spend more time with her Papa. She was still holding her Papa's hat on her chest. She wept and whimpered, and her tears kept dropping like broken beads.

"If I could get another chance at life, I am willing to exchange it with anything. Just let me see my Papa again. I want to hold his hand, sit down with him, and have a heart-to-heart talk once again," Nina said to herself. She kept mumbling and weeping. Her tears fell in a continuous stream.

CHAPTER TWENTY-FOUR

June 1982

Tel Aviv, Israel

On the way back from her father's funeral on the train, Nina started to write a memorial article about her dearest Papa. She tried to write every scene from Berlin to London, and then the port in Genoa and sailing went through the Red Sea and so many crazy things that happened in Shanghai ghetto with Papa. She was writing and crying, then crying and writing alternatively, without stopping.

An old gentleman was sitting next to Nina's seat, who peeked at her at first, and then he stared at her and surprised her by saying, "Oh, Dear, are you all right?"

"I am fine," Nina lifted her head to answer the gentleman.

"Why are you crying so much? Whom do you write for?" He asked two questions together.

"I am crying for my father. I am writing for my father too," Nina answered with tears.

"Ah, a good daughter," the gentleman said. He gave Nina the thumbs up.

"Thank you," Nina answered politely.

204 - JOHNSON WU

"The sorrow of love," the old gentleman said with a quiet voice and then turned to his view outside the train window.

Nina also looked out the window. The yellow birch leaves were moving backward fast with the speeding train. Nina was reminded of a piece of music that her Papa used to play on a violin called "Trauer der Liebe" (Sorrow of Love).

With the beautiful violin melody, accompanied by the moving train's rhythm, Nina kept writing the memoir of her Papa all the way home.

***

After all the sadness for lost loved ones, Nina concentrated all the energy on her musical career. Every morning when the sun was rising, Nina stood by the Jordan River and played with passion on her flute. Every evening with the sunset, Nina sat by the river and practiced again. She practiced her flute tirelessly, every day, every week, and every month for years.

On many occasions, Nina played her flute in different locations and ceremonies, such as for a friend's wedding, someone's graduation party, or in retirement homes. She participated in a few competitions in the Tel Aviv area and received some awards for her musical performance. She was often invited by local communities for their concerts. Her flute playing was recognized as a unique style. She established an outstanding reputation as a musician.

When practicing her music, Nina realized playing the music was not only for other people's pleasure and celebration but also for her own emotional healing. Whenever she felt sad, she would play. If she felt happy, she would play. Sometimes if she felt bored, she would play and increase her spiritual energy. Nina also enjoyed listening to music. Music was her best friend, accompanying all aspects of her life.

Nina met many friends in the musical world, people like herself who loved music. Likewise, she met many musicians who devoted themselves to different musical instruments such as piccolo, clarinet, harp, accordion, cello, ukulele, mandolin, oboe, trombone, and xylophone, and so on. Sometimes, when the friends got together, they would willingly form a band to play different types of music: classical, modern, jazz, and traditional Jewish music.

During the pursuit of her musical career, Nina grew in her own wisdom and understanding. She recognized that the person who would practice a musical instrument and develop the ability to play would also develop a certain degree of mental concentration. That would also develop critical motor skills, indicating good physical agility. According to general social norms, people who can play a musical instrument are usually classified as a noble class. If that person is a woman, she would be recognized as gentle, classy, and more educated lady.

During this time, Nina attended as many different concerts as she could. In addition, Nina learned to play other instruments besides the flute, such as piano and violin. She even learned how to conduct the band.

Five years later, Nina had her most outstanding performance. She played the flute with magnificent success at a Tel Aviv concert. Nina reached to the top of her music career when she played the repertoire "Flight of the Bumblebee" with an unbelievable superior skill. This music is challenging to play, but her performance was outstanding. It was a tremendous accomplishment to play the song with a sophisticated style, melodically. Since then, Nina has earned a solid reputation as a flutist in the musical community.

Nina was selected by the Israeli government to represent her country by going to Europe for a unique musical event. She performed her flute with her colleagues and had a wonderful time with her international peers.

Nina's photo was on the front page of the national newspaper. She was playing her flute passionately in the picture on the newspaper printed. Later on, Nina was chosen for a national band to welcome a foreign president in a formal government ceremony.

After Nina had established her excellent reputation, she had many students who wanted to learn the flute from her. Because of their enthusiasm to work with her, Nina became a music teacher naturally.

While teaching one of her students, Olivia, Nina learned that human potential is unlimited for learning and being creative. She thought people should do anything to increase their creative skills to achieve better results. She also realized how important being polite and respectful for all learners.

"You have to be patient, calm, cheerful, and confident when you practice," Nina said to Olivia, who was a 15-years old girl. Nina recalled she also learn to play flute at that age, but it was in Shanghai ghetto, learning bamboo flute from Hason.

"Okay," Olivia nodded.

"You need to maintain your health and preserve a healthy living environment, which will enhance your learning ability and creativity," Nina added that she meant physical and mental health is essential for the student to succeed.

Nina thought she might be over meticulous in picking up almost every flaw of her student's mistakes during her teaching. She could not stand any wrong notes or sloppy playing techniques. But she recognized this was her character. She was the same way with her children. As a result, her students, including Olivia and her parents, often worried that Nina was too harsh with her criticism during her teaching sessions.

"Please take it easy on my daughter," Olivia's mother often said.

Eventually, Nina developed a relatively easy-going teaching style. She understood that every person had a unique character. They always have different learning abilities, some fast, some slow, some paying more attention to the skill development, and others to the music style. In fact, everyone has a different understanding of the essence and meaning of music. Therefore, playing perfectly was almost impossible. Flawlessness essentially did not exist in this world.

One unique idea Nina passed on to her students was that excellent performance depends on harmony, not competition. Musicians created harmony by working together, not trying to outshine each other. Nina emphasized to her students that they need this attitude to obtain a successful musical career. This mentality was readily accepted by many of her students.

Feeling content with the achievements in her life, Nina looked back on her past. She did not want to dwell on her wounded heart. Life was indeed like the river; the water slowly washed away the vicissitudes of life.

Nina recalled an ancient Chinese poem she learned in the Shanghai ghetto, "Frosted autumn leaves are much redder and more beautiful than early spring garden flowers." Nina thought of herself just like the red leaf bitten by frost on the cold days. She was still a beautiful and elegant woman. Nina had become much more mature in the windy, rainy, and sunny climate. Now she was more grateful for those challenging life experiences. She believed that she could make significant progress without anxiety. She was learning to understand more about life with more positive energy.

While Nina had her successful musical career, her life was hectic. She was responsible for raising her daughters and had a good relationship with both of them. They remained reasonably close.

The older daughter Anna's first marriage failed. She divorced and remarried within two years. Even though her physical health was not very good, Anna had a good husband and a beautiful daughter, Amira. Nina loved her baby granddaughter very much.

The younger daughter, Bela's marriage did not last for a year. She had always been unhappy in her emotional life. She went through a difficult divorce.

Later, Bela traveled to her mother's hometown, Cologne, in Germany. Bela enjoyed her time by the Rhine River with sunshine and music. She also took the opportunity to visit her favorite German author Heinrich Boll's status in the city. Bela still admired Boll's story about the classical conversations between a smartly dressed enterprising tourist and a shabbily dressed local fisherman. Bela believed that she would choose happiness, not money if she must make a choice between the two.

Bela's life changed at the Christopher Street Day of Cologne Pride celebrations. As she walked with so many people, celebrating pride in gay and lesbian culture, she realized in her heart and spirit she was a lesbian. That was why her marriage failed a man. This revelation was totally unexpected to Bela. With this new awareness, Bela celebrated with all her lesbian friends on Cologne Street for Christopher Street Day. After that, Bela made up her mind firmly, "When I'm back to Israel, I will find myself a female partner and establish a family."

And Bela did. She lived with her partner in a small city outside of Tel Aviv.

***

It was a magical summer night in 1988. The moonlight shone on the water. Nina was playing the flute by the Jordan River. She looked at the twinkling starlight in the azure sky. Nina had an epiphany all of a sudden. She realized her fifty-eighth birthday was coming. "Life already has offered me many challenges but also many chances to survive. I have to make my life happy!" That night the music inspired her and awakened her deep longing for happiness. Her heartbeat was faster when she thought about love again. "I can create a new life somewhere."

Nina believed her happiness was not only for herself but also for her father and mother. She remembered how her parents used to make sacrifices in their life for her happiness during the war. Therefore, she decided she owed them to get rid of any negativity in her life and make every effort to be happy.

Nina asked herself the primary question, "What is the essence of happiness for her?" Sitting on the bank of the Jordan River, Nina knew that the essence of happiness is to love and be loved. It is the meaning and purpose of life.

Nina read a book that told her that "Love can happen to anyone at any age." She knew that not everyone would understand her journey, which was okay. So she decided to pursue a better and happy life. Suddenly, she felt reborn. Everything seemed to be brighter for the future. She would make herself happy and make the best of this life wherever she was.

She decided she would start to look for a partner from that exact moment. She didn't care what anybody else was going to say about her life. She would look for someone to love. She believed someone would appear, match her in harmony, and become her genuine love.

Like the Law of Attraction, Nina's positive attitude brought very positive experiences into her life. Nina met Sam Weinberg on a kibbutz tour in Tel Aviv by coincidence. The fateful trajectory was magical. Sam was a tall man from America with a bright smile. They had a friendly but brief chat at that time. Sam was surprised that Nina could speak English with a pure British accent.

Sam was an excellent professional swimming coach in New York City. He was proud to mention to Nina that one of his students had won the American National Swimming Competition's gold medal. In addition to swimming, Sam also liked to take pictures with his Canon camera. He showed Nina some fantastic images of various animals he shot with his long-focus lens.

Nina was surprised and delighted when Sam played the harmonica wonderfully during the tour party. Sam played a very touching song, and Nina wondered why his smile was so familiar. Suddenly, she realized Sam's smile was exactly the same as Hason's, the boy she loved in Shanghai. Nina instantly knew she liked this man.

Nina and Sam started communicating by mail after Sam went back to the US, then phone calls became frequent.

"Can I invite you to visit me?" Sam asked.

"Sure," Nina said.

"Would you be able to come to New York next week?"

"Sure!"

Nina did not think she would have an unbelievable life later because of this decision.

PART V

THE HUDSON RIVER

CHAPTER TWENTY-FIVE

September 1989
New York, U.S.

N ina arrived in New York from Tel Aviv precisely a week later. It was an autumn afternoon in 1989.

"Welcome to New York!" Sam picked Nina up at the airport.

The breeze from the Hudson River was gently blowing Nina's hair. Her face was rosy in the chilly air.

"I didn't know what kind of gift I should bring you," Nina gave Sam a small box. Even though she had come all the way to New York to be with Sam, they were still new in their relationship. She did not want to give him anything that exposed her feelings for him too soon. So instead, she chose a gift that was somewhat neutral but meaningful.

"Thank you very much!" Sam opened the gift box. He found a hand-shaped plate painted with a circle of green leaves, colorful flowers, and a dove picking up a green stem in the center. Below the dove was a printed word, "Shalom" (Hebrew: Peace).

"Beauty and peace, Shalom," Sam read out the word and stared at Nina.

"Shalom for the country and people," Nina said. The gift had a universal and personal meaning for Nina. She had come here to look for peace and love at this time in her life.

"Absolutely," Sam smiled back at her.

Their laugh was accompanied by the seagulls' squawk over the Hudson River. A pair of seagulls was soaring over the water towards the Statue of Liberty, standing far away over the river.

Nina and Sam strolled along the Hudson shoreline. They walked side by side in the October air, talking about their life.

Sam suggested, "Let's sit on a bench, facing the Statue of Liberty for a while."

"It is lovely beside the river," Nina answered, her hair dancing around her ears with the wind.

"Should we visit the Statue of Liberty tomorrow?" Sam suggested.

"Sure," Nina was happy to go.

The following day, they sat in the front of the cruise ship and looked at the Statue of Liberty in New York Harbor. The water of the Hudson River sparkled beautifully in the sunlight. The air was fresh, with a gentle breeze. A group of seagulls followed their cruise ship, soaring and screeching.

"Nina, can you imagine how many new immigrants entered the United States through the Statue of Liberty," Sam said. He walked shoulder by shoulder with Nina inside of the museum.

"I wonder what kind of feelings they had when they came through this place," Nina asked Sam.

"Those people left all that was familiar to them to come to this extraordinary land. It must have been very stressful," Sam guessed.

"They also had great hopes," Nina added.

"Sure, even though the new immigrants were escaping poverty and suffering in their home country, their hearts were full of expectations for a new life. This was a new beginning for them."

"Yes, the essence of human nature is to escape pain and pursue happiness," Nina agreed.

"Absolutely, it is this inner vitality for pursuing happiness that gives us all kinds of creative ability," Sam said.

Sam lifted his camera and shot a few pictures of the Statue of Liberty with Nina.

Thursday morning, Sam took Nina to visit the Museum of Modern Art in the city. Sam tried to show her the most famous places in the city. They spent a lot of time inside MoMA. They enjoyed the paintings of Monet and Picasso and other well-known painters in the museum collections.

When Nina stood in front of an oil painting named The Starry Night, she stepped closer to look at it. She recognized it as Vincent van Gogh's masterpiece.

"This is Van Gogh's painting about the light at night," Nina said to Sam.

"Yes, someone was saying this is one of the most recognized paintings in western culture, which makes it one of the most valuable paintings in this museum," Sam said.

"Among all the artists, van Gogh struck me the most," Nina said.

"Vincent was poor and frustrated when he was alive. His works were bought and sold only after his death. Vincent's sunflowers had been sold at a dazzlingly high price, about forty million dollars," Sam said.

"Wow!"

"Although Vincent's expressive brushwork was characterized by bold colors and was very dramatic, he only sold one painting in his lifetime. He suffered from mental illness and poverty. He shot himself. It is a pity that a great artist suffered so much," Sam said.

"It is a real tragedy," Nina was sorry for Vincent's suicide.

Obviously, Sam didn't know Nina's personal history yet. He could not fully understand her response to Vincent's suicide, but he did think she seemed a little tired. He suggested they sit down on a bench in the gallery.

"There are so many intelligent people in this world who do win the power of money," Nina sighed.

"On the other hand, the power of money has indeed produced many tragedies in history," Sam said.

"That is true," Nina agreed.

"There are also many touching stories about another aspect of the world because of love, not because of money."

"Yes. Let me ask you a controversial question. Love or bread, which is more important in life," Nina asked Sam.

"I have heard a saying that if a person is truly in love, he could do everything well. He could be more creative and earn more bread because he has that good energy," Sam answered.

"That is true," Nina said.

After the museum, Nina and Sam went into a restaurant near the Hudson River to have a lunch. When they finished dining, they saw an old street person with tattered clothes at the door. He wanted to come into the restaurant but was blocked by the restaurant manager.

"You cannot enter our restaurant," The manager said to the old man.

"Ah?" The old man did not expect that. He most likely wanted to sneak into the restaurant and maybe get some leftover food from the customers.

"You are not allowed to come inside this restaurant," the manager repeated his order.

"Ah?" The old man was embarrassed

"I am sorry, but this restaurant is expensive," the manager said.

Sam walked over to the old man and the manager. "Good evening, gentlemen. Can I say something?" Sam talked to both men for a few minutes.

"Hello Sir, I am willing to bear all the cost for a meal and tip for this gentleman tonight," Sam smiled at the manager and held his hand out to the old man. The two men looked at Sam, surprised.

"That is fine, Sir," the manager said.

Sam took a few bills and put them into the old man's hand. The man was still leaning on the door.

"Thank you!" Sam paid the bill, smiled at the old man, and walked into the windy street with Nina.

Nina had observed Sam's natural generosity and was touched. She recognized him as a very caring and sincere man. She considered him to be a man of good character. Nina made up her mind. She knew Sam was the right man for her. She even remembered her Papa doing the same thing in a Shanghai restaurant before they left for Israel.

The next morning, Sam took Nina to New York's Central Park for a walk. They watched people coming and going. There were a lot of boys and girls holding hands and even old couples doing the same. The atmosphere of the park was lovely, even romantic. They found a bench to sit down and talk.

"Look at those boys and girls, and those men and women," Nina said to Sam.

"Yes, they must be pleased with each other." Sam looked at them passing by.

"I would like to ask you a question. What is the most important factor in a relationship between a man and a woman?" Nina asked Sam.

"I think it should be tolerance," Sam replied with confidence.

"Then, what is your understanding the tolerance?" Nina continued to ask.

"I believe that tolerance is accepting and appreciating the other person's differences from you," Sam replied.

"Oh," Nina looked into the distance as she thought about this idea.

"Tolerance encourages others to share different feelings and opinions. Tolerance is to think about the circumstances from the other's point of view," Sam said.

"It can be difficult to understand another's different ideas. It is even more difficult to accept different values. It can be very difficult to respect people who have a different mentality," Nina said.

"True, tolerance is a lubricant for people to get along."

"I agree," Nina responded.

Nina and Sam walked along Wall Street in the Manhattan financial district. First, they watched the famous sculpture of a bronze charging bull on Broadway. Then, they went for coffee and talked about stocks and business.

The streets were full of businessmen, looking very important, rushing around.

"Why didn't you become a businessman?" Nina asked.

"It seems to me businessmen are generally oriented to making money. So they have to have a strong pragmatic attitude," Sam replied.

"So, what kind of person are you?" Nina asked with a smile.

"I am not sure. But my friend once concluded I could not be a businessman. I am too easy-going, which is not what you need for business."

"I like easy-going people," Nina said. She stared at Sam for a second.

"They say I am too focused on technical details. But, unfortunately, most technical people don't have a strong money sense," Sam said.

"So, that is why you become a swimming coach?"

"That is true." Sam laughed.

Nina and Sam went to a suburban park near the Hudson River on the weekend. It was a lovely, sunny day, and many people were there already. The aroma of meat cooking on the barbecue grill near the river was enticing. The park was open to people to set up their camps for the weekend as well as day visitors like Nina and Sam. The atmosphere was festive, with families, children, and dogs enjoying themselves. Nina and Sam found a place to sit. They bought something to eat and chatted, enjoying the leisure of a summer day.

"The tantalizing aroma of these barbecues reminds me of a significant thing about my ex-wife. I call it a pork incident," Sam mentioned to Nina.

"Tell me, please," Nina was interested.

"My ex is not Jewish, but she did understand about the Jews not eating pork. In the early days of our marriage, she cared about my feelings, and she tried not to eat pork in front of me. Then, as our emotional attachment faded, it became a kind of pain for her. She didn't care about my feelings anymore," Sam said.

"What happened?"

"She would buy pork and throw it on the kitchen table with a bang. She made her pork ribs with sauce. She did not try to spare me at all.

Once, she asked me, with a little provocative tone, do you want to take a bite?" Sam said

"That is really hurtful," Nina expressed her thoughts.

"Not caring about my feelings is the key factor," Sam said.

"Sure," Nina agreed. She had her own awful experience, so her voice was a little emotional.

"Let us walk a little in the park," Sam suggested, wanting to change the subject. It was getting too heavy.

"Yes, let us enjoy the fresh air and beautiful sunshine," Nina agreed.

CHAPTER TWENTY-SIX

October 1989

New York, U.S.

O n the following evening, Sam played some western cowboy music with his harmonica. It was fantastic. Nina was stunned. She did not know Sam was able to play the harmonica with a variety of techniques. He was excellent at the vibrating tone. That night, Sam played a lot of original harmonica music for Nina. The elegant, melodious, and passionate harmonica music left a deep impression on Nina. The common interest in music between Sam and Nina quickly drew two lonely hearts together.

On the last day of Nina's visit to New York, they again went to the bank of the Hudson River.

"Can I ask you some simple questions?" Sam stared at Nina with a grin.

"Sure," Nina said. Nina found herself staring into his mesmeric gaze. She smiled back at Sam and combed her fingers through her hair.

"Look over there. Why is that white cloud so white," Sam asked, pointing to the sky above the Hudson River.

"That's because the sky is astonishingly blue," Nina replied.

"That is because two people are delighted, so the sky is bluer, the cloud is whiter, the wind is warmer, and even the Hudson River is more cheerful," Sam said.

"Are you saying you have a crush on me?" Nina asked. She had a blush on her cheeks.

"No, I don't have a crush on you," Sam shook his head with a smile.

"Then, what is it?" Nina looked at Sam, surprised.

"I think I have fallen in love with you. I am serious," Sam said. He gazed at Nina affectionately.

"Really," Nina's face was getting redder, but her heart was full of happiness because she knew she loved this exquisite and cheerful gentleman too.

"Nina, you are so beautiful," Sam said.

"I want to hear you say that every day. That is what has driven me to come all the way from Tel Aviv to New York," Nina said.

"Will you marry me?" Sam was suddenly down on one knee in front of Nina and magically took out a small box with a diamond ring, presenting it to her. He prepared well for this moment.

Nina did not expect Sam to propose marriage to her that day. She was so delighted and excited about his proposal.

"Yes, I will," Nina's eyes were full of happy tears.

Nina stood up, reached out to Sam, and took the little box with the diamond ring with trembling hands.

"I love you, Nina," Sam stood up and held Nina's hand.

"I love you too, Sam," Nina said softly.

They did not kiss passionately and did not hug each other madly either. They only held hands and stared at each other with longing. Yet, through their eyes, they knew the passion of their love. "Our hearts are united together, forever."

They kept a magical silence for a long time. The love that comes from the heart speaks a universal language, with no necessity for speech. They saw the love, felt the love, smelled the love, and heard the love without words.

Nina looked out into the distance, over the Hudson River, towards the entrance to the New York Harbor. She saw the Statue of Liberty, the goddess of freedom, carrying a book of laws in her left hand and holding a torch aloft in her right. Nina's vision was blurred by her tears. She thought of her two previous marriages, which failed for different reasons. She was puzzled by the thought of them and was grateful to savor and enjoy this new genuine love she felt for Sam.

"Sam, what is true love after all?" Nina murmured. She looked into Sam's eyes first and then looked at the sailboats on the Hudson River.

"True love should be without any conditions." Sam tried to explain his understanding.

"True love means being willing to do all the things in life for the one who is loved, right?" Nina also wanted to state her opinions on true love.

"Yes, true love means wanting to bring out the best in each other, to want the other to achieve their best potential, and to help them make their dreams come true," Sam said.

"I agree. With true love, you are your best self, and I can be my best self," Nina looped her hand around Sam's arm.

"Shall we go home now?" Sam suggested to Nina.

"Let's go," Nina nodded happily.

* * *

In the year 1990, Sam and Nina had a beautiful wedding ceremony in New York City.

They organized photographic activities before the wedding banquet in different parts of New York City, particularly in Central Park and near the Hudson River. They had many memorable pictures taken in many beautiful poses. They tried on different costumes creating unique and stunning scenarios. The professional photographer said, "I've never had such a joyful shoot with newlyweds, even at your age. You are classier than all the young people. Maybe it is because you are older and you have accumulated wisdom. You both look regal and avant-garde."

During the marriage ceremony, Nina and Sam performed with their musical instruments. It was an exceptional combination, flute with harmonica. They played the fantastic and romantic song, Scarborough Fair. Their friends applaud enthusiastically with the performance's rhythm. They said Nina and Sam had lovely cooperation and harmony on the stage. Their smiles were natural, and their stance was elegant.

A lot of friends and relatives attended the wedding. Sam's son came with his wife and two sons. They all were pleased.

Nina felt a little disappointed that her two daughters made excuses for not coming to the wedding. They were not happy that their mother was leaving Tel Aviv for New York. But they sent lovely gifts and congratulations on the marriage.

Nina and Sam chose California for their honeymoon. They had a lovely time chatting on the plane as they flew across the country. When they arrived in San Francisco, Sam took Nina to the famous Wayfare Tavern downtown. They tried the unique popovers and enjoyed watching the other couples in the restaurant.

The second morning they went to Yosemite National Park. Nina and Sam were amazed by the beauty of the place with its wonderful waterfalls and ancient giant sequoias. They met lots of other loving couples on the trip.

They arrived at the next destination, Las Vegas, that evening. There were neon lights everywhere in that city. They were not interested in gambling but enjoyed the elaborate shows. Nina was very impressed by Bellagio fountain water musical show in front of a magnificent hotel.

Then they visited the Grand Canyon. It had spectacular scenery. They stood at Lipan Point, where they could view a wide array of rock strata in the inner canyon. Then, suddenly, the beauty all around them was spoiled by an incidence about a woman who took her life by jumping off a cliff nearby. Nina could not believe it and was saddened that some people came this way to die.

After their trip, Nina began her new life in New York as a private music teacher. They lived in Lower Manhattan. They enjoyed their newly-married life.

Nina and Sam were both teachers, and both had many students. However, they held different philosophies about competition. For instance, Sam thought that competition was important in life. If a student joins a swimming competition, he must try his best to defeat the other swimmers. In contrast, Nina believed her students should strive for the perfect musical performance. But even in a competition, Nina's emphasis was on pursuing an expression of harmony, balance, and a sense of satisfaction. The purpose is not to beat their peers but to be the best they can be.

Nina loved Sam's personality. He was kind, humble, and consistently cheerful. She loved his ability and willingness to do many household tasks and his knowledgeable analysis of the world. And Sam, in turn, loved Nina very much. With open communication and practice, their intimacy grew and enhanced their love.

Nina felt free to ask Sam to pleasure her in new ways. He looked at her with love and longing. Then, he started kissing her face, both ears, then her neck. He kept hugging her and rubbing her back, and gently his hand touched her front, and she sensed some kind of shivering. Nina kissed Sam back on his lips. They had a long and joyful kiss. Nina became excited and aroused. Once Sam came into her, she felt so much pleasure she hugged Sam tightly. They moaned together until both of them flew up to the top of their happiness.

CHAPTER TWENTY-SEVEN

February 1990
New York, U.S.

N ina and Sam had their own independent professional lives. However, they respected each other and never interfered with the other's work routine. Personally, they supported each other. Nina often felt love from her husband through his affectionate smile or a gentle touch.

Nina had quite a few private students to learn flute from her. One of the students was a 14-year-old boy, Adam Graham. He came to class with his grand aunt. The boy loved the flute very much.

Sam continued his career as a swimming coach. He had a position in the Athletic & Swim Club at 7th Avenue in the city.

One weekend, Nina and Sam strolled on Fifth Avenue. All the famous shops showed their best products in the store windows. When Nina saw an advertisement for the sports brand "Michael Jordan," she thought straight away about the sport her husband was involved with. She turned to Sam and asked, "I watched you diving the other day. Are you ever afraid of jumping from such a height?"

"Not at all," Sam replied, "This self-confidence is a kind of spiritual power that comes from being well-trained. Bravery is based on confidence in the heart. That is what I tell my students all the time."

"Oh!" Nina nodded.

Sam was an excellent and dedicated swim instructor. He spent a lot of time studying swimming techniques, even in his spare time. He had taught and trained numerous students, among them some who won national swim championships in the national level.

"What is your secret to training a champion swimmer?" Nina asked.

"I research and study to find out how each individual student can improve their swimming techniques," Sam talked professionally.

"You do?" Nina looked at him.

"Sure. I developed a quick turn maneuver so the swimmer doesn't lose time turning into his next lap," Sam nodded his head and smiled at Nina with pride.

"Tell me more about it, please," Nina said. She was excited to know the details of his innovation.

"That is the method of turning over when a swimmer reaches the opposite wall. It allows him or her to maintain momentum, keeping or even increasing speed. I call it Somersault Turnover."

"Somersault Turnover," Nina repeated the name.

"That is an important factor for my students to achieve wonderful results and win championships," Sam enjoyed talking about it.

"I remember you mentioned three of your students won the national championships, isn't that right?" Nina asked for confirmation.

"Yes, you are right," Sam answered, "I tell my students it is useless to change the swimming pool or the coach. If they are serious about competitive swimming, only thing they can do is to combine their natural talent with lots of practice and mastery of innovative swimming techniques."

Besides his swimming coachwork, Sam's hobby was photography. He liked to go into the countryside to shoot nature scenes and wild animals. Nina loved to go with him on these trips. They always enjoyed being together. They loved the freshness in the suburbs and the surrounding area.

Nina also joined various music clubs and participated in many concerts in the area beside her teaching work. In addition, she was periodically invited by the musical association at Yale University in New Haven to present flute seminars. As a result, she made a lot of friends there.

One autumn weekend, Sam drove his SUV on highway-95. They were on the way to Connecticut. Nina would see a friend from her musical circle, and Sam would take photos of birds.

Driving fast along the highway, the colorful trees sped by with the Hudson River visible in the far distance. Then Nina saw a woman standing by a car, which pulled over by the roadside. She looked so distressed, a real tragic character. The woman reminded Nina of a person she once knew.

"Have you ever heard about the tragic character?" Nina asked Sam.

"What is that?" Sam was a relaxed driver, using only one hand on the steering wheel. The traffic was not heavy anyway.

"My ex-husband, Dan, had a cousin, Eva," Nina said, "She was an example of a tragic character."

"What kind of life did she have?" Sam asked, looking down the highway.

"Eva had an easygoing husband. They started off with a good relationship. But Eva had a nervous personality, always wanting things to be perfect. Her lust for money and sex made Eva reckless and merciless. She even showed signs of paranoia. The couple got into lots of fights because of that. They argued about almost everything," Nina said.

"This kind of marriage won't last," Sam said.

"Yes, things deteriorated between them. Eva ridiculed her husband. He did not even want to respond to her. In the end, they were divorced."

"That is understandable," Sam said.

"There was more to Eva's life," Nina said. "Be careful of the sharp turn, Sam!"

"Don't worry, Honey. I'm good," Sam looked at the road and held his steering wheel with both hands.

"Eva did not learn from her experience of marriage and divorce. Instead, she was even more careless in her new relationships. Eva dated a few men and chose a plumber with strong muscles. They got married ridiculously fast," Nina said.

"Wow, she was lucky to find the man she was looking for," Sam said.

"You are wrong, Sam," Nina told her husband," Eva discovered that her new husband used heroin soon after the wedding."

"That is terrible."

"That was not the only terrible thing," Nina said.

"Big fights," Sam asked.

"Yes, he not only beat Eva up but also threatened to kill her. He said he had already killed someone before."

"What?" Sam was surprised and tried to hold his steering wheel steady.

"The man told Eva that he killed a previous girlfriend about thirty years ago. He had spent a few years in prison because of it. He had kept this secret from Eva," Nina said,

"Oh gosh, that is a horrible secret," Sam said.

"Once Eva confirmed that her husband had indeed killed his girlfriend, she divorced him," Nina said.

"Eva really is a tragic character," Sam said.

"After all those traumatic events, Eva isolated herself from friends and family. As a result, no one, including the so-called best friends, cared about her," Nina said.

"That is sad," Sam said.

"I can imagine that no one will come to see her when Eva is sick. And when she is dying, she will die alone," Nina said with a deep sigh.

"That is a real tragedy," Sam said with sympathy.

"I have heard that a person with a tragic character, no matter how and what choices the person makes in life, will never be lucky," Nina said.

"That sounds awful," Sam said.

"It is because of personality problems, or defects, which lead to poor judgments," Nina said.

"It is a true pity for those people," Sam said.

"All their judgments and understandings are wrong. No matter how they choose, it will turn out badly for them. They will have a dramatic, sad fate for their entire life."

"That is true, Honey," Sam said.

* * *

A month later, Nina was coming back to New York City from New Haven, Connecticut. She had just attended a music club meeting organized by a Yale University professor. She gave a speech to many flute enthusiasts and answered many questions. The more complicated the questions, the harder she tried to explain. Nina spent quite a lot of energy on the meeting that day.

The winter in New York State was brutal. However, the morning was full of sunshine when Nina drove on the Joe DiMaggio Highway along the Hudson River from New York to New Haven.

Snow started to fly in the afternoon. The temperature dropped drastically. The water in the atmosphere cooled to form hexagonal snow crystals. A lot of single snow crystals condensed into snowflakes. Countless snowflakes were flying down from the sky. The precipitation was a combination of snow, ice, and rain.

The northern area of New York and New Haven looked like a white snowfield. Heavy snowstorms form black ice, covering the road. Highway 95 twisted through the snowy country like a giant python crawling slowly from New Haven into New York. Nina's car was clutched in the middle of that iron snake.

There was more traffic on the highway that day. A huge truck driving in the next lane was wobbling and making Nina extremely nervous. Her face was flushed, and her back and neck were sweating because of the stress. Then, another fuel tank truck drove beside her vehicle. It was longer and bigger. It distracted her. Nina was frightened and a little lightheaded.

Suddenly, Nina heard a fierce explosion and the terrible sound of metal crashing. A vast fireball rose above the white snow-covered field in front of her, accompanied by rolling smoke. Nina made an abrupt brake spontaneously.

She had no idea what hit her car. It was so sudden. She completely lost control of the car as it spun across the highway. She didn't even realize she was involved in a multi-vehicle accident.

Nina was confused and had severe dizziness and enormous pain in her left arm. She was imprisoned temporarily inside the crashed car.

After rescue personnel arrived, Nina and the other accident survivors were sent to the nearby hospital.

Nina shared a hospital room with two other women injured in the road accident. She had a dislocated shoulder. Another woman had a fractured leg.

The next morning, the sun shone into the ward, providing a warm, comfortable feeling. The wind was blowing fiercely outside, the temperature falling. The hospital's indoor heating was extraordinarily strong. As a result, Nina had an illusion of the sunlight being extra-warm. People were more likely to have an illusion after being traumatized.

Nina still felt pain in her left shoulder. She had to remain in the hospital for three weeks. During that time, she became friends with Jenny Grafane, the woman in the next bed. They developed a very good friendship.

Later, Sam told Nina how lucky she was to survive such a massive accident. It involved thirty cars. Eleven people had lost their lives on the spot. The rescue efforts were equally great, with many police officers and numerous ambulances, including three orange emergency ambulance helicopters. Black ice caused a series of crashes, blocking the highway and causing many crashes.

The accident taught Nina again that anything could happen at any time in our life.

CHAPTER TWENTY-EIGHT

September 1995
New York, U.S.

Nina and Sam had rented out one of their rooms to a medical student from Shanghai. Hai Chen was an outstanding student, pursuing a graduate degree at Columbia University's Medical School in New York.

Nina always remembered Papa telling her that she needed to be grateful to the city of Shanghai for saving their family during the war. Papa told Nina the United Nations discovered that more than twenty thousand German-speaking Jews found sanctuary in Shanghai. No other city harbored as many German Jewish refugees as Shanghai did. Because of her life-saving experience in the Shanghai ghetto, Nina wholeheartedly wanted to help this student from Shanghai.

Nina helped Hai Chen financially and oriented him to the city: where to shop, how to use the subway, and other means of living in the city. Hai Chen turned to Nina if he had any questions about life in New York.

"I actually grew up in Shanghai. I was there from age nine to nineteen. So I grew up fifteen inches in those ten years," Nina said to Hai Chen.

"Which part of Shanghai did you live in?" Hai Chen was interested.

"My family used to live on Wayside Road. Where are you living in Shanghai?" Nina asked.

"My home is at Zhoushan Road," Hai Chen answered.

"I knew a park called Zhoushan Park in the Hongkew area," Nina refreshed her memory.

"Nina, you must be Jewish?" Hai Chen inquired.

"Sure." Nina nodded.

"Oh, the park you mentioned must be Huoshan Park. It is very close to my home," Hai Chen said.

"Really," Nina felt how small the world is.

"I know there are two special things in the park about Jewish people in Shanghai during the war," He said.

"What are they?" Nina asked.

"An old building used as a Jewish refugee shelter is in the park."

"How do you know that?" Nina was very interested.

"I remember seeing the sign briefly on the building. It offered a thank you to the people of Shanghai for taking in Jewish refugees in WWII. The Israeli government funded the building repairs for the purpose of the commemoration."

"I recalled the refugee shelter in that park," Nina thought about it.

"Another is a marble plaque in Huoshan Park, especially for Jewish refugees," Hai Chen said.

"Do you remember what is on it?" Nina was eager to know.

"Sorry, I don't remember what it says exactly. But I have a photo with the marble plaque on my computer. Let me find it for you." Hai Chen hurried into his room.

It was a Tuesday evening. Nina sat on a chair in the porch. She enjoyed the warm breeze at dusk while her thoughts flew to the memories of Shanghai time.

Nina remembered that Papa had brought her to that park the first time. Later she went there with her friend Mei Lin to jump the ropes. She even came to this park with Hason, who once caught a noisy cicada in the woods there. Nina lost two of her best Chinese friends in the war. It was nearly a half-century ago. Time passed by just like a river current. Nina felt her eyes tearing up.

"Are you okay, Nina?" Hai Chen saw Nina's emotions when he came back with his laptop.

"I have so many memories about the Shanghai ghetto. I was only a young girl," Nina told Hai Chen.

"Let me show you a picture of me in Huoshan Park." Hai Chen opened up his computer in front of Nina.

"Could you enlarge the words of the marble plaque beside you?" Nina requested because her vision was blurred.

"Sure."

When Hai Chen amplified the photo, Nina could see three languages on the plaque: Chinese, English, and Hebrew.

She started to read slowly:

"The Designated Area for Stateless Refugees. From 1937 to 1941, thousands of Jews came to Shanghai, fleeing from Nazi persecution. Japanese occupation authorities regarded them as "stateless refugees" and set up the designated area to restrict their residence and business. The designated area was bordered on the west by Gongping Road, on the east by Tongbei Road, on the south by Huimin Road, and on the north by Zhoujiazui Road. Hongkou District, People's Government."

"This is exactly Shanghai's Jewish ghetto." Nina's voice was a little hoarse.

"I understand it was tough at that time for you and your family," Hai Chen said.

"We never knew we traveled across the sea, over 7000 km, only to fall into the clutches of the Japanese army, the Nazi's ally," Nina sighed.

"I learned in school that we Chinese went through eight years of war with Japan, the Sino-Japanese War," Hai Chen said.

"Unlike some of the Jewish ghettos in Europe at that time, the Shanghai ghetto was not fenced off," Nina said to Hai Chen.

"Ah," he nodded.

"You know that if a Jew escaped in Europe, they had to go into hiding or were caught, even be killed. But we could study, play, and do business in Shanghai," Nina said.

"I heard that most Jewish refugees in Shanghai survived the war."

"Yes. The majority of Shanghai's Jewish refugees survived, while six million Jews were murdered during the Holocaust in Europe."

"Six million people have been killed?" Hai Chen asked.

"Yes. That is why a historian regarded our survival as the 'Miracle of Shanghai,'" Nina said.

"Most of our young people don't have enough knowledge of history. Nina, thank you for letting me know more about the history of my city," Hai Chen said.

* * *

Happy times always go fast. Eight years fly by quickly in New York.

Nina was happy with her life. Her two daughters, Anna and Bela, came to New York a few times, keeping their good connection despite past disagreements.

Nina loved it when Anna brought her daughter to spend time with her. Nina was pleased to see her granddaughter growing up to be a decent and lovely girl. Bela had come for only two short visits. They all had gotten along very well with Sam.

Nina was good at keeping connected to people she cared about. One of those people was one of her best students, Adam, the young flutist who came to her when he was only fourteen.

One weekend, Sam and Nina drove into Manhattan to meet Adam, who was a grown man working in the city right now.

A pair of seagulls flew over the Hudson River, dancing and singing above the waves.

"Sam, I wonder why I have a particular love for the water?" Nina watched the waves on the Hudson River.

"Nina, that may be because the river current is like human life," Sam said.

"Yes, you are right. The river is so energetic and so dynamic. It may look quiet, but it can surge powerfully," Nina said.

"You are right. The river has many changing moods. Sometimes it is furious and fast; other times, it can be as still as glass or lazy with gentle ripples," Sam agreed.

"Even though water is colorless, odorless, and tasteless, it is the basis of all living things. It also forms rich habitats like rivers, lakes, and oceans," Nina said.

"Water is a wonder, isn't it?" Sam said.

"Definitely, when the sunlight hits the water, it will show us all its colors, which is incredibly beautiful," Nina said.

"You mean the beauty of the rainbow?" Sam asked.

"Yes," Nina was delighted.

"There have always been rivers in my life, no matter where I lived. I remember the Rhine in Germany was kind of gloomy. The Thames in England looked warm under the night lights. The Huangpu in China, with the sunset, looked beautiful. The Jordan in Israel was a mix of colors. Now, here in the United States, the Hudson looks lovely." Nina smiled, thinking of her great love of water.

"Yes, our life is just like a river," Sam said

"Many of the world's major cities sprang up on the banks of rivers. Many people think of rivers simply as waterways, which crossed on the way to another place. Still, rivers sustain our lives in multiple ways beyond connecting the world together. Rivers nurture us, supporting us with water, food, irrigation, transportation, and power. Rivers also provide us with cultural and economic opportunities. They are the inextricable links between history and ecology," Nina stated.

"The river is a good metaphor for human experience. Our lives follow their own unique path just like the river does," Sam followed Nina's thoughts.

"Right, where is this river rushing to?" Nina asked.

"To the boundless, limitless, and vast sea," Sam said with awe.

That evening, after visited Adam, Nina and Sam walked the streets of Manhattan in a pleasurable silence. With colorful neon lights reflected on the road, they enjoyed the romantic healing music in gentle rain. They enjoyed the unique beauty of twilight in the city.

"What a peaceful and beautiful place Manhattan is," Nina said.

"In fact, rainy Manhattan is often accompanied by strong winds, blowing your umbrella inside out in minutes. It is not so peaceful and beautiful most of the time. It is just because you are here that the city is beautiful tonight," Sam said.

"Wow, thank you for saying those kind words to me," Nina was delighted to hear Sam's admiration, "I believe there are always challenges in different life stages, but this is a treasured time for us when we can be happy and secure with each other. Don't you think so?" Nina asked Sam.

"I agree," Sam nodded.

Nina and Sam never thought something horrible would happen to them right here in Manhattan.

CHAPTER TWENTY-NINE

September 2001
New York, U.S.

I t was Tuesday morning, September 11 of 2001, around 9 o'clock. When Nina cleaned up her breakfast dishes, she watched the early news on TV as usual. The TV host reported a vast explosion near the World Trade Center. The reporter said a small commuter plane might have hit one of the tall buildings.

Nina was very concerned because her best student, Adam, worked in the World Trade Center. She and Sam had visited him a few weeks ago. Nina put down her dishes to pay attention to the news, worrying about Adam.

The TV showed some of the devastations of what was happening. Nina saw a large hole in one of the World Trade Center buildings with black smoke and flame shooting up. The newscaster repeated over and over that a plane had crashed into one of the towering buildings. They showed flames jumping from the building immediately after the explosion.

It wasn't clear whether it was the north or south tower that was involved with the explosion. Nina remembered that Adam seemed to work in the north tower. She tried to call him. Her hand was shaking so much that she had difficulty punching in the right numbers. She got no answer. Then she tried again.

Nina was too nervous to hold the phone steady. Adam's phone kept ringing with no answer and then voicemail. Nina kept dialing. Finally, Adam picked up.

"Are you all right, Adam?" Nina tried to keep her voice calm.

"I am okay. The smoke alarm is going off in our building right now, but we don't know what is happening?" he said.

"CNN has reported your building has been hit by an airplane. It is on fire right now. You have to leave the building now," Nina tried not to shout.

"I did feel the building shake a few minutes ago, but I can't see anything from our office window," Adam told Nina.

"But your building is on fire!" Nina repeated.

"Someone from the Center's management will control the fire. Don't worry, Nina," Adam said calmly. Nina could hear a lot of noise in the background.

"From CNN's live report, the huge fire is spreading. I think you are in danger. You have to go outside right now," Nina insisted.

"Thanks! Nina! Let me go out to the lobby to see what is going on. Please don't hang up the phone. Keep me posted on what the updated news is," Adam said.

Nina was grateful he was taking her warning seriously. Adam was a bright boy. He could play the flute beautifully, and he won several awards for his playing.

"For sure, Adam, Just go and check up on the situation. I am here to talk to you until you are safe," Nina knew that Adam got an advanced cellular phone called BlackBerry from his Canadian friend.

"Someone has just come back to the office saying the elevators have stopped working." The noise behind him was increasing.

"Then you have to walk down to get out of the building," Nina was almost yelling now. She was getting more nervous when she heard CNN reporting that the other World Trade Center tower had been hit by another airplane.

"But I am on the 80th floor, Nina!" Adam said.

"You need to leave now. This is a big fire in your building," Nina had trouble speaking. She was so frightened for Adam.

"I can't hear you," Adam shouted. Nina could hear someone yelling close to him in the office.

"Adam, you have to get out of that building right now," Nina roared.

"Wow, Wow! The floor downstairs has collapsed..." Adam shouted.

"You must go out right now," Nina yelled.

"What? What?" Adam's voice disappeared. There was a crashing sound in the background.

"Adam! Adam! Adam!" Nina kept calling his name while she stared at CNN live. Not hearing him made her more anxious and worried.

"Oh Nina, Oh my God," Adam's voice was becoming panicked.

"What's happened, Adam?"

Nina did not get an answer. Instead, she heard a massive explosion. Then all of a sudden, Adam's phone went dead.

Nina was desperate after calling Adam's BlackBerry almost every two minutes and getting only non-connected busy signals for forty-five minutes.

She did not know what to do. She was panting and sweaty as her anxiety grew. Finally, she called Sam.

"Sam, the World Trade Center is on fire from an airplane crash. Adam is there. I just spoke to him, but his phone died. The phone calls can't get through at all," Nina was almost crying.

"Don't worry, Honey! I will come home immediately," Sam said.

"What should we do now?" Nina asked.

"I am coming back. You wait at home," Sam's voice was calm.

Nina felt a little better after this phone call with Sam. She sat down on the sofa to rest, but her eyes were still glued to the TV screen.

Nina saw something falling off the tower building, but she did not know what it was. Nina stood up to get a closer look at the images. She unmistakably saw a person jump out of the burning window from the World Trade Center. Nina covered her mouth and cried, "Oh, gosh!"

The horror she was seeing brought back the bad memories of her own horror, standing on the rooftops in Berlin with her mother, watching the Nazis burning their synagogue. The smoke and the fire were so similar. She seemed to hear the roaring of the airplanes and the whistling of the bombings over the Shanghai ghetto. The painful and terrible memories made Nina heartache.

Nina watched as CNN news continuously showed the explosions in the twin towers. Then, unbelievably she saw one of the towers collapse to the ground, followed by a massive fire and an enormous amount of smoke. About a half-hour later, she saw the North Tower collapse. She thought about Adam, thinking he was there, hoping he wasn't there.

CNN continued to repeat the scene of devastation, with buildings falling like matchsticks and people jumping to their death out of the burning buildings. Nina had to stop watching. Her pain was so great, she could not bear the heartbreaking pain anymore.

When Sam finally came back home, he hugged her tightly.

"I was speaking to Adam and told him to get out of that building. Then I lost his BlackBerry signal." She was distraught and frustrated by her helplessness.

"Do you remember what CNN live reported at that time?"

"Let me think. When I was on the phone with Adam, I could see another airplane crashing into the other Twin Tower," Nina said.

"Nina, is Adam's office in north Tower?" Sam asked.

"I am confused about whether Adam works in the North Tower or South Tower. I tried to remember, but I'm too upset now," Nina answered.

"Oh, don't worry, Honey! We will find out."

"I kept calling and calling his BlackBerry but only got a busy signal."

"Oh, Honey," Sam hugged Nina's shoulders.

"I don't know what happened to him. But, I'm so scared for him. Sam."

"Adam will be fine, don't worry."

"I don't know what we should do now," Nina said.

"Let us get more confirmed information before we do anything," Sam said.

"If Adam got out of the Twin Towers, he would certainly call me back," Nina said and looked out of the window restlessly.

"We need to wait for more information," Sam said.

"There must be a reason Adam hasn't called me back," Nina said. "You know, I saw both Towers collapse. No one could live through that."

"I saw some people walk out of there. They looked like they were coming out of a chimney, covered totally with dust on their clothes, their faces, and their hair," Sam said.

"Adam lost his parents and his aunt and has no siblings. He will only contact us if he comes out of that burning building." Nina presumed in a sorrowful voice.

It took a long time for Nina to fall asleep that night. She woke up at midnight, shaken by severe anxiety. She did not go back to sleep that night.

The next day, in the early morning, when Nina opened the window, she was surprised to find snow on her window ledge. It was still coming down, and lots of it. But when Nina lifted her chin to look up into the sky, she was startled. It was not snowing at all. What she was looking at was actually the ashes from the burning Twin Towers of the World Trade Center. The ashes had been blown with the wind all over the Manhattan area, some landing on Nina's window ledge.

Nina touched the white ash with her trembling hand. She cried uncontrollably because she thought about Adam right away. Those ashes could be from Adam, even though Nina kept pushing away this idea from her mind.

Nina and Sam went to lower Manhattan to look for Adam the following day. They could see the cloud of smoke over Manhattan when they drove over there. Nina and Sam walked down the messy streets, covered with debris and rubble and a strong smoke odor. When Nina breathed in the burning air, she remembered the same smell from the Kristallnacht in Berlin street, that was more than sixty years ago. The same terrible feeling made her suffer dreadfully.

Nina remembered how she had followed her mother and walked on Berlin streets that morning after Kristallnacht. They stepped on the broken glasses and smelled the almost exact same burning smoky odor. All the memories made Nina shiver. She held onto Sam's arm tightly.

The closer they got to the site of the Twin Towers, the thicker the smoke in the air. It made their noses sting, and they started to cough. She could see the white and gray ash floating through the air. She knew the ash came from the destruction of the two towers, but it could also be from the bodies murdered inside the towers. Nina was grateful Sam was with her, and she held onto him even tighter.

US Army soldiers with rifles guarded the site and blocked Nina and Sam's way. One soldier directed them to a nearby hospital for information about any person missing from the World Trade Center.

There were thousands of desperate people on the street looking for their loved ones. Nina and Sam followed them into a building. In the huge lobby, people had posted pictures of loved ones on the wall. Nina wished they could put Adam's name and picture on one of the missing person posters, but they came in such a rush to find Adam they did not think about bringing a photo of him.

Nina was shocked by the quantities of photos. There were people of every color and ethnicity in the photos on the wall. She was overwhelmed by the fact that those depicted on the wall could be lost forever, including her best student Adam, who was almost like her adopted son. Nina felt a vast sadness. Sam patted her shoulder and squeezed her hand, which gave Nina some consolation.

A woman suggested Nina could fill out the missing person report instead of a photo for the wall of missing victims. She found the table set up for this purpose and filled out the missing person report form for Adam. The woman at the help table told Nina that the rescue efforts were still going on, and they should keep their fingers crossed that their missing person could be found.

About a few days later, however, the authorities decided to stop looking for survivors because they said nobody would still be alive in that rubble after so many days. This decision was heartbreaking for Nina and Sam because it meant they were never ever going to see Adam again, dead or alive.

Nina could not stop thinking about the catastrophic possibilities for Adam. She just could not take it all in. Nina started to sob in despair. Her hands were trembling. She leaned her head on Sam's chest. Sam hugged Nina's shoulders, stroking her gently.

Nina assumed Adam fell from the 80th floor in the Twin Towers while she was talking to him on the phone. When she thought that Adam could be burned to death in those fires, she could feel her chest tighten. She could not stop crying.

Nina remembered her Chinese girlfriend, Mei Lin, who had been burned to death by the Shanghai ghetto bombing during WWII. Nina's legs could hardly hold her upright. They trembled so much with her sobbing.

Sam led Nina outside. He comforted her as best he could, caressing her shoulder and rubbing her back until she was calmer.

A few weeks later, Nina and Sam went to the Ground Zero ruins, the new name everybody called the site of the collapsed Twin Towers. Before dusk, a few people had already lit candles near Ground Zero to remember their loved ones. Nina asked Sam to get a candle. They joined the group of people to pray silently. Nina's tears streamed down. When Sam's right hand held the candle, and his left hand held her hand, more tears rolled down Nina's face.

Following September 11, 2001, people across the United States repeatedly watched the images of the two civil aviation planes colliding into the Twin Towers. The collapse of the World Trade Center was broadcast by CNN all day long. The smoke and dust were everywhere, covering everything. It looked like the end of the world, creating an insurmountable fear in Nina's heart.

Sam got government report, which stated, "We know that 2977 people were murdered in the attack on the Twin Towers." The terrorist attack of 9/11 was the worst in American history. Besides the Twin Towers, other skyscrapers were destroyed, many Wall Street elites died, and financial companies suffered irreparable losses. The old saying is, "The show must go on regardless of what happens." But after 9/11, even New York's Broadway was shut down. There was almost no one who did not feel the profound impact of this devastation.

New Yorkers commemorated the lost souls of 9/11 with two super-strong clusters of blue light. Nina always thought about Adam when she looked at these two blue lights at Ground Zero.

Nina told Sam that she could not stand the atmosphere anymore in New York City. She said she was overwhelmed in this depressive environment, most specifically because of her profound grief for Adam's death.

Nina and Sam took solace in music. It was the only thing that helped to heal the grief and sorrow they felt. Everything had already been said so that they sat quietly listening to the soothing strains of the music they loved. Sometimes as Nina listened to music, she cried silently, tears falling without a sound. Eventually, the healing music helped Nina and Sam.

CHAPTER THIRTY

November 2001
New York-, U.S.

M r. Perlman's violin melody of "Schindler's List" continued to reverberate in Nina's brain.

A friend in Manhattan gave Nina and Sam tickets to attend a concert in Carnegie Hall. They listened to the performance by the famous violinist, Mr. Itzhak Perlman, who wore black silk Chinese-style clothes. He played the theme from the film "Schindler's List." The violinist's music wept for the millions of people who perished under the Nazis. The pure, clear tone of Mr. Perlman's violin made Nina's heart tremble. The melody was tragically beautiful, as if sobbing, mourning, shrieking, and whispering.

Nina was deeply touched by Mr. Perlman's musical performance. She remembered her father wore the exact same style of black clothes in the Shanghai ghetto. She remembered all she had lost in the war. She thought of her grandmother and her uncle Allen. As she thought about her grandmother, missing her, her eyes brimmed with unstoppable tears. Nina's eyes were still wet with tears when they walked out of Carnegie Hall.

Nina and Sam walked along 7th Avenue. Once they reached Central Park, Nina wanted to sit on the park bench to rest for a while.

"I've watched Steven Spielberg's movie Schindler's List three times. I had been touched every time," Sam said to Nina.

"I watched Schindler's List five times. Oskar Schindler bravely saved the lives of 1,200 Jews during the Holocaust. I had even visited his grave in Jerusalem and put down my stone to his memory. The Israeli government named him Righteous among the Nations," Nina said.

"He is a hero to me," Sam said.

"Did you know there are also British Schindler, Swedish Schindler, Japanese Schindler, and Chinese Schindler?"

"To be honest, I don't know," Sam said.

"Mr. Nicholas Winton is a British Schindler who rescued 669 Jewish children. Mr. Raoul Wallenberg is a Swedish Schindler who saved 4500 Jews. Mr. Chiune Sugihara is a Japanese Schindler who saved 6000 Jews. Dr. Feng Shan Ho is a Chinese Schindler who heroically saved more than 2000 Jews during the war. Dr. Ho is the gentleman who saved my family," Nina said.

"Wow, you remember all these Holocaust heroes," Sam said.

When Nina lifted her chin, she suddenly saw the blue lights from Ground Zero far away in the direction of the Hudson River. She thought about the 9/11 attack and the death of Adam. She started to tear up again.

"Honey, let us go home now," Sam put his arm around Nina.

That evening, Nina heard the sound of a flute playing a sad song somewhere near their home. A week later, Nina played with her own flute a memorable and heartbreaking musical piece in the dusk.

The sadness related to the events of 9/11 kept bothering both of them in the following months. Nina had difficulty sleeping. She was always hyper-alert and easily startled. Sam would find her often staring outside at nothing. In the end, Sam started to consider moving out of New York, a sad place for both of them.

Sam suggested they should execute an often-talked travel plan, to visit their northern neighbor, Canada. It was close enough they could drive there by car.

Sam discussed with Nina that he was interested in moving to Canada. He suggested they look for a life away from the hustle and bustle of the big city. Instead, they ought to find a place with a combination of city and nature.

They drove along Highway 87, stopping in Albany, the New York state's capital, to visit one of Nina's friends, Jenny Grafane. They met in the hospital after that terrible traffic accident a few years ago. Nina was cheered up by visiting her friend.

In the woods near Jenny's residence, in a suburb of Albany, Nina and Sam were thrilled to meet a family of white-tailed deer.

Sam, always with his camera ready, shot the deer from different angles. Nina whispered, "Keep quiet," She saw the younger deer looking very alert, both ears up, and its eyes opened wide. It was wonderful to be close enough to see them wandering around green grass. The younger deer looked at Sam with amazement. His companion chewed the soft grass, the sweet fresh leaves. The father deer lifted his ears to listen for any danger. After all, sometimes, there were coyotes in the woods. Father deer led his family to the other side of the forest. He stopped to look back to ensure the family followed. The stag had a natural sense of responsibility for his family. When he came to a small creek, he did not hesitate to jump into the water, then others jumped in after him. Within a short moment, the deer family disappeared into the depths of the indigo woods.

The water splashed up as the deer jumped in the creek, catching the golden setting sun. The whole experience was so beautiful. Sam was delighted to have captured them with many photo shots.

"Why did you and Jenny connect so well?" Sam asked, heading to Jenny's home.

"Because Jenny is a cheerful person, she helped me a lot in the hospital," Nina replied.

"Oh, I understand," Sam said.

"I know a Chinese proverb that says if you plant melon seeds, you get melons; if you plant beans, and then you harvest beans," Nina said.

"Oh, I heard that before."

"I would like to extend this proverb. My version is that you plant love, you harvest love; if you plant hatred, you get hatred."

"Where did you learn this?" Sam asked.

"In the Shanghai ghetto," Nina said.

* * *

Nina looked out the car window when they went through the US-Canada border on the well-known Rainbow Bridge. She found the river running fast. It reminded her of the Huangpu River with its endless waves. Nina thought about Shanghai. She thought about Hason.

Nina stared at the green grass beside the road. Every blade of grass was coated with dew. The dewdrops sparkled and reflected beautiful colors in the sunlight. It was reminiscent of the most memorable time in her life when she was with Hason on the bank of the Huangpu River. Nina remembered clearly that the morning sunlight reflected on the heavy sparkling dew on the green grass near the Huangpu River in the very same way as here. Nina's eyes filled with tears, but she kept watching the sparkling dew even through her tears.

Nina's mind was all over the place after the door of her emotions had been opened by the dewdrops. She wished Dan had never known her. She wished Adam had never died. There was so much to regret. Nina cried more. She needed a tissue to wipe her cheeks.

"Our lives are just like rivers. The water goes under and over all different kinds of bridges and hurdles. Sometimes it's smooth, but other times it's rough. There is always something that happens during the journey, which is exactly what happens to human beings in this world," Sam said.

"I'm sure that people want to survive, but they also want to live, to be happy, and to enjoy their life," Nina said.

"Time will heal everything," Sam said.

"My father said the same thing," Nina nodded. "But time doesn't heal everything. People just forget things over time." Nina's mode was pessimistic today.

"Sometimes, we need to let some memories fade away with time," Sam said.

"But the reality is different. People can still experience the acute pain of previous emotional trauma. A scar in the heart is difficult to heal. It can never be forgotten."

"You could be right," Sam said.

"Every time I smell burning, I immediately feel sad," Nina said.

"The experience of 9/11 will hang over us as long as we stay in New York."

"Where are we supposed to go in this world?" Nina asked.

"We can think about moving to the North," Sam was delighted to have an answer.

"You mean to immigrate to Canada, not just to visit there?" Nina inquired.

"What do you think?" Sam asked.

"Let's see," Nina agreed.

They discussed the idea of immigrating to Canada seriously. But they didn't know where to live. They visited Canada's largest city, Toronto, but they found it too big and too noisy. They toured around looking for the right place. They wanted a peaceful environment with natural beauty. Nina and Sam went to the capital city of Canada and visited the suburban area of Ottawa. They saw the wild deer running in groups, a pair of wild turkeys feeding in the field, lots of Canadian geese flying over the river heading south. They even saw a fox standing on top of rock in the mountain. It was a good and promising omen for their future.

Nina and Sam discovered that Canada was a beautiful country with lots of natural environments and wildlife. They were seeking a quiet life to help them heal from the trauma they experienced in New York. The natural beauty of Canada indeed attracted both of them. They watched the spectacle of salmon returning from the sea. When Nina gazed at the salmon swimming up against the rapid and robust current, she suddenly thought about a famous quote from The Great Gatsby, "So we beat on, boats against the current, borne back ceaselessly into the past."

Nina realized that they have to make an effort to swim in life's sea, despite the past, and they have to seek a peaceful and quiet life.

"I think we made the right decision to move to Canada." Nina turned to her husband.

"Absolutely," Sam stared at his wife with a passion.

This was another new beginning for Nina. She never anticipated she would face another life-and-death challenge in Canada.

PART VI

THE OTTAWA RIVER

CHAPTER THIRTY-ONE

October 2002
Ottawa, Canada

In the beautiful autumn of 2002, Nina and Sam immigrated to Ottawa, Canada.

They had chosen the Ottawa River as their setting for immigration destination because the Ottawa suburb met all their needs. Nina and Sam wanted to live at the junction between the city and the countryside. The place they at last found was a tranquil location with mountains and water. It had an abundance of natural scenery, the air was fresh, the area was tranquil, and there was no skyscraper to be seen anywhere.

They bought a charming house situated right by the edge of the Ottawa River. Moreover, their waterfront house, although rural, has a convenient distance to town. They could see all kinds of natural scenery from their new home.

Nina loved living in the place. In the spring, she could hear birds singing. In the summer, flowers bloomed in the park, and they could fish and swim in the river. They could hike amid the colorful maple leaves in autumn, and there was lots of snow for skiing in the winter.

Nature was just at their back door. Sam had lots of opportunities to shoot with his camera a variety of wild animals: wild turkey, fox, coyote, whitetail deer, black bear, and even moose. He was fascinated by them all. Nina developed her own garden for flowers and vegetables.

Sam loved Nina so much that he took over most of household tasks in their home, such as paying the bills and even doing the taxes himself. Nina, at last, became a worry-free woman. She could enjoy sleeping until she woke up naturally for the first time in her life. It was like a beautiful fairy tale.

Nina slowly built up her private music classes for students wanting to play the flute. Her reputation as an excellent teacher grew. Her students performed in various concerts in the Ottawa area.

Sam participated in the Canadian National swimming competition himself. He used his own technique to increase his speed, but it caused him some dizziness because of his age. He found his dizziness probably from an imbalance in the inner ear labyrinth. So, Sam got some acupuncture treatments and regained his balance. Without any vertigo, Sam, using his new technique, won first place in his age group in a provincial swimming championship. He then joined the Canadian National Swimming Championship in Montreal and won second place in his age group.

Nina was so happy about Sam's achievements. Sam told her about the oldest swimmer in his age group was 102 years old. The gentleman declared the secret to his longevity was cleaning his teeth with salt water after every meal for more than eighty years.

The leaders of the local community center wanted Sam to coach the other younger swimming coaches. He would be responsible for guiding coaches at all levels of experience. Sam was delighted about this opportunity. It fits with his professional expertise. He could give back to the community and share his knowledge. Nina was also pleased to see her husband enjoying something he loved.

***

Time passed as fast as the water flowing in the Ottawa River. By the year 2010, Nina would be eighty years old. Yet, Nina's heart was full of happiness and love.

Nina has lots of ideas based on her vast experience in life. She decided to cherish these ideas by writing poetry to record her inspiration. Nina remembered she wrote a poem for Hason when she was in the Shanghai ghetto, which was a long time ago. She kept developing and enjoying her skill in writing poetry since her first winter in Canada. Sitting with Sam before a log fire, Nina relished the joys of her warm and cozy home. She put more logwoods in the fireplace. Nina put her pen and paper on the dining table, and she wrote:

Fluttering Early Spring Snow Dancing

Crystal snowflakes are fluttering to welcome the spring's coming,
The plump buds of purple lilac flowers are preparing for the spring bloom.
The thickness of ice in the swimming pool indicates the frozen harsh winter weather,
The wood fire is jumping endlessly in the fireplace, warming us all.
Could I ask you, "Where are you rushing to, Ms. Brown Squirrel?"
Could I request of you, "Would you please send this poem to my love, Mr. Ruby Cardinal?"
At the moment of flowers blooming and willows in green in the remote southern villages,
It's time for the frozen ice and snow to melt in this northern land.

One day, Sam suggested they revisit Toronto and arrange to go to Niagara Falls again. Nina felt precisely the same. She wanted to travel.

Sam told Nina that he wanted to take her to a place where she could see the full view of the city. He drove his SUV from Highway 401 to the Don Valley Parkway (DVP). The scene along the DVP is beautiful, especially in the fall. Nina was delighted by the breathtaking beauty of the maple leaves with colors ranging from red, yellow, green, brown, and purple. Although it was almost noon, a thin layer of mist floated in the valley. It looked like the whole valley was a marvelous oil painting. Nina felt it was poetic and romantic.

At that moment, Sam pushed a button on the car radio. A piece of romantic flute music flooded the car. It was the British folk song, Scarborough Fair, a favorite of Nina's. Besides loving the romantic theme, Nina appreciated her husband's loving gesture in choosing this music for her. Nina was pleased about the genuine love between Sam and herself.

Sam took Nina to the Canadian National Tower (CN Tower) in downtown Toronto.

"We had been here before?" Nina asked, smiling.

"Sure, but today is something special," Sam answered with a secret smile.

"What is it?" Nina guessed something pleasurable maybe in store for them.

"You will see," Sam kept his subtle smile.

While they waited for the elevator, the speaker in the waiting area introduced the CN Tower, "This Tower is a landmark in Toronto. The tower is 1,800 feet high. It was the tallest building in the world until last year."

The elevator swiftly took them to the top floor and revolving restaurant. Sam gave his reservation number to the waiter, who guided them to a table close to the windows. There they could see the whole city as the restaurant rotated 360 degrees.

As soon as Nina sat down, Sam took out a card, put it in front of Nina, and said, "Happy Birthday, My Love!"

"Oh, thank you, Honey!" Nina was surprised and happy. She almost forgot today was her birthday.

Nina took out the birthday card from a cream-colored envelope decorated with a large red rose. She also found a gold necklace with a heart-shaped pendant surrounded by small diamonds.

Nina was so happy that she wanted to reach across the table to kiss his face, but instead held and kissed Sam's hand. She gently said with emotion, "I love you, Honey!"

Sam took many pictures for her to celebrate this moment. Nina felt loved, with the sweetest love from the sweetest man.

Nina saw other loving couples in the restaurant snuggling together, whispering their loving words.

The restaurant moved so slowly Nina was not aware it was moving until Sam pointed out some landmarks of the city, especially the Lake Ontario.

Sam spoke to the waiter about the meal specially prepared for them. He requested the chef to cook the steaks separately, so they would be delicious, just the way they liked them. Well done for Nina, while Sam wanted his steak rare.

They were sipping red wine and watching the sailing boats on the lake. Nina noticed a small airport on an island at the edge of the lake.

"Look, there is an airport over there," Nina pointed in that direction.

"Yes, it is one of the smallest airports." They could see a plane landing and then another plane taking off.

It was a sunny day. Nina could see the silver plane reflected on the water, which caused a flutter of warm feelings in her heart.

"I've never seen an airplane flying below my feet. It is so interesting," Nina said. She sounded like a little girl, not an eighty-year-old woman.

"Me too," Sam laughed.

As the restaurant rotated, they got a good view of the city. There were large swathes of green, lots of trees, many houses, and high-rise buildings.

They saw the buildings and the traffic below and felt the energy in the city. They talked about how people, themselves included, loved the urbanization in a big city. And they talked about also loving being close to nature. They liked some of both worlds, from urbanized civilization to suburban naturalism.

The waiter came over to speak in Sam's ear, and Sam nodded his head. As Nina wondered what it was about, the speakers on the wall were suddenly playing the classical Happy Birthday song.

The waiter presented her with a big birthday cake, with "Happy 80th Birthday Nina!" on it.

Sam stood up and faced Nina, singing, "Happy birthday to you, happy birthday to Nina, Happy birthday to you!"

Everyone in the restaurant clapped their hands and sang the birthday song together. Nina was so touched her eyes filled with happy tears.

She stood up, saying, "Thank you! Thank you!" She almost forgot to blow out the candles until Sam reminded her to make a wish.

Nina let the waiter and Sam share her sizable birthday cake with nearby couples in the restaurant.

Nina appreciated Sam's arrangements to celebrate her birthday in such a unique way, celebrating in the tallest building in Canada.

Nina wrote a poem to thank Sam for the birthday dinner at the CN Tower. She quietly slid the poem into Sam's notebook in his bag.

Thanks! My Love!

Gently
You are coming, lovely big man.
Cheerfully
We are celebrating in the CN Tower.

Rotating 360-degree restaurant
Sing our love song in the biggest city in Canada.
Gorgeous CN Tower
Witnessing our love from the highest sky in Canada

Overlooking the sparkled ripples from the Lake Ontario
Watching the airplane take off from the Central Island
On our marvelous night skylight

I received the best birthday gift from my love.

Genuinely appreciate your smile, your heart, and your passion.
Your smiling is as bright and sparkling as the stars.
Your heart is as clear and generous as the lake.
Your love is as extraordinary and majestic as this Tower.

The next day when they visited Toronto Chinatown, Nina learned about the Dragon Boat Festival a few months later.

"Sam, I want to see the Dragon Boat Festival," Nina told Sam. Because of her years in the Shanghai ghetto during the war, Nina was interested in all activities related to Chinese culture. Sam also wanted to see the dragon boat race.

"Sure, let us arrange to come back at that time," Sam replied and put the leaflet in his bag.

After several months, Sam and Nina drove five hundred kilometers from Ottawa to Toronto to watch the Dragon Boat Festival organized by the Chinese communities.

The festival was on Center Island, in Toronto harbor, so they took the ferry over. There were lots of excited people waiting for the races to begin. Nina was dressed in a colorful dress, carrying a purse to match. She looked very pretty, and Sam took lots of pictures of her. In the background, one could see Canada geese and the many rowboats on the lake.

There were so many people gathered to watch the races. All the benches were already occupied. Sam and Nina didn't mind standing in the grass near the river. The excitement of the crowd was infectious. Loudspeakers were broadcasting traditional Chinese music.

"I didn't know so many people loved the dragon boat race," Sam said to Nina.

"They do it because it is so exciting," Nina said.

"I was told the dragon boat race was indeed a sport, just like swimming," Sam said.

"Yes, it originated in China about two thousand years ago."

"Look over there. The dragon boats are decorated with the heads and tails of Chinese dragons."

"Today should be the longest day of the year," Nina guessed and put her index finger on her temple.

"Why do you say that?" Sam asked.

"Because the ancient dragon boat race is supposed to occur in the summer solstice holiday, which is the longest day of the year," Nina answered.

"Ah, you did good research about the race before you came here," Sam admired her.

"You bet!"

"I understand western culture believes the dragon is a demon. Why use a dragon as a symbol?" Sam asked

"For the Chinese, it is the exact opposite. The dragon is considered a great spirit of strength and power. Therefore, only the emperor could use the dragon as a symbol in ancient times," Nina explained.

Nina was interrupted by the announcement from the loudspeakers. The Dragon Boat Race had started. Each boat had ten paddlers, as well as the steersman and the drummer. The loudspeakers introduced each boat, representing different local communities. Sam quickly realized the drummer was the leader of each boat. The drummer set the pace for the paddlers with his drum beats, hand signals, or loud orders. Sam saw that the dragon boat race was a competition like the swimming, which he was familiar with.

Nina and Sam were thrilled and amazed by the excitement of the crowd, applauding, clapping, and shouting, "Come on! Come on!" They were happy to join in.

"All the paddlers need to work together to make the boat move fast," Nina explained what she understood of the sport.

"Yes, the key person is the drummer. All the paddlers have to follow the rhythm of his drum with their strokes," Sam said.

Nina and Sam were delighted after watching the race. They were pleased to take part in the Dragon Boat Festival.

After a brief lunch, they strolled around Island Park. Sam also photographed a pair of seagulls that landed on the guardrail at the lake. The seagulls kissed each other and then flew away side by side, like Nina and Sam walking hand in hand.

Near the edge of this Island Park, Nina saw a large group of lake birds flying over the water. "Sam, you are a bird specialist. Do you know what these birds are called?" Nina asked Sam, testing him.

"Those are pelicans," Sam replied confidently.

Nina watched the pelicans barely touch the water as they flew over the water. They were skillful and very concentrated. A small white yacht passed by in front of them. The flying birds and sailing yacht created the most beautiful scenery on the misty water. Sam was excited and used his camera with a telescopic lens to capture the birds. Nina could hear continuing sounds of the shutter. She knew that her husband was quickly taking multiple photos of the flying pelicans.

"Look over there. More birds are coming," Nina pointed to the far distance.

"Wow, I've never seen so many huge birds in such a large group before," Sam said while still shooting non-stop with his camera.

The birds kept coming, a few hundred or thousands, flying over the Lake Ontario. It was spectacular. Sam was thrilled to be able to take photos of the magnificent pelicans.

"Where are these birds going?" Nina asked.

"I don't know. It looks like they are going in the direction of New York," Sam answered.

"Ah, we have come from the US to Canada. They are from Canada going to the US." Nina thought it was interesting.

"Life is paradoxically amazing!" Nina added.

CHAPTER THIRTY-TWO

July 2011
Ottawa, Canada

Aﬅer the dragon boat festival, Sam and Nina drove their SUV along the busy highway 401 to Niagara Falls.

"I am just wondering why the majority of the foreign vehicles on the highway come from Germany or Japan, two countries defeated in WWII?" Nina asked Sam as they drove along Hwy 401.

"Wow, you've made a fascinating observation. But, to be honest, I do not know why. But I know Germany and Japan both make excellent quality automobiles," Sam replied.

"The ordinary people in Germany and Japan do good quality work, excluding the war criminals, of course," Nina said.

They had visited the famous falls a few times before on both sides of the US and Canadian border. Nina stated, "I prefer to view the falls from the Canadian side. The falls are larger and more spectacular. They are gorgeous."

"When I watch the vast amount of water dropping more than 188 feet vertically, I think the Canadian Niagara Falls must be the most beautiful waterfall in the world," Sam agreed.

Since they arrived at the destination at dusk, they went directly to the hotel. After some food, they fell asleep on the sofa. They were both exhausted from the long and exciting day.

Interestingly, they both woke up at two o'clock in the middle of the night. Nina felt wide awake. She asked Sam, "Do you still feel sleepy after a six-hour nap?"

"Not really," Sam stood up and walked around the hotel room.

"Do you want to see Niagara Falls at midnight?" Nina suggested.

"Why not? Let's go right now," Sam thought this was a superb idea, "Let me bring my camera," Sam did not want to miss any opportunity to take good photos. Then they headed towards Niagara Falls.

They were the only people there. Compared to how crowded it was during the day, it was peaceful at night. They could see the American Falls pouring vast amounts of water over the edge, making much more noise than the daytime.

It was the busiest sightseeing location in the daytime, full of people, but now only two persons. Suddenly Nina saw a pair of skunks walking around the sidewalks under the dim light of the streetlamps. She waved to get Sam's attention, pointing at the skunks.

Sam tried to take photos of the skunks, but it was too dark. He was still happy to be able to see these animals so close. The two black and white fluffy animals took advantage of the night when the tourists were all gone, meandering and enjoying the falls themselves. Obviously, the skunks were looking for food. The night was a safe time without the interference of humans.

Sam stood in the walkway in front of skunks. He loved being able to study their behavior. He created a whole scenario of their lives. They looked like they were not scared of any person because they may think the night belonged to them. This pair of skunks was meandering. They were most likely a couple since they stayed close together. If one walked forward too fast or too far, and the other did not follow close enough, the first skunk would wait and look back. It seemed to say, "come on, guy, hurry up." The skunk behind seemed to say, "Okay, why do you not wait for me a little more." Sam was amazed at these beautiful animals' communication at midnight.

Then, the first skunk suddenly found a human standing in his way. It showed no fear at all.

"Hello, Buddy. Why are you here? It is midnight, the time for animals, not humans." The skunk walked around Sam and continued to search for his food. Sam guessed that the skunk was not frightened of him because it held a powerful weapon.

"Why are they not afraid of us at all?" Nina asked.

"It is because skunks have a famous defensive weapon."

"What is that?"

"It's called skunk's spray. When a skunk feels threatened, it will wiggle its fluffy tail up high to send a warning first," Sam said.

"And then?"

"If necessary to protect itself, the skunk will spray an offensive liquid with a bitterly awful odor onto the attacker," Sam said.

"Really?" Nina was surprised.

"You will have a chance to smell this notorious odor sometimes later. People say the foul odor is strong enough you could even smell it from five kilometers away. I am sure you will never forget it once you smell it," Sam explained.

"But they look pretty, and their behavior is wonderful," Nina said. She liked the animals.

"Yes, they only defend themselves when they feel threatened," Sam whispered.

"That sounds very reasonable," Nina said.

"But they will use the spray with a high degree of accuracy on any attackers," Sam added, "Even big animals like wolves, coyotes, or foxes are scared to attack skunks because of their fear of being sprayed. It's a powerful weapon."

"Good for them! These small and fluffy animals," Nina said.

"By the way, you should understand that the chemicals of its spray could cause severe running nose, violent eye irritation, or temporary blindness. So you should never ever try to threaten them," Sam said. However, he believed it was unnecessary to warn Nina since she loves these small animals.

"Sure, Thanks!" Nina thought she was not a child, but she loved Sam's way of treating her like a child.

Nina and Sam had a fun night at Niagara Falls because of the two skunks.

When they passed by a casino with flashing neon lights, Nina asked Sam, "Do you remember that we didn't go to the casino when we were in Las Vegas a few years ago?"

"Sure, I did not want to ruin our honeymoon at that time," Sam responded.

"Have you ever wanted to go to the casino to try your luck?" Nina continued.

"Frankly, I have never been inside a casino," Sam said, "I don't even know what it looks like, except for what I've seen in the movies," Sam answered.

"Do you want to go inside and take a look," Nina said. She was always interested in trying something new.

"I agree. Let's go!"

"But we are not going to gamble."

"That is for sure."

Despite the late hour, the casino was still open. The security personnel on the door told them that the casino was open twenty-four hours a day, seven days a week.

Sam and Nina looked around. There are only a couple of people still in front of the slot machine, their eyes were red, and they looked exhausted. There was no one at the roulette and card tables.

Nina and Sam did not know how to use the different gambling machines. They saw only a few casino staff, but they were busy collecting the money from the devices.

"That's all the casino do. They only collect your money," Sam pointed at the staff with his lips, but he spoke quietly.

"I can see that some people will find this entertaining, but you will never win money from the casino," Nina said.

It took them only fifteen minutes to see all they wanted of the casino. At least now, they knew what the casino looked like inside.

Once they were back home in Ottawa, Nina was pleased to discover Sam was also a brilliant handyman. He was inspired by the cute he saw small cabins on the way. So he decided to build a tiny house.

They choose a vacant lot by the Ottawa River to build a tiny house together. They bought lots of materials such as wood and metal joints and necessary tools from the nearby Home Depot. Sam already had a well-stocked toolbox. There was a hammer, five regular screwdrivers, four Phillips screwdrivers, scissors, pliers, different winches, an electric miter saw, table saw, and chainsaw. Sam even used his chainsaw to cut some trees in their lot to build their house.

Even though it was not easy to build a tiny house, it was an excellent experience for both of them. It was not only a new endeavor for them both but also a rewarding achievement. When they took a break from work, Sam looked at the Ottawa River's waves in the distance, "I am feeling terrific about this kind of activity in such a fresh environment. Don't you think so?" Sam asked Nina.

"Sure, compared to living in an overcrowded and polluted big city," Nina was pleased with the beauty and peacefulness.

A big bird was flying over the river slowly. It extended its wings gently, in no rush at all.

"Life is a choice. We make our choice for a peaceful life or a bustling life, don't we?" Sam asked Nina.

"Yes, most of us make our choices by our emotions, instead of by logic, even for the most important life decisions," Nina said.

"I'm aware of this ironic phenomenon. The logical components often only account for twenty percent in determining people's decision-making. That is why we often see so many irrational events occur in our daily life," Sam said.

"But everyone wants to improve their lives and improve life for their loved ones," Nina said.

"That is why the wisdom of life is worth seeking," Sam said.

"We must pass on these life lessons to our next generations and learn from our life experiences," Nina said.

"You are right. Should we get back to work?" Sam asked.

"Sure, let's finish the east wall today," Nina suggested.

One morning, Sam showed Nina where the beaver had gnawed down a considerable willow tree near the creek during the night. In just one night, a small creature did such a massive job. Nina was amazed by the determination and the hard work of the beaver.

After working on their tiny house for nine weeks, Sam had a severe headache for more than a week. He worried he might have a brain tumor because the pain in the right side of his head was so intense he could not sleep for seven nights.

Sam went to his family doctor, who also suspected he had some neurological disease. The pounding headaches and nightmares made him depressed, so he thought his life would be over soon. However, Sam did not tell Nina that he was afraid he had a brain tumor that may kill him soon. He did not want to scare her.

Sam thought about the many dreams he had not realized yet. He had so many things he wanted to do, to enjoy more time with his family, especially to enjoy the beautiful love with Nina. Sam was sure he was not ready to say goodbye to this world yet.

Surprisingly, a group of blisters broke out on Sam's forehead two weeks later. The doctor, in the end, diagnosed him with Herpes Zoster. It was a severe type of shingles because it involved the optical nerves. Even though Sam still suffered stinging pain, his panic about dying was relieved. He also felt blessed. He escaped a possible severe disaster in his life.

During the treatment, he had a lot of side effects from the chemical drugs. The experience made him realize that any synthetic drug could make the symptoms worse. Finally, he gave up most of the chemical medications and used only natural medicine, recovering completely.

Nina remembered talking to Sam about the choices between natural medicine and western medicine and the strong western influence on science. Sam always thought western medicine should be better, but Nina preferred a more natural approach. She felt that natural therapies and other alternative treatments would have fewer side effects on the human body.

Nina and Sam also had conflicting attitudes toward modern culture versus traditional culture. It was the conflict between the value of science and the belief in the healing power of nature. Nina had some deep-rooted bias. She loved all things natural.

Nina never knew that this specific preference would dramatically impact her life later.

CHAPTER THIRTY-THREE

October 2013

Ottawa, Canada

After Sam recovered from his severe shingles, Nina suggested her husband take a refreshing trip to Nova Scotia for birdwatching. They drove about 20 hours on and off from Ottawa to Nova Scotia, visiting several places on the way.

"Sam, look, there are a lot of wild roses on this island," Nina said to Sam.

"That is why they named it Brier Island. The wild brier rose was growing all over the island," Sam said.

"They are not easy to grow up here in this rocky terrain." Nina had sympathy for her favorite rose.

"Those are volcanic rocks called basalts, and this island is actually made up of those rocks," Sam did his pre-trip research as always.

The next morning, they watched the fascinating sunrise, the sun like a beautiful red wheel, jumping above the horizon. Nina felt touched by the rising sun because it gave enormous warm energy to her heart.

A flock of seagulls flew across the sky, above the waves. They were highlighted in the blue sky with white clouds. What a splendid picture!

Nina tapped Sam's shoulder. He was so transported by the beautiful scenery he forgot to take a photo of the fascinating sunrise.

Because Sam loved photography, he naturally became a birdwatcher. He learned the different types of birds by reading books and watching birds with their friends. He could tell Nina what a bird was called and what kind of habits they had. Sam taught Nina how to use binoculars for birdwatching on Brier Island on this trip. According to Sam's research, there were different types of birds on this island.

"Sam, what is the name of those birds?" Nina asked Sam by pointing to the flying birds near the seashore.

"Oh, those are called storm-petrels," Sam said.

They watched a group of storm petrels dancing on the surface of seawater, playing, and searching for food. When Sam was busy shooting photographs, Nina enjoyed birdwatching by herself.

Nina noticed the storm petrel had a white waist and scissors-tail. The birds were chattering loudly with each other during their flight. They extended their wings, flying with the wind, gliding up and down freely, looking very elegant and relaxed. Nina imagined they were several petrel families, and they came here together for a nice picnic today.

Nina followed the storm petrels along the seashore. When a giant wave splashed on her, the name Maxim Gorky popped up in her mind out of the blue. She thought of his famous poem, "The Song of the Stormy Petrel."

"Between the sea and clouds, the stormy petrel was proudly soaring, like a bolt of black lightning." That was the only sentence Nina could remember. She stopped walking and looked at the dancing storm petrels, and she tried to think about where she learned about this poem. Was it from the English teacher in the Shanghai ghetto? Or was it from her Russian musical friend in Tel Aviv? She couldn't recall at all.

Nina was so happy she saw a real storm petrel on this island. But they were not in a fighting mode that day, probably because there was no real storm on this sunny morning. Nina was still impressed by Gorky's poem.

"Where are you going," Sam caught up to her.

"I am watching the storm petrels. Look and listen. They are dancing and singing."

"Wow, is that wonderful?"

"The island is an important stopover point for many migrating sea birds. There are also many species of seabirds, shorebirds, and waterfowl on this island," Sam said.

"Let's go and see!"

Nina became more enthusiastic about birdwatching than her husband. She was watching a pair of birds chasing a boat.

"Why are these seagulls so big?" Nina asked.

"Because they are not seagulls," Sam said.

"Then, what are they?"

"These are called albatrosses."

"Ah, these are the famous albatrosses."

"They are one of the largest seabirds which can fly," Sam said, "Do you believe these two albatrosses are a married couple?"

"Are you serious?" Nina thought that Sam was just making a joke.

"Yes, albatrosses do a mating dance before they get married, then males and females bond together for their lifetime," Sam said.

Nina thought about herself with Sam, just like albatrosses, bonding together for a lifetime.

"Wow, I admire their lifestyle," Nina said with respect.

"Humans should learn from them, don't you think so?" Sam asked.

"Sure." They both laughed.

Later that day, they saw eagles, wild ducks, warblers, gannets, and shearwaters on Brier Island.

In the evening, they sat on the chairs at the back of the lodge. Sam brought the harmonica with him, and he played a famous song called "La Paloma." Nina closed her eyes to appreciate the melody. The harmonica's beautiful sound brought to mind the bird song Nina had heard that day. The notes were circling, flying forward and backward, gliding side by side, soaring up and down like the storm petrel.

Nina thought life should be like this: traveling together, seeing the world, and enjoying life's beauty.

Nina and Sam enjoyed their trip to Nova Scotia.

* * *

Three months after the Nova Scotia trip, Nina sat by the Ottawa River in their backyard. She stared at the river going forward with waves, and her thoughts flowed. It has been said any river is an excellent metaphor for humanity because of its living nature. Rivers have peculiar characteristics and personalities. They can be quiet or noisy. They can be gentle or aggressive. The water is sometimes clear and soft; other times, it is rough and dirty. Human beings have similar characteristics. All the water from rivers had nourished her life and gave her an adamant personality.

All rivers are nourished by their environment. They can be buffeted by the wind. They can be dried up by the scorching sun or flooded beyond their banks by torrential rains. They become solid in the cold. Rivers, in turn, nourish the environment they travel through, carrying the vegetation and wildlife from insects to fish and large mammals. Rivers are an essential means of transportation, floating large cargo ships to small pleasure crafts. Rivers give life, but they can also take it. We need to learn to acknowledge and respect the rivers in our lives.

People love rivers because each river has its own story.

Nina was sitting on their back deck in the evening when she saw an ominous purple cloud hanging over the river. It was similar to clouds she had seen years ago in Tel Aviv before her father died. Nina felt a cold shiver in her heart. Then a gust of wind came, and it swept away the purple clouds. The night air was crisp and clear. The stars in the sky were twinkling again. The layers of the stars added immeasurable depth to the darkness in the sky.

Accidentally, Nina found some small nodules on her legs. When she touched the nodules, there was no pain and no itch. She went back inside the house to look carefully at her legs. They were covered with many hard and rough nodules.

Nina immediately thought something terrible had happened to her.

CHAPTER THIRTY-FOUR

January 2014
Ottawa, Canada

Nina was panicked.

"Skin cancer?" Nina's heart sank once she thought those bumpy nodules could be cancer.

"Oh, I just reached the best stage of my life," Nina's emotions were in turmoil.

Nina wished Sam was home, but he went to Toronto for an international wildlife photography show. He would not be back until the tomorrow afternoon. She went to bed but could not fall asleep at all. Her thoughts were all over the place, keeping her awake. Nina thought mostly about her father and mother. She also recalled her panic when she lived through the terrible bombings in the Shanghai ghetto. She could be killed at that time. That was nearly seventy years ago.

The next day, Sam came back home, and he hugged Nina first and gave her lots of comforting words. However, the most convincing point he made was that there was no diagnosis by the doctor about the nodules yet.

They went to The Ottawa Hospital. It was close to their home. The doctor in the hospital counted the nodules on her legs. Nina had twenty skin nodules in different sizes on each of her legs. Nina was so surprised she had a total of forty nodules. The doctor said he could not do anything about them at the hospital. He referred her to a dermatologist. He got her the earliest appointment, the following Tuesday, with a skin specialist. However, a diagnosis couldn't be made until Nina had a biopsy. The dermatologist arranged for Nina to have a biopsy to confirm the final diagnosis.

This was the beginning of Nina's anxious waiting life. She had to wait to see the dermatologist, then wait for the biopsy, then wait for the diagnosis, wait for the treatment, and wait for the therapy results. However, she felt she did not have the patience for all those waiting. Although Sam kept telling her it was only a skin issue, Nina still felt anxious about her illness. Once Nina calmed herself down, she thought about the tough life she went through during the war and recognized she had survived all of that. She tried to regain her strength for this new fight against severe disease.

Nina was pleased with the dermatologist. He was a pleasant, older gentleman. He said he did not want to presume a diagnosis before the biopsy. His assistant took a few skin samples from Nina's legs. Nina felt the biopsy procedure was not too painful, and Sam drove her back home. Her dermatologist said she needed to wait about two weeks for the pathological report.

To her surprise, the first challenge came relatively soon after Nina made up her mind to fight this illness.

The second day after the biopsy, Nina's whole body broke out in a red itchy rash. It started on both her legs and then developed onto her abdomen and chest, later moving up onto her face. Sam had to take her to the emergency department in the hospital. The ER doctor said the rash could be an allergic reaction to something. Because her rash was acute and severe, the doctor ordered some injections as well as oral medications.

The two weeks passed quickly. Nina went to the Ottawa Hospital early and alone on purpose. She wanted to pick up her biopsy report by herself. She consciously did not want to give any stress to Sam, although he would know it sooner or later. She also wanted the space to think things over by herself.

A senior doctor told Nina that the biopsy showed the severe skin lesions on her two legs were indeed skin carcinoma.

Nina held the pathological report. The paper felt like a piece of heavy metal, as if it was a living malignant tumor itself. She sensed her heart cramped and aching. Although she had prepared for this result, she was still shocked by the bad news that she had skin cancer.

When Nina came out of the doctor's office with an unsteady gait, she went directly to a nearby park. She felt so dizzy that she could not walk properly. When she found an available bench in the corner of the park, she sat down clumsily. She believed her dizziness was just because of her sleeplessness last night. After sitting down for about five minutes, she understood her whole situation.

The diagnosis of any malignant tumor is like a death sentence. Everyone knows that the consequence of a cancer could lead to death.

"My life will sink into darkness soon," Nina thought. She realized that she was already more than eighty years old, much older than her parents when they passed away. Nina thought her life was in the twilight of her time on earth. Life is so vulnerable, so easy to be damaged or even destroyed by any number of possible harmful forces.

Nina could not help thinking about her father. Albert's doctor told him, "Your cancer is an aggressive type. You probably only had three months to live." Thinking of that, Nina started to believe her situation would be a similar scenario.

On the park bench, Nina kept asking herself, "Do I only have three months to live? What am I going to do now?" She was under high-level psychological and emotional stress, which made her physical fatigue much worse. She felt she was once again in danger of dying. The mental pressure was enormous. Nina desperately needed the help of her loved ones.

All of a sudden, Nina saw her father's encouraging eyes. Papa reminded her, "You have survived premature birth and escaped from the Nazis in Berlin, fleeing to London. You fought and got away from the Japanese soldier in Shanghai. You avoided the dangerous violence from your ex-husband in Tel Aviv. You went through the horrible terrorist attack in New York. Now you are plagued by cancer." Her Papa whispered in her ear, "Sweetie, you can overcome this challenge." Nina closed her eyes, saw her father's encouraging eyes again, and knew he was with her.

Nina realized that at that moment, "Life has two basic driving forces: fear and pleasure. Whatever happens to me, my life must carry on. I must face reality, whether it is tough or easy. I will never give up!"

At last, when Nina calmed herself down, she sent a text message to her husband.

"The biopsy report is cancer. I am now sitting in the park beside the doctor's office. Please come to pick me up. Thanks!" Nina sent a text to Sam.

"Honey, Do not move! I'm driving there to pick her up immediately." Sam called Nina at once and told her to stay in the park.

When Sam found Nina, he hugged her for a little while, held her hand, and said in a quiet voice, "Let's go home Honey!"

There were a lot of cars on the road that day. They had been stopped at almost every traffic light. There was virtually no green light for them at any of the intersections. Nina thought the red lights were just like cancer, wanting to stop her life.

Sam tried to concentrate on his driving, so they kept silent in the car, which was unusual for them. But, for sure, Sam was as upset about the biopsy report as Nina.

Nina's mood was slightly better about ten minutes later, even though she still looked upset and tired. Sam vacated his right hand from the steering wheel and patted Nina gently. Again, Nina felt her husband's concern for her through his gentle action and caring posture.

When they got home, Nina sat on the sofa. Sam made a cup of tea for her and coffee for himself. Then he sat next to Nina, not opposite her as before.

"Honey, thank you," Nina took a sip of tea, "Although I have known of this possibility, I am still shocked."

"I know, my dear, don't worry! We will fight this together," Sam put his arm around her shoulder.

"But my heart still feels heavy. I don't know what to do," Nina said.

"I will arrange for the examinations and the treatment. I will call our family doctor to refer you to an oncologist today," Sam said.

"Okay," Nina said, but her voice was still uncertain.

"First of all, you have to lift yourself up. We need the energy to face this cancer and overcome it," Sam said with confidence.

"Yes, I will get out of this frustrating feeling," Nina said.

"My dear, I understand that when a person is depressed, the immune function will be depressed too. That will make it difficult to fight this cancer," Sam went on, "We both must have the courage to overcome the illness."

"Honey, with you, I am not afraid of anything," Nina felt much better.

"We can overcome any challenges in life if we have confidence," Sam gave Nina more encouragement; "You need to eat and sleep well for the future fight."

"Yes," Nina reached out and held Sam's hand.

Sam embraced Nina's shoulders again. Their hands passed their inner strength to each other. Nina's eyes were also misted. This is the power of love, which can overcome all the challenges.

Nina could not fall asleep that night. The howling of the coyotes in the woods sounded like a child crying in terrible pain. Nina thought, "I want to alleviate the fear of death and maximize the quality of my remaining life. But, in her deep thinking about the meaning of life, Nina realized that life is not only what we see and hear. Life could continue beyond our five senses. Maybe that is one of the essential meanings of life.

Bad luck comes together sometimes in life. The following day, Nina's trigeminal neuralgia flared up, probably brought on by her insomnia for so many nights and the enormous stress of a cancer diagnosis. The left side of Nina's face was pounding with severe nerve pain. She could not even get up from her bed. Nina felt the physical pain had reached the extreme.

Sam immediately gave her painkillers and antibiotics. Nina was reassured, knowing there was always a caring hand and a strong heart to support her life in any difficulty.

When Nina heard Sam leave the house, she felt very alone and thought about her death more seriously. She was still under the nagging pain from her trigeminal neuralgia.

Nina wondered if the cancer cells were eating her up right now. It was the first time she felt she was dying after the shock of the diagnosis.

Nina could not fall asleep, so she finally sat up and leaned her body on a large cushion decorated with loving hearts. Nina remembered the words of a philosopher who said that when a person is born, they may face death at any stage of their life. A courageous person will die for the truth, but a sincerely brave person dares to live for love.

"For love, I will survive," Nina decided. She made up her mind firmly.

Nina thought about Sam, and her heart was grateful because she believed that she had received true love. Nina understood the test of true love is how it manifests itself when you are faced with suffering or setbacks. At this critical moment of her life, true love gave her enormous courage to survive.

Nina thought about what her life had been like so far. She loved and had been loved. She did many good things in her life, trying to make the world better in the future. When she thought about her granddaughter, she smiled as if the beautiful girl was standing in front of her.

Nina remembered what her father told her in the Shanghai ghetto. When a person is suffering, he has no right to be pessimistic. If a suffering person is pessimistic, he will lose the courage he needs to face the difficult reality. Without the strength to fight against suffering, his suffering will be even greater.

In the midst of this crisis, Sam stood beside her and cared for her. He gave her strength and confidence. The most important thing was to support her in having the courage to overcome any difficulties and win the battle.

Even though Sam gave Nina lots of encouragement, he was very anxious about his wife's diagnosis of cancer.

Sam accompanied Nina for a walk in a nearby park in the afternoon. While Nina sat on a bench to rest in the sun, he excused himself to walk in the woods for a while.

Nina indistinctly heard Sam crying in a quiet corner of the woods from a distance. Nina understood her husband wanted to release his stress by himself in a peaceful place. Sam was crying so hard in the woods that he had to bend forward to catch his breath. Nina felt her heart aching. She felt Sam's genuine love for her. If a person truly loves another person, the threat of losing that person would double the pain. Nina's eyes were soon brimming with tears.

At the end of the woods, the sunset was red, and the whole forest was aglow with the gorgeous color of the setting sun. It was warm and encouraging. A group of Canadian geese flew gracefully over his head. They were lined up in the vee formation they are famous for, flapping their wings, climbing higher into the sky, and full of vitality.

When Sam walked out of the woods, he was full of confidence. He knew that he would put all his efforts into caring for his true love. Sam came and sat beside Nina. He told Nina that he had figured out various ways to overcome these current difficulties. For example, they should consult multiple doctors, including family doctors, oncologists, and surgeons. They should explore various kinds of tests, as well as natural remedies and oxygen therapy. They should contact friends to provide helpful diet therapies known for their anti-cancer benefits.

With Sam's confidence and plans, Nina felt she had much more courage to fight this cancer with hope, optimism, and great love!

CHAPTER THIRTY-FIVE

March 2014

Ottawa, Canada

Nina and Sam took a train to Toronto on a wet drizzly day. They were going to the Princess Margaret Hospital, the best cancer hospital in the country, to see a famous oncologist referred by her family doctor.

Nina and Sam arrived at Princess Margaret Hospital. They, at last, met the famous oncologist, Dr. Green, who looked very distinguished with white hair and dark-rimmed glasses.

Dr. Green began the appointment. "I had reviewed your referral from your family doctor. The biopsy indicates skin carcinoma." Then, Dr. Green pointed to the table in his office, "Nina, please lay down. I'd like to check your leg lesions first."

After the examination, Dr. Green said, "I am afraid to say these skin cancers are still growing."

"Dr. Green. We need your advice for treatment," Sam said with urgency, as Nina got up from the examination table.

Once Nina sat down again, Dr. Green stated, "Basically, we have four treatment options for this type of cancer. The local treatments are surgical removal of the cancers or radiotherapy. The other choices are chemotherapy or some alternative medicine."

"Dr. Green, is the surgical treatment to cut off the skin cancer?" Sam asked politely.

"Your understanding is right," Dr. Green said.

"Surgery is unbearable for me. It was proved not suitable for me," Nina responded.

"Nina had a severe skin reaction to her whole body after the biopsy, so she is still upset about that," Sam explained.

"Dr. Green, would chemotherapy be beneficial for me?" Nina asked anxiously.

"So far, chemotherapy for this type of skin cancer has been not very effective," Dr. Green said.

"I've read about a new drug that can cure cancer in the newspaper. Is there any new medicine that could be used for my wife?" Sam inquired.

Dr. Green said, "The new drug treatment you saw in the media is a breakthrough in the research for cancer treatment. But, unfortunately, that information was published in academic journals, and it is a long way from when it will be ready for use by patients."

"How about using alternative medicine?" Nina asked.

"I am the only one who have an open mind for alternative medicine in this hospital, but I am not the person to answer your question. You have to find an expert to consult about your specific medical condition," Dr. Green said frankly.

"Make no mistake, I would never recommend treating cancer using alternative medicine only," Dr. Green emphasized, "Alternative medicine may impact the cancer patient's health, but must be used the right way."

"Dr. Green, what do you mean the right way?" Sam asked.

"Alternative medicine should be used in conjunction with modern medical techniques," Dr. Green said.

"Thanks for your advice! We appreciate your open-minded approach," Nina said.

"You are welcome," Dr. Green said, "Let me prescribe you some cream for your dry and itchy skin, but this is only symptomatic treatment."

"Thank you so much! Dr. Green!" Sam said.

"You can call my office or email me if you have any further questions." He gave his card to Nina.

Nina and Sam went back to Ottawa on the train, discussing the next steps for the treatment for her cancer.

"What are we going to do now?" Nina turned to look at Sam.

"One thing for sure, we need treatment for this skin cancer right now," Sam said, "We cannot wait any longer since we waited for the doctor's appointments, waited for the biopsy, waited for the report, and waited for the specialist."

"You are right. While we are waiting, the cancer is growing," Nina said.

"Now we understand that if you cannot do any surgical, radiation, or chemotherapeutic treatments, we need to quickly find out which alternative medicine is good for you when we are back to Ottawa," Sam said. He could always come up with an action plan, which is one of the outstanding qualities Nina loved in him.

Nina and Sam calmed down after Dr. Green's consultation. Nina was able to look at the challenges and possibilities logically and reasonably. They analyzed the advantages and disadvantages of each treatment plan. Faced with different types of treatments, the biggest problem was choice. Any choice does not guarantee to be the correct one.

"The focus should be on what we value most. Which one is better for me?" Nina asked.

"Whether it is modern medical treatment or alternative medicine, we need a brave and wise choice," Sam replied.

"I feel the surgical operation may not solve my skin problem because the previous biopsy procedure already caused me a severe allergic reaction," Nina stated.

"Yes, even if we don't know what caused the rashes, we should not consider surgical procedure right now," Sam agreed.

Nina believed that any surgical treatment, radiotherapy, and chemotherapy were not compatible with her body. So, at last, she decided to try traditional Chinese medicine.

"I want to contact my favorite doctor, Dr. Lu. He specializes in traditional Chinese medicine and has a good reputation in the Ottawa area. Hopefully, I can make an appointment to see him in the next few days. What do you think?" Nina asked.

"Good idea. We need to get some advice from Dr. Lu first," Sam agreed.

"Sure," Nina gave Sam a lovely smile.

The train traveled, running fast towards Ottawa, carrying Nina and Sam home. Nina brooded over her life, looking out the train window, watching the trees speed by. She thought her life was just like the train, speeding forward, and eighty years had passed by quickly. So many things in life came and went and then became history.

Now, this cancer has invaded her life. The shadow of death was hanging over her, threatening to grab her into hell like the ugly Japanese drunken soldier did a long time ago. "I am not scared of this ugly ghost lingering around," Nina told herself. When the death threat came, Nina's inner strength and determination for survival far exceeded the fear of dying. She decided that she would never give up her life, but she was ready to face death.

"What is the meaning of life for me now, facing with possible death?" That was a question that had often come to Nina's mind lately. Nina decided she would decisively fight this cancer, whatever the consequence, good or bad. She was also determined that she would enjoy the last journey of her life. Every minute of life is worth cherishing. When you turn the kaleidoscope of life, besides the color of fear, the cherished parts of life are even more vibrant.

The train was still running like the wind, and Nina saw that Sam had dozed off.

He was exhausted.

Nina believed that a natural approach to treatment was the lucky way for her, according to her personal experience in the Shanghai ghetto.

CHAPTER THIRTY-SIX

March 2014

Ottawa, Canada

Several days later, Nina went to see her Chinese medical doctor. Dr. Ying Lu was a medium-sized man, well dressed, always paying attention and listening to his patients. He spoke gently and firmly. After obtaining Nina's medical history about the skin condition, Dr. Lu made his routine pulse and tongue diagnosis. Then he checked Nina's legs carefully. Finally, he asked Nina's permission to take a few pictures of the nodules on each leg, notably the prominent ones. He would need the photos for comparison.

"Nina, you had forty cancerous nodules, twenty nodules for each leg. Which treatment have you already tried?" he asked Nina after the examination.

"Besides the biopsy, I only used some cream on the legs," Nina answered.

"Can you offer a treatment option, doctor?" Sam asked.

"Oh, before we talk about the treatment option, let me tell you what the Chinese medical diagnosis is for Nina's condition first," Doctor offered Sam a smile.

"What is your diagnosis?" Sam inquired.

"The Chinese medical term is Qi Deficiency with Blood Stasis," he stated.

"Could you please explain it to us, doctor?" Nina was confused about the medical terminology.

"This is a Chinese medical term," he leaned toward them. "Qi deficiency means that Nina's immunity is weak. It is the major cause of cancer. Cancer occurs and grows because of a weak immune system."

"I understand my immunity hasn't been strong for years," Nina nodded her head.

"The blood stasis is the basic reason your normal cells have mutated into cancer cells. They have been damaged due to circulation blockage," the doctor continued his explanation.

"This is the first time I heard of the cause of cancer. It is fascinating," Sam said.

"In fact, the Qi theory was created more than 2000 years ago. Now I'm using modern medical language to explain it briefly," he said.

"So, what is your advice for using this Qi theory for Nina?" Sam was puzzled about the Qi theory.

"This will be the basic treatment principle for Nina's skin cancer," the doctor said with a confident tone.

"Doctor, I have heard that you cured cancer patients before. I also truly believe in the peculiar curative effect of herbal medicine. But, to be honest, my husband is skeptical. Could you please give us more explanation about the herbs?" Nina requested.

"Sure, I understand that. Chinese herbs have been used for over 2000 years. The herbal formula should be decocted together in water, which is the traditional and the best way to use the herbs," the doctor paused and sipped a little water from his cup. "For Nina's herbs, one group will be to nourish her Qi and another to clear her blood stasis."

"Do you mean to improve my immune system and to get rid of the cancer cells?" Nina asked.

"You have an excellent understanding!" The doctor praised Nina, "My expertise lets me assess your medical condition, select the two groups of herbs, and decide the best dose."

"Wow, that sounds great," Sam said. But, he was convinced by the doctor's detailed explanation, "Are there any side effects from the herbs?"

"The herbs are natural, like whole food, so there are no side effects. The only thing is that the decocted herbs taste very bitter," Dr. Lu said.

"I do not mind any bitterness," Nina declared and looked at Sam for his support.

"Doctor, we want to try the herbal formula," Sam said.

"Yes, doctor," Nina confirmed.

"I will prescribe an herbal formula for you," the doctor said, "Please read the preparation instructions carefully first."

Nina felt optimistic about using herbs to combat cancer because she always tended to use anything natural in her life. In fact, Nina's personal connection with Chinese culture from her experience in the Shanghai ghetto made her believe the Chinese herbs would save her life. Many years ago, Nina was saved in Shanghai during the war. Nina also had a good experience in London when her eczema was healed by drinking herbal tea.

Nina gave her hand to Sam and let him hold it in his warm palm. She knew it was important that Sam should understand and support her choice of herbal treatment.

"Nina, let me show you some herb samples from your formula," doctor put a plate containing some colorful plants on his desk.

"Oh, these herbs look beautiful," Nina said. She appreciated the arrangement of the multi-color herbs on the plate.

"Look at this light yellow root. It is called Astragalus," the doctor pointed to a few long strips of roots, "This is the best herb to enhance the body's immune function by improving the Qi."

"Oh. What are these colorful plants?" Nina pointed to another of the herbs.

"These herbs with rich colored roots are called Spatholobus Suberectus Dunn," The doctor pointed out a flower-like herb with many red stripes, "This herb not only can invigorate Qi and promote blood circulation but also has very good anti-cancer properties."

"I like these herbs," Nina said. She found herself developing an unbelievable preference for these herbs even before treatment.

"This herb is called Cortex Phellodendri Chinensis, and that herb is called Common Burred Rhizome. They all have powerful anti-cancer functions," he said.

"Doctor, how many types of herbs are in this formula?" Sam asked with curiosity.

"Today, I only gave Nina ten herbs with each package. Next time I will adjust the herbs according to Nina's condition."

"Do you mean I won't get the same herbs each time?" Nina asked.

"You're right. The formula will change in dosage and herbs with the change according to your body condition. This is the best feature of Chinese medical herbs. Its advantage is that the treatment is adjusted to match an individual's medical condition. It is very dynamic. Its disadvantage is that it can't be mass-produced to be sold commercially."

"I think it is logical and reasonable," Sam said.

Nina and Sam left Dr. Lu's office with a week's supply of herbs. Nina confronted her first challenge of taking them. They had a particularly bitter flavor. She told Sam that the herbs' taste was not just bitter. There was also a pungent smell too strong. It was not easy to take them at the beginning of treatment.

As the patient, Nina put all her hope and effort into every step of the battle against cancer. After taking herbs for a few weeks, Nina slowly overcame the bitter flavor and got used to the herbs' smell. But unfortunately, she was disappointed that she did not see any improvement in her skin cancer.

Nina went to the clinic weekly. Knowing that natural medicine methods are usually slow, she was determined to be patient and persistent in herbal treatment. In the meantime, Nina also followed the doctor's advice regarding her lifestyle. For example, her diet had no alcohol, no seafood, no spicy food, no animal skin, no deep-fried food, less coffee, less sugar, less salt, more water, more dark-green vegetables, and more fresh fruits.

Nina needed regular relaxing exercises, paying attention to a fresh air environment, and avoid pollution from the busy street. Nina required more than seven hours of sleep. She had to go to bed at routine times in a quiet, warm, and dark environment. Nina reduced stress in her life to the minimum.

During the treatment process, Nina tried to find the reasons for her skin cancer. Nina recalled that when she was young in Tel Aviv, she used to be in the sun all the time. The doctor considered this may be the most direct cause of her skin cancer. At that time, it was fashionable to spend a lot of time at the beach sunbathing under the strong sunlight. Everyone wanted to darken their skin with the sun to look healthy and beautiful.

The doctor told Nina, "A proverb says, where will the hair grow if your skin has gone? Which means where is the beauty if life disappears?"

"That is true. To look beautiful or to destroy life, "Nina learned a hard lesson about sunbathing after her skin cancer.

Later that month, Nina understood that exposure to sunlight will dramatically increase skin cancer incidence. If the ozone layer is damaged, then the incidence of skin cancer will also increase. Many young women go to the so-called tanning salons to get a suntan from a sunbathing machine. Nina wanted to shout to these girls. Please don't be stupid because you have significantly increased your risk of skin cancer. One day, you will regret it from the bottom of your heart as much as I regret it today. Sunlight causes skin cancer, just like smoking cause lung cancer, or eating pickled things cause stomach cancer.

Nina also realized that her immune system was damaged by many life stresses, such as her failed marriage and losing loved ones. All those factors harmfully damaged her physical and mental health. However, the traumatic death of her ex-husband, who shot himself, affected her the most.

"Doctor, how does suntan cause skin cancer?" Nina asked.

"Okay, Nina. Here is my theory about cancer formation," the doctor said. He leaned his body onto his chair. "Although there are various reasons for cancers, such as genetics, radioactive damage, or certain chemicals, I believe most cancers are caused by inflammation."

"Inflammation," Nina was puzzled.

"For example, liver cancer is from chronic hepatitis; stomach cancer is from chronic gastritis; lung cancer is from chronic bronchitis; colon cancer is from chronic colorectal inflammation; cervix cancer is from chronic cervix inflammation. For your situation, skin cancer is also due to the mild inflammation of your skin caused by sun exposure," the doctor said.

"Wow, you have done deep research into the cause of cancer," Nina said. She admired the doctor very much.

"If we could eliminate inflammation in the body at an early stage, the cancer incidence will be greatly reduced, which will also reduce cancer mortality. A lot of herbs could do that, getting rid of the chronic inflammation from the body," the doctor continued.

"I quite like these herbs now," Nina said.

When Nina drank her herbal medicine, she always imagined that all the cancer cells would be eaten up by her recovered immune system. Therefore, she was convinced that it was practical and feasible to treat her cancer with herbal medicine.

In the meantime, Nina felt her husband's support was hugely beneficial to her immune function and helped her recover smoothly. Nina had heard from one of her doctors that when you have loved ones facing your suffering with you, your inner function will become much more robust. When your immune function becomes strong, your immune system's macrophages can phagocytize the cancer cells, eating up the deadly cancer.

Nina continued to see the doctor regularly for months, rain or sunshine. She never missed an appointment. Then, finally, she started to see a remission of her skin cancer. The first thing Nina noticed was the cancer growth had stopped. Then, Nina was thrilled to see that the cancers had disappeared one by one. Nina's confidence and compliance with the treatment was paying off.

In the end, all the skin cancers were absorbed totally from both legs. After eleven months of herbal treatment, Nina's skin cancers disappeared completely. The doctor had taken pictures of her legs every week to record the progress and the healing. In Nina's case, it was confirmed that herbal medicine can completely cure certain skin cancers. Its pharmacological effect was to improve immune function and eliminate cancer cells.

Nina understood that her immune function improved during treatment and was crucial for her healing successfully. But she still had a big question for Dr. Lu.

"Where did the cancers go?" she asked her doctor with a confused tone.

"Excellent question," he was smiling, and he replied, "In fact, those cancers were absorbed by your body."

"Really," Nina was more confused by the doctor's answer.

"It is the Qi in your body eating up all the cancer cells," the doctor said, "It is also the Qi in your body that will prevent cancer from coming back."

"Wow, how can Qi do that wonder?"

"The Qi concept is pretty confusing for most people, even in the medical field, mainly because people cannot see, smell, hear and touch the Qi even though it, in fact, exists," the doctor leaned his body on his chair. "I spent the last forty years researching Qi theory from an ancient medical book called Yellow Emperor's Internal Classic. The book was written in 2711 BCE. It stated that if there is sufficient healthy Qi inside the body, pathogenic factors have no way to invade the body. However, once the pathogenic factors get into the body, the Qi is certainly deficient."

"Wow, forty years' research," Nina said.

"Only recently, I found Qi's material base. It is called the Interstitium," the doctor said.

"I never heard about it. What is the name again?" Nina asked with curiosity.

"Its name is Interstitium. It is composed of the extracellular matrix. It is one of the human organs. A professor from New York University called it an "open, fluid-filled highway," the doctor had a good memory.

"A fluid-filled highway in our body is Qi?" Nina was amazed by the idea.

"This is exactly like the concept of Qi. The Qi always moves and functions around our body quickly and effectively. The Qi distributes nutrients into our system's cells, just like the interstitial fluid does in our body. Someone even called this interstitium network of fluid-filled spaces a newfound organ."

"Do you think this new organ Qi has a relationship to cancer?" Nina did not fully understand what the doctor said, but she loved to hear that good news.

"Yes. Your skin cancers have been absorbed by this interstitium," he said.

"So, I should thank this Qi for saving my life," Nina was pleased to say.

"I remember an ancient Chinese medical book stated that a small fire in the corner of a room could be extinguished with one bucket of water. However, a fire in the whole house might not be able to be put out by one hundred buckets of water. That indicates the importance of early treatment or prevention," the doctor said.

"If cancer usually takes five to ten years to develop and to metastasize so it can show its symptoms and destroy the body, we should do something five or ten years earlier to prevent it. Supposing inflammation somewhere in the body is a possible cause of cancer. We need to clear the inflammation much earlier to prevent cancer," the doctor seemed to say to himself, and his voice was gentle and firm.

"An excellent idea," Nina applauded.

"Based on this idea, I have a prevention strategy for possible cancer," he said.

"What is it?" Nina asked with great interest.

"I think anyone with a high risk for cancer such as familial cancer history or chronic infectious illness should take a harmless preventive treatment as early as possible. It might be needed for only a few weeks. That means it needs only one bucket of water," the doctor smiled with an easy grin.

"One bucket of water," Nina repeated and tried to digest the doctor's idea.

"I call it 'A Bucket of Water Theory.' According to this, an herbal formula would be developed to nourish the Qi and clear the inflammation. I believe this is the best way to reduce the mortality of cancer. And the use of the herbal formula is a harmless and low-cost way," the doctor said.

"I hope more people can hear this theory," Nina responded.

CHAPTER THIRTY-SEVEN

May 2016

Ottawa, Canada

Nina followed Dr. Lu's advice, doing exercise regularly. She loved yoga the most. One day after yoga class, her peers requested her to do the powerful handstand pose that she used to do before.

Nina placed her head and both hands on the yoga mat. She swung her two legs upwards and held them straight and stable in the air. She held the upside-down position solidly.

"One, two, three," her peers counted how long she could hold the position.

"Fifty-eight, fifty-nine, sixty," Nina held the headstand position firmly for sixty seconds!

As an eighty-six-year-old woman and a recovering cancer patient, Nina impressed everyone. All her classmates were cheering and clapping for her in the gymnasium.

The community center leader passed by and saw Nina's energetic show. She was impressed with Nina's recovery from cancer. Later that day, she phoned Nina and invited her to give a speech to tell her story of survival, "Is there any possibility you could give a speech to a large group of our community members?"

"Sure," Nina replied, "My life has experienced so many hardships, but these tribulations now have become my treasure. I want to share my experience with other people. I hope I can help them somehow."

"Thank you, Nina," the leader said.

"You're welcome," Nina said, "I want to promote the spirit of surviving. By doing that, I will feel that my life is much more meaningful," Nina accepted the invitation with joy. She was willing to share her information with the world, to improve people's health and life.

Nina used to play flute solos on the stage, but she never made a speech in front of so many people. She asked Sam which subject she should talk about. Sam suggested she borrow a topic from Dr. Lu, "Save Qi and save life!"

At the beginning of her speech, Nina showed the photos the doctor gave to her, showing her leg conditions before and after treatment. That was from forty cancer nodules to none.

"I am here to share my story about my fight against cancer by saving my Qi," Nina said. "Qi is vitality energy. Qi is a healing power." She tried to explain using professional words first since she had learned many medical terms during her illness.

"During the eighty-some years of my life, I have experienced various hardships. I fled from the Nazi and Japanese soldiers in WWII. I lost loved ones in the Middle-East War. I lost my marriage with a devastating divorce and lost my parents to illness. I lost my best student in a terrorist attack. I almost lost my life to terrible cancer last year. But I have survived, so I can stand here to speak to everyone today," Nina said. Everyone applauded.

"I am here to promote a healthy lifestyle: Save Qi, save life!" Nina emphasized. "Saving Qi means to keep healthy with food, sleep, exercise, and relationships. Saving Qi means discovering and treating any illness at an early stage without delay. Saving Qi is the basis of happiness and longevity. Life is a never-ending battle at any stage. I have to do the best

I can for the people I love. I've learned to view suffering as an inevitable life experience."

"Nina, did you feel nervous when you found out you had cancer?" An audience member asked.

"Sure. I was not only nervous also depressed. I isolated myself, not wanting to associate with anyone. It is a tendency in human nature when frightened to retreat. My husband knew that true love is not shown by lip service but by actions. The major test is always at a critical time. He gave me much-needed love, caring, and firm support. He told me we will overcome this cancer together," Nina paused, "What determines why one patient survives for five years and another for six months may depend on the biology of cancer, on proper and prompt treatment, but more on the right lifestyles."

"I hope everyone has a healthy and better life! Thank you!" All the audience clapped loudly.

* * *

Later that month, Nina accompanied Sam to Toronto for a swimming championship. That evening, Nina walked to Earl Bales Park. The evening sun lit up a family picnic area, the warming sunlight touching the green grass. Two girls dressed in red were playing with the Canadian geese on the grass. They were chasing the geese, or the geese were chasing them. A group of boys was playing rugby. They were running, jumping, and shouting. A young couple was jogging on the park trail with a golden retriever.

Nina strolled along and turned into the monument area in the park. She saw a woman who was looking at pictures on the monument walls. Nina said hello to her.

"Hello," the woman answered, "Thinking about the war is unbearable," The woman said. "Is that all about the Second World War?" Nina asked.

"Yes, most people here have been murdered by Hitler," she said.

Nina looked at the names placed beside the pictures on the wall. To her enormous surprise, Nina recognized the name of someone who was from China. Nina could not believe her eyes, "Feng Shan Ho!" His name had been engraved on the black marble stone in Earl Bale Park of Toronto, right here in Canada. In the memorial monument, Feng Shan Ho's name was on the "Righteous People among the Nations" list.

"This Chinese gentleman saved my family's life," Nina said to the lady. She was so excited and tried to tell the story about Dr. Ho's life-saving visa and her life in the Shanghai ghetto. "Without Dr. Ho saving my life, I would have been one of the victims of the Holocaust, like my other family members."

The two women walked over to the long bench in the park and sat down to admire the sunset. The sky glowed red in the west as it fell behind an enormous pine tree. It looked like a giant red ball being held in the tree. The young boys were still playing rugby on the green grass. On the sidewalk, an old couple held hands and walked in the direction of the marvelous sunset. The entire park was stunningly beautiful.

* * *

In autumn 2018, Nina received an invitation from the city of Berlin, Germany. It was for original Berlin citizens who participated in the Kindertransport Program in the Second World War. The letter indicated that the German government would pay 2,500 Euros to each of the Kindertransport Program's "Kinder" (child) who is still alive. This symbolic monetary token was to mark the program's 80th anniversary. The current government wanted to recognize the immense psychological trauma these children suffered because of the Nazis. Nina thought that the children of the perpetrators of the Holocaust should not be responsible for their parents' actions, although the Holocaust had killed almost her whole family. History has also showed Nina that hatred and discrimination are doomed to fail.

Nina realized it was almost eighty years since she left Berlin. She had a lot of sweet and bitter memories from her childhood there. The most unforgettable and horrible event was, of course, Kristallnacht. Up until now, she never had an opportunity to go back Germany. During the war, she had to escape from Berlin to protect her life. After the war, her family did not want to go back there. When her life was so busy raising her children in Israel, she did not think about it. In New York, sometimes she thought about going back, but it never happened.

Nina decided she would accept this invitation to go back to Berlin after nearly eight decades. Sam could not go with Nina because he was committed to training the swimming coaches for five local communities. Nina promised Sam that she would take good care of herself during the trip to Germany.

A special committee from the Berlin city council had already organized the trip with the schedule of events for the visitors. They would visit Berlin's historic sites, important monuments, and famous parks during the week. In addition, they would treat the former Berlin citizens to musical concerts.

To her tremendous surprise, Nina realized that she had lost the ability to speak German from the first moment she arrived at Berlin airport. Fortunately, she retained her ability to understand the spoken language she heard. She listened to everyone who spoke fluent German, but she just couldn't talk at all.

Nina felt so embarrassed that she could not speak German anymore. She was amazed. Here she was in Berlin, her own city, and she could not speak the language. She could not open her mouth to speak the language of her birth. Nina always thought of herself as a multi-linguistic person. She could not believe this was her situation, especially since she was in Berlin. She was very frustrated about the reality of her losing her mother tongue in her hometown.

"What's happened to me? Nina! This is your native language," Nina said to herself. She felt so perturbed that she stayed in the back of the group at the reception desk at the five-star luxury hotel in downtown Berlin.

Once she dropped her luggage in her hotel room, Nina closed the door and started to cry, first quietly sobbing and then sadly whimpering.

Then, finally, she sat on the sofa in the corner, curling her back, and covered her face with both hands.

In trying to understand how she lost her ability to speak her native language, Nina reviewed her eighty-eight-year life like watching an unbelievable movie. Nina had lived by six of the most famous rivers in the world. She realized that her life had an incredible connection with those rivers. She was born by the Rhine River in Germany. She spent her early childhood by the Thames in England, escaping from the Nazis just before WWII. Then she spent her youth living in the Shanghai ghetto by the Huangpu River, fighting Japanese soldier. Later as an adult, she lived near the Jordan River in Israel, struggling with a devastating divorce. Next, she had an incredible experience on the Hudson River in the United States, confronting a terrorist attack. Finally, she had settled near the Ottawa River in Canada, recovering from deadly cancer.

On the sofa in the hotel room, Nina recalled the German spoken noise of the boys and girls in her elementary school. However, after that terrible rainy morning in 1938, when she left Berlin, Nina very seldom heard German spoken for nearly eighty years. "I was only an eight-year-old girl when I could speak German," Nina cried. She felt such pity for the little girl she had been who was exiled from her native country. "I was only eight years old, only eight years old," She repeated.

Nina recalled how difficult it had been to learn to speak English in the early days in London. She had just escaped from Berlin. She never imagined that English would become one of her main languages for most of her life. She appreciated her foster parents, John and Mary, for patiently teaching her English. Nina was saddened once she thought about her foster parents, who died in the Blitz in London.

Nina spoke only English and Hebrew in the Shanghai ghetto. She tried to speak a little Chinese and a bit of Japanese but did not speak German at all. Her father hated anything related to Germany so much that he did not allow anyone to speak German at home. So they spoke Hebrew to each other. Nina was grateful to her English teacher, Ms. Beresford, in the Shanghai Jewish School, for so many fascinating English lessons, as well as the special treat of being invited to dinner at her home. Like Nina's father said to her a long time ago, people will never forget what you do, whether a good or bad thing.

Thanks to her father's hard decision against the German language, Nina could speak Hebrew well when she landed in Israel. And Hebrew became her primary language in her adult life. She also continued to read books in English but did not use the German language at all.

When Nina immigrated to the US and Canada, she used English chiefly. However, she spoke to her daughters and granddaughter in Hebrew. She never even realized she had lost the ability to speak German because she never had reason to speak it.

Whatever happened, one thing would never change, and Germany would always be her country of birth. There was a repeated reminder when she used or renewed her passport.

"Germany, ah, Germany, You have a painful and loving part in my heart forever," Nina thought with agony.

Nina went to bed that first night without eating any food because she did not want to be bothered by the language issue in the hotel cafeteria. If anybody asked her any questions, how would she answer them? For a person who never had a chance to speak in German for almost eighty years, what would you expect of her? Nina tried to forgive herself. Anyway, she was exhausted from the traveling and the embarrassment of the lost language, and she plummeted into a deep sleep on the comfortable hotel bed.

During her sleep, Nina dreamed of her mother holding her hand, walking on the rooftop in Berlin on the Night of Broken Glass. Walking and running, she felt unbearable exhaustion. She heard the horrible yelling and sound of glass-smashing. She could still smell the awful burning smoke. Then Nina saw her mother standing on Berlin Street and waving at her, "Auf wiedersehen! Auf wiedersehen!" Nina was waving back to her mother, "Auf wiedersehen! Auf wiedersehen!"

Nina woke from her nightmare, her pillow wet with her tears.

She tried to drink a sip of water, but the sound of "Auf wiedersehen! Auf wiedersehen!" was still in her ears. It was her mother saying

"Goodbye" to her at the most critical moment in her life. Neither mother nor child knew if they would ever see each other again.

Nina tried to drink another sip of water on the night table. Her mother's voice crying "Auf wiedersehen, Auf wiedersehen!" still resounded in her mind.

Nina suddenly remembered her mother saying those exact words, "Auf wiedersehen! Auf wiedersehen!" in the last phone call she had with her from the hospital in Tel Aviv. Nina was now full of regret, thinking about the same words her Mama repeated. At that time, she did not know these were her mother's last words to her. "Auf wiedersehen! Auf wiedersehen!" Her mother was saying "goodbye forever" to her. When she thought of that, Nina cried out, "Mama, Mama!" She covered and wiped her eyes with the back of her wrists.

"Auf wiedersehen, Mama!" Nina leaned on the pillow, repeating the German words to her mother in the middle of the night at the best hotel in Berlin.

"Auf wiedersehen, Mama!"

All of a sudden, Nina realized she was speaking German. She said, "Mama, Ich liebe dich!" Nina was telling her mother she loved her in German. She knew she could speak German now. She was sure that it was her mother who gave her the power to recover her native language in her dream, miraculously.

On the second day, when she joined the tour of Berlin, she could speak German better and better by the hour. She could talk to anybody on the street or in the shops. Nina communicated with different kinds of people with no problem. Her German-language ability had recovered entirely.

The tour took the group to the Oberbaum Bridge, crossing over River Spree. Nina vividly remembered the time she held her Mama's hand as they walked across the same bridge.

As arranged by the city authorities, Nina and other former citizens went to the Holocaust-Mahnmal (In German: Holocaust Memorial), the Memorial to the Murdered Jews of Europe located in Berlin. Nina knew that Berlin had one of Europe's largest Jewish populations before WWII. Its underground "Place of Information" holds approximately 3 million Jewish victims of the Holocaust. The monument is in Berlin's Friedrichstadt district, close to the Reichstag building and the Brandenburg Gate, near the Tiergarten. Nina had been told that the memorial's location was near Hitler's underground bunker.

Although the architect Peter Eisenman stated the monument's design had no symbolic significance, Nina still felt uneasy and confused when looking at the sculptures. Her mind was on her family members, particularly her dearest grandma. When Nina randomly touched one of the sculptures, her eyes flooded with tears immediately. Her emotional response was so strong. The massive concrete stelae in the memorial blocked out all the street noise from Berlin. Nina only heard her grandma's soft and firm voice inside her ears.

Grandma gave Nina the seeds of her resilience and endurance at a young age. Nina felt her grandma's blessings were always with her, everywhere and all the time. Finally, Nina lifted her head and looked at the blue sky. She put her right hand on her heart and said, "Grandma, my life is excellent. Thank you for your blessings from the heaven! You are in my heart forever!"

Nina visited the famous W. Michael Blumenthal Academy, located opposite Berlin Jewish Museum. Nina was surprised to learn that Mr. Blumenthal also lived in the Shanghai ghetto during WWII. His family traveled from Berlin to Shanghai and then to the US after the war. Mr. Blumenthal even served as United States Secretary of the Treasury under President Jimmy Carter. As a historian stated, the Shanghai ghetto saved many well-known people in the war.

The other unique memorial that impressed Nina was the copper plates engraved with the name of murdered Jewish citizens on Berlin Streets. Nina found his uncle Allen's name on one of these memorial copper plates. Unfortunately, uncle Allen had been murdered by the Nazis right there on that site. Nina kneeled down there and touched the copper with her hand. She felt as if she were touching uncle Allen's hand again, which was warm and supportive as always. Nina truly appreciated her uncle's critical help in saving her family during the Nazi regime.

CHAPTER THIRTY-EIGHT

September 2018

Ottawa, Canada

After visiting Berlin, Nina decided impulsively to visit Cologne, her birthplace. It was also the place she had the best memories of time with her grandma by the Rhine River.

"Compared to Ottawa, Cologne is very close to Berlin," Nina said when she told Sam about her travel plan over the phone. In fact, Sam supported her idea very much.

In Cologne, Nina saw people sunbathing and reading in the soft sunlight beside the Rhine River. She thought of her beloved grandma. She missed her so much. How many times had she brought Nina to this river bank where they would lie on the grass enjoying the sunshine?

Nina cried softly, "It was the war that destroyed everything. It was Hitler's Nazis that destroyed everything."

Nina knew she would not know anybody in Cologne because Hitler had murdered everyone she had ever known in this city, whether her family members, relatives, or friends.

It was the older generation who had suffered during the war.

Today, the new generations in Germany have a peaceful and happy life. Nina saw a group of students carrying their school bags, jumping and singing on the pavement by the river. It was a beautiful scene with happy people. Colorful tulips and lines of trees along the Rhine make Nina smile gently.

Suddenly, Nina saw a familiar face in a group of young girls walking toward her. She thought she must be getting so old that her vision was getting worse every year. Nevertheless, she laughed about her degenerating sight deceiving her. She continued to walk and watch the Rhine River and thought about her mother and grandmother.

"Mama, Mama!" A familiar voice was heard over the crowd. When Nina looked around, she could not believe who was standing in front of her.

"Bela, ah, how come you are here?" Nina was amazed and so happy to see her daughter. She never thought she would meet Bela in Cologne by the Rhine.

"I am here for my friend's wedding," Bela said. She hugged her mother.

"You have a friend in Cologne?" Nina asked. She touched her daughter's face.

"Yes, she helped me a lot on Nick's Day last year," Bela answered. She was also excited to see her mother here. "Mama, let me show you around the city like my friend did last year for me," Bela put her hand inside her mother's arm.

It was lovely for Nina to have her daughter beside her, walking and chatting along the Rhine. Bela told Nina that Cologne held the famous Christopher Street Gay parade every year. It never occurred to Nina that her daughter would be involved in it.

For the following two days, Bela accompanied her mother sightseeing in the city. Although Nina had been born there, she didn't know much about the city at all. On the other hand, Bela adapted and learned about this new place very fast as a young person. The only place Nina recognized was the Hohenzollern Bridge. Bela showed her mother how this bridge had been turned into the Love Locks Bridge by many lovers who put their love locks on the bridge. In the meantime, Nina told Bela her memory of the Rhine River when it was frozen near the Hohenzollern Bridge a long time ago.

Nina did not expect to have such a perfect time with her younger daughter in her birthplace, Cologne. Bela was relaxed and eager to please her mother, telling her all she knew of the city. This was a real contrast to Bela's rebellious attitude towards her when she lived in Tel Aviv. When Nina mentioned to Bela that she would go to Tel Aviv before going home to Canada because her sister, Anna, was going to have a gallbladder operation there, Bela immediately decided to end her holiday early and go with her mother back to Tel Aviv. Nina was happy to see Bela becoming a considerate daughter.

Once Nina and Bela were back in Tel Aviv, Bela's pleasant holiday mood was slowly faded. Instead, she started to argue about almost everything with Nina again.

They visited Anna in the hospital. She had an amazingly easy key-hole operation to remove her gallstones. After that, Nina and Bela went back home.

Nina tried to bridge the gap between her and her daughter. She wanted to give her some wisdom she had learned over the years. She told Bela, "Life should be built on honesty to yourself, loyalty to your family, and decency in the society. Life is favorable to those who follow their personal dream. When an issue comes up, life always has two choices: leave it or deal with it."

Bela nodded her head.

Nina said, "Fear humbles me to alert, and humility motivates me to work harder. Success is the result of hard work. Being unsuccessful is the result of not enough hard work."

Bela continued to nod her head.

"To maintain a good relationship, you need to give first, and then think about taking. The best relationship comes from forgiving and forgetting," Nina said. She looked at her daughter.

They discussed Bela's future studies because Bela planned to change her career again.

"If you want my advice, Bela, you should think about becoming a social worker or a web designer," Nina suggested.

"I don't know if I really want to pursue those types of jobs."

"Bela, you need to understand that parents love their children without any conditions," Nina said. "Whatever you do, if you are happy, I will be happy."

"Unconditional love, what are you talking about? There is no such thing in the world," Bela said.

"I'm only thinking of you. You need to build up a career. It is the time in your life to do that," Nina said.

"To be honest, Mama, I don't want to think about anything right now. Maybe tomorrow," Bela was not interested.

"Yesterday was history, tomorrow would be a mystery, and today is a gift. So please master the moment of today, Bela." Nina made her speech to her daughter again.

"No more lectures for me, Mama!" Bela ended their debate and left home, slamming the door.

Nina was upset about Bela. She had a hard time understanding why Bela, as an adult, still behaved like a child, slamming doors and leaving the house in a temper.

Some people may never grow up at all, Nina thought.

Nina was upset and sat down on the sofa. She found a small skin nodule on her left leg. She was surprised, "Is cancer coming back?" The idea was shocking. She knew she was exhausted from traveling in Germany, and she was worried about both her daughters. She indeed missed Sam now, even though they often talked over the phone or exchanged emails. Nina wished he was with her right now. She would call Sam again that evening.

"If you feel your daughters are causing you too much stress, why not visit your friends there or think about coming back to Canada a little early?" Sam suggested.

"You are right, Sam. I may come back to you early but let me visit my friends here first because I don't know when I will come to Tel Aviv again," Nina said.

"All right, Honey. Please keep me updated on your leg condition every day. Honey, go and cheer up with your friends," Sam said.

The following day, Nina visited an old friend who lived near the location of their previous farm. Nina saw a crow on a leafless tree by the Jordan River, barking like a dog. Nina stood there and listened to the crow. All her terrible memories about Dan came rushing into her mind. In the Shanghai ghetto, Nina knew the crow was a bad omen, and its cawing may be a warning signal for some imminent danger. Before Nina could figure out the threat, the bird flew, leaving the barren tree and disappearing into the vague mist over the Jordan River.

That night, Nina couldn't sleep again. Once she dozed off, Nina saw her ex-husband, Dan, coming into her room with a horrible bloody face, slurred drunken voice, and a pistol spewing blue smoke in his hand. Nina woke up in a panic with palpitations. She was soaked with sweat. She was afraid to sleep again, fearful of the nightmare returning.

On the second day, Nina developed a fever and a severe cough. In addition, she noticed she had lost her sense of taste and smell. She waited for another day but finally reluctantly called her daughter Anna, asking her husband to take her to the hospital.

The doctor in the hospital said Nina had a severe cold with bronchitis. He prescribed some antibiotics. In the meantime, the doctor also found three nodules on her left leg. One of the nodules started to bleed slightly. He warned Nina the leg nodules were more alarming than her bronchitis. Nina was terrified.

Anna came to see her mother promptly once she knew Nina's cancer might be back, although Anna had not fully recovered from the gallbladder operation. They contacted and discussed with Sam and decided Nina should return to Canada as soon as possible. Anna was crying about her mother's situation. Nina did her best to comfort Anna.

"Anna, don't worry, I will be okay."

"Mama, I don't like the word cancer at all," Anna said. She held Nina's hand.

"Don't worry! Last time I had forty cancerous nodules on both legs. But this time, I only have three," Nina said, recovering her optimistic attitude.

"I should call Bela to come to see you before you go back to Canada," Anna said.

"You don't need to call her. Besides, she is too far from here," Nina said, although she missed her troublesome daughter all the time.

Nina overheard Anna's phone call to Bela. Anna told her younger sister everything about their mother's medical condition and cancer, including the possible prognosis for someone of her age. Anna implied they wouldn't even have a chance to walk with their mother anymore if the cancer got out of control.

Then Nina lay on the bed, thinking about her Bela, worrying about her situation.

The following day was a cold, wet day when Nina went to Tel Aviv Airport to fly back to Canada. After saying goodbye to Anna, her son-in-law, and her lovely granddaughter, Nina still had low mood. At the airport, Nina kept turning her head to look back. She seemed to expect someone would appear.

Nina heard the announcement that her plane was about to board. She hugged her granddaughter, Anna, and her son-in-law one by one for one more time. Nina looked back over her shoulder again. The loudspeaker in the airport kept announcing that her airplane was boarding. Nina turned to walk toward the gate.

"Mama, Mama!" Nina heard a loud calling behind her back. She knew it was her Bela.

Nina turned and saw Bela running on the airport's rolling elevator towards her, waving her hand and calling, "Mama! Mama, Mama!"

Suddenly, Nina stared at her daughter as if seeing herself, her eyes brimming with tears. She was jumping out of the gray car and running towards her mother on a Berlin street, calling "Mama! Mama, Mama!" She was reliving the day she left Berlin for London without her family in 1938.

Nina's eyes flooded with tears.

"Bela," Nina only managed to call her daughter's name once because she was crying.

"Mama, Mama, Mama!" Bela called.

Nina had to squat down, and Bela helped her up.

"Mama, I love you!"

"I love you too, Bela!" Nina said, struggling to stand.

Nina and Bela were hugging each other with tears and laughter. The other three family members also joined in happily.

On the plane, Nina flew through the colorful clouds. The rain had stopped. She closed her eyes and drifted into a sweet dream.

Nina saw her grandma hiding her doll Mini in Rhinepark by the Rhine River. John and Mary were waving to her by the Thames, and Papa and Mama were meeting her in the port of Genoa. She saw Hason playing a bamboo flute near the Huangpu River. Then she saw David wearing a brand-new army uniform by the Jordan River. She could see Adam having a picnic by the Hudson River. Sam was taking her to a beautiful park near the Ottawa River. Then she and Sam were looking for Dr. Lu everywhere...

All the important people in her life were there by the rivers that had meant so much to her.

When Nina arrived in Ottawa, Sam picked her up at the airport. After visiting Dr. Lu for three more months, Nina was cancer-free again.

***

The sunset tinted the sky with a rosy hue. The ripples on the Ottawa River were bathed in burgundy. In the far distance, the trees on the mountain were multicolored. Two brown boats were floating on the river nearby.

"I have a shocking discovery," Sam said.

"What is it?" Nina asked.

"Let's draw a 600km horizontal line from Ottawa to Tobermory of the Bruce Peninsula. Let's call it Wow Line. The north of Wow Line occupies 90% of the provincial land, but only 6% of Ontarians live there. However, the south of Wow Line barely makes up 10% of the provincial acreages, but more than 94% of Ontarians inhabit here."

"Wow, 6% of people live in 90% of the land."

"Furthermore, it seems the people in the north of Wow Line live a longer life than the south."

"Why?" Nina asked.

"It may be because they breathe fresh air 24 hours a day and 365 days a year. So every cell of their body is full of fresh energy."

"That's reasonable. Everybody knows fresh air contributes to longevity. Still, not everyone gets it on purpose all the time, even if fresh air is free," Nina said.

"All right let's sit on the deck outside and get more fresh air," Sam suggested.

Sam sat on a wooden chair on the pale-yellow log deck, smiling at Nina. She played a cheerful love song with her flute on the river bank. Nina smiled back at Sam, then started to dance gently. Her husband stood up and joined her. They kissed once in a while and kept dancing. With the lovely and peaceful dance steps, Nina recollected Nietzsche's famous saying, "We should consider that day a loss if on which day we have not danced at least once." Nina slowed down her dancing and picked up a pen, recording her sparkling inspiration:

Let us dance

Let us dance in the morning glow,
Let us dance on the riverbank where the sun shines,
Let us dance in the bright moonlight,
Let us dance every ordinary day.

The rivers travel to the sea, surging forward gallantly,
Our life shall be staunch, permeated with passion.
No winter will last forever,
No spring will never come.

We long for peace in wartime,
We understand war in peacetime.
With love, we could survive any toughness,
With music, we would be happy with any challenges.

November 7, 2018
Ottawa, Canada

Nina was invited by the Prime Minister of Canada to attend the federal government's official meeting. The Right Honorable, Mr. Justin Trudeau, made a formal apology speech about the turning away of the MS St. Louis in 1939, historically known as the Voyage of the Damned, which happened just before the Second World War erupted.

So many war survivors and their families participated in this meeting. Nina became emotional when she heard the woman who sat beside her crying. She had flown over from the Netherlands. Her name was Vera. Triggered by the contagious emotions, Vera's sobbing made Nina's eyes fill with tears. Nina could indistinctly see her father and mother waving at her through the dazzling teardrops in her eyes.

Nina remembered her Papa told her about Aunt Rose in the Shanghai ghetto. She took the MS St. Louis before Papa and mama left Berlin in 1939. But Aunt Rose didn't enter Havana, Cuba, as her family planned. Instead, after being refused sanctuary and turned away, Aunt Rose landed in France. She was murdered after Nazi Germany invaded France in June 1940. Nina still recalled her Papa's words. "Each goodbye could become the last one during a war."

After several emotional moments inside the Parliament buildings, Nina stepped outside. She felt better when the gentle breeze touched her face. The autumn sunlight spread on the green grass of the vast front lawn of the gorgeous Gothic revivalist building. Even at the age of eighty-eight, with gray hair, Nina still walked lightly and with elegance. "How do we long for peace in wartime? How do we understand war in the time of peace?" Those were the thoughts Nina kept thinking about when she walked out of the Canadian Parliament building.

On the lawn of Parliament square, there was a water fountain called the Centennial Flame. Nina walked close to watch the red fire jumping around with the blue flame on top of the fountain. She continued to think about war and peace. She stared at the dancing fire and thought, "If the fire is for war, then the water is for peace. We love peace, what is why we always lived by the water."

Vera came over, and they walked to a nearby park. They leaned on the iron railings, taking in the vista of the Ottawa River from this elevated perch.

"Look at those Canadian geese," Nina pointed to the geese in vee formation over the river.

"Ah," Vera sighed profoundly and gazed at the geese flying until they were out of sight. "Where are they going?" she wondered.

"Look over there. A motorboat is racing on the river."

"You mean that white boat?"

"Yes. It is churning up the water, making white foam in the middle of the river as if it was dividing it in half."

"You are right," Vera said.

"The people from this side of the river speak English, and on the other side, they speak French. Originally, I spoke German," Nina told Vera.

"I come from Germany too. I injured my back in a bombing during the war," Vera used her right hand to form a clenched fist and kept patting her lower back.

"I experienced a terrible bombing in the Shanghai ghetto in the war," Nina faced Vera.

"Shanghai ghetto? I never heard about it," Vera was surprised.

They sauntered to a long bench in the park and sat down to appreciate the dusk. The arduous setting sun became a giant red ball hanging on the substantial hemlock trees. A group of white pigeons flew over the luminous water of the Ottawa River.

Nina looked into the far distance as she described her horrific story of the bombing in the Shanghai ghetto by the Huangpu River...

AUTHOR'S NOTE

Though this novel based on true events of many real people's stories, please bear in mind this book is a work of fiction. All incidents and dialogue, names, organizations, dates, and all characters are products of the author's imagination and not to be construed as real, and not intended to depict actual events or to change the entirely fictional nature of the work. In all other respects, any resemblance to persons living or dead is entirely coincidental.

ACKNOWLEDGMENTS

First, thanks to my editor, NYT bestselling author, Caroline Leavitt, for your professional revising the manuscript and your encouraging words about this novel "The story is thrilling!"

Special thanks to Jim Bensimon for your enthusiasm for the book and invaluable advice from the Jewish point of view.

I am very grateful to the inspiration from Naomi Zahavi, Lily Lieberman, and Esther Seemann, for sharing your incredible experience. I truly appreciate your positive spirit for your heroic life. I'm also indebted to many of my Jewish friends for their real-life stories and their encouragement for this book, especially, Menashe Yarkony, your amazing energy is a wonder for me.

I would like to thank Heather Conrad for your extremely helpful editorial suggestions and fantastic eye for plot development. I really appreciate your great effort of polishing my novel, most importantly for your enthusiastic and consistent support.

Thanks to Percy Zhen for your initial supportive attitude for the book. Thanks to my beloved first readers Long Zhang, Eva Richardson, Andrew Kim, Kristen Bedard, and Lily Moshe who provided important feedbacks for the book. Many thanks to Amanda Evans, for your time and effort for the book editing ideas.

Thanks to Nicolette Oakwell-Margan, Jennie Davidson for your encouragement and support for this book.

Thanks to Jian Chen, the curator of Shanghai Jewish Museum, for the nice communication about the book.

Many thanks to my son for your time and effort for editing the book. Thanks to my stepdaughter for your helping to carry numerous books from the library.

Special thanks to my brother for taking so many pictures of the place used to call "Shanghai Ghetto" for my book's reference.

And last, but most certainly not least, many thanks to my wife, for your enduring love, your faith in me, and your ongoing support and encouragement in every endeavor I have pursued.

Most of all, huge thanks go to my readers!!

CPSIA information can be obtained
at www.ICGtesting.com
Printed in the USA
LVHW100316300123
738186LV00002B/279